The Syndicate 3:

Carl Weber Presents

The Syndicate 3:

Carl Weber Presents

Brick & Storm

www.urbanbooks.net

Urban Books, LLC
300 Farmingdale Road, NY-Route 109
Farmingdale, NY 11735

The Syndicate 3: Carl Weber Presents
Copyright © 2017 Brick & Storm

ISBN 13: 978-1-62286-584-0
ISBN 10: 1-62286-584-7

First Trade Paperback Printing November 2017
Printed in the United States of America

10 9 8 7 6 5 4 3 2 1

This is a work of fiction. Any references or similarities to actual events, real people, living or dead, or to real locales are intended to give the novel a sense of reality. Any similarity in other names, characters, places, and incidents is entirely coincidental.

Distributed by Kensington Publishing Corp.
Submit orders to:
Customer Service
400 Hahn Road
Westminster, MD 21157-4627
Phone: 1-800-733-3000
Fax: 1-800-659-2436

Prelude

Claudette

Back in Atlanta . . .

Kingston had pulled me into his office the day before and had sat me down and told me that I had gotten a call. That delicious husband of mine had literally squatted down in front of me, taken my hands, and told me that I needed to take this call. He had sweetly told me to forget about any anger that I had toward the person who called me and just to listen. . . .

"She's a Miss Beautiful Supreme. A girl that others wish that they could be." He smiled as he sang a little of Stevie's "Ebony Eyes" to flirt a bit and to calm me.

My King made me laugh because he'd always sing those lines to me while looking at me in a manner that only he could: with a slight lick of his lips, a mischievous glint in his eyes, a flash of his pearly whites, and twin indents in his cheeks.

I remembered him smelling like sweet grass, the warmth of the sun, and his favorite cologne. My sweetheart wore camel-toned work boots, casual jeans, a white tank. He was taking off his work gloves. He had been working outside on the house when he got called to his office by young Snap. He called for me, and I came into the room with ice water, a sandwich, and some of my plans for work in the house for him. I remembered the way the sun broke through the stained-glass window of his office and bathed him in soft light. My man was illuminating, and it wasn't just his magnetic personality. It was his aura.

My Kingston had a brief smile when he saw me. He always did, but it faltered with his next words. "Dette, come sit with me for a moment."

Kingston Francis McPhearson was my everything, so I didn't question why he was asking me to sit with him. Maybe he had something he wanted to teach me, or maybe my man wanted to feel a little bit of Claudette.

I watched him casually walk over to his desk with that sexy, confident manner he had before he sat behind his desk. I made my way over to sit near him in a long-back old chaise chair that I loved—one that he never let anyone sit in.

He stopped me with a, "No, right here, woman, where your throne is. You know betta."

Heat rose to my cheeks. Always did when he flirted with me. I happily went on over, sat where he patted on his thick-toned thigh, and relaxed.

I knew something wasn't good. We always had a way of communicating without words, knowing the secret thoughts of one another without sharing. So, the sadness, with a glint of anger, in his eyes let me know something wasn't right.

My King gently ran his hand up and down my spine. His other hand found its way against my folded hands on my lap. We laced our fingers together. He put my hands to his lips and looked me in the eyes.

"Ain't never been any other woman but you, Dette. You own me, all of me," he told me.

"You own all of me, too." I laid my hand against his cheek, loving the feel of the slight stubble on his strong jawline. "Like two stars in the black night . . ."

"I'm always by you," he said, *finishing for me.*

That simple saying had always been ours. When I looked in King's eyes, I felt his lips meet mine and fit just right. I loved all that man, all of him.

"I always feel a part of you with me no matter where I am," I said.

"Good, because like I always tell you, one day you'll need to remember that I'm always with cha no matter what."

I loved when he let his accent come out; it felt like home.

"And I told you not to tell me stuff like that. I hate when you talk in finalities. It hurts. So stop it, King, and tell me what's running in your mind that got you talking like that. You're worrying me, and you know how I get when that happens."

"Uh-huh. You try to get your gun to shoot me in the foot if I start vexing you, or your blade to swipe at me."

I laughed at his goofy jokes, then gave him a stern gaze.

King squeezed my hand and pulled me closer as his voice deepened even further, betraying his playfulness.

"What's wrong now, Kingston?" Nerves had me standing up. "I always get calls. What's different about this call that has you looking like that?"

King followed my movements but didn't let me move too far from him. He hooked his hand around my waist and had me sit in his chair. He squatted in front of me.

I watched as he stared toward a picture of us on our wedding day. It sat on the fireplace mantel, facing his desk. We were so young and happy in love and lust. It was the finest moment in my life. Loving Kingston.

"Ghosts are the main difference with this call, my Dette. We . . . you have a situation that you need to handle." Only my Kingston could make me swallow my pride *and do something, such as talk with the person whom I called a blight on my soul. Only my husband could make me forgive as a lesson in learning how to work with those we called the enemy, though this person was different from the ones we dealt with in the Syndicate and in our designated area.*

Only my lover and best friend could calm the rage in a storm. So, in listening to my husband, I returned the call that would put a chill in my heart and have me flying down the highway toward a place I had left when I was twenty years old: good ole Creek Town, Georgia.

"Claudette! What you doing round here, gal? Been a long time since I done seent ya pretty self."

It was the summer of 1985. The wafting scent of burning sweet wood, blended with spices and the savory addition of meat, brought me back to my youth. Rows of old wooden houses were cloaked in sporadic bushes of ancient trees and other plants. Other homes were bare and falling apart, with rusted fridges, cars, and other metal objects lying about. From their porches, people were watching me. They were either sitting on the stoop or standing, with one hand holding their sloping tin roof.

Kids played all around, some running up and down the unevenly paved streets while others rode their bikes. Some played basketball. A few played hand jive, while others took turns in double Dutch. Small that it was, my home was busy with life, and it made me happy that it hadn't died in all these years.

Constrained anger had me on edge, while a tinge of red scabbed over my eyes. In other words, a sista was pissed and ready to kill. I was as hot under the collar as a pussy in heat, okay?

I was thirty years old, with a gun hidden against the back of my purple, wide-legged cropped pants, a switchblade under my white top—in the bra—and a personal vendetta needing to be handled. While I walked up the sidewalk to my childhood home, B.B. King could be heard crooning on the radio in the old juke joint down the street. It was a place where I used to wait tables at as a teen. A place where I was also wooed by my husband, Kingston. The memories of those days helped me keep a calm center while I visited this old home of mine.

"Ain't doing nothin' but brang'n' some trouble to a motherfucker who did some foul wrong, Miss Jenkins." Being back in my familiar surroundings had me returning to the natural Southern drawl of my birth.

Sun in my eyes, I turned to address Miss Jenkins, who was chewing tobacco, while shielding my eyes from the bright glare with my lace-covered hand. "You wouldn't know what I'm talk'n' 'bout, now would cha?"

"Still ya daddy's chile, huh?" Miss Jenkins said with a sweet smile on her face. She sat with the ends of her blue dress bunched up on her lap, revealing smooth, toned brown legs and her white house shoe–covered feet. In her hand was a sharp knife, one that was cleanly slicing thin slivers of apple. "I see ya got ya some fancy taste now too and a handsome young man, huh?"

A gentle laughter came from me. Miss Jenkins was being nosy, but she also was making sure that I wasn't breaking the community code and bringing in a threat. Since it had been a while, I figured that I'd entertain her curiosity in the only way I knew how: by avoiding her questions.

"Yes, ma'am, I am still my daddy's child. He always taught us how to handle business and keep our shadow protected," I said, glancing toward the young brotha by my side.

Miss Jenkins followed my gaze. The blade that had been in her hand disappeared as she laughed. "Mm-hmm.

*You ain't lied 'bout that one, baby girl. Yo' daddy taught
y'all just right. Mm-hmm . . . I just like how han'some
that protection can be."*

*Tall like a willow tree and built lean but sturdy like
a brick wall, my shadow kept his expressions stoic. His
skin was smooth and flawless, and he had a shadow
of dark, soft hair on his jaw. Because of the weather,
he wore a white linen shirt that had the sleeves rolled
up around his arms. Suspenders were attached to his
brown trousers. Miss Jenkins's chuckle made me look
up at the man by my side. My husband had made him
promise to protect me, even at the risk of his own life,
while down in this little sweltering town.*

*"Don't give this boy the big head," I said with a light
chuckle. "He's just protection. Ain't that right, Snap?"*

*I studied how Snap's taunt jaw relaxed and a cool
breeze of a smile spread across his handsome angu-
lar face. Snap reached for the screen door of my family
home. When I looked past his shoulder and behind that
screen door, there stood someone whom I had been pre-
paring myself to see, the person who had called to tell me
about our old friend's daughter, Toya, having been raped.
Raped by a bastard who had, in my youth, been a
well-feared hoodlum, one who had married the bitch I
had written off from my life.*

*As I squared my shoulders, I readied myself. This
poltergeist had called me to help end the blight that she
had stupidly let in her life and to avenge our fifteen-
year-old god-daughter. As Snap stepped back from the
door, I stood there in silence. The sun soaked into my
skin. Sweat slipped between my breasts.*

*My lush black hair, which was slicked back into a
ponytail, with a large puff in the back, started to become
wild in the humidity. And through it all, Snap stayed by
my side. From his body language, I could tell that he felt*

the anxiousness in me, the constrained anger, the flashes of hurt, and the unspoken "How could you?" pointed toward the person behind the screen. Because of it, and as trained as he was, I knew that he was watching the same person behind the screen as I was.

It was then that I wished Kingston was here and not tied up in Syndicate business.

When Snap shifted his hand, he reached up and tilted toward Miss Jenkins the hat that sat on his head. He then opened the screen door and said, "Yes, ma'am. That's my job."

Chapter 1

Shanelle

The cries of a baby woke me up in the middle of the night. Life in the McPhearson household had changed drastically. It had been one whole year since our foster mother, Claudette McPhearson, had been gunned down on the street. One whole year since we'd found out she was not the woman we had thought she was. On the day of our mother's funeral, we found out that she had been the leader of a crime ring called the Syndicate. Since then, our lives had played out like a crime mob or gangster movie.

Mama Claudette had raised us like we were her own children, all the while giving us the skills we would need to control one of the biggest criminal enterprises since the Commission, which had been the governing body of the top five mafia families in New York at one time. It had been a hard pill to swallow for those first few days—hell, for those first few months—but we'd done it. Javon had done it.

In a few short days after learning the truth of who Mama Claudette was, Javon had taken the Syndicate and turned it on its head. He'd taken out the Irish, who, we'd initially thought, put the hit out on Mama, and had brought in the Commission to have a seat at the table. My husband was a mastermind, and Mama Claudette had known this, which was why she'd tagged him to be the one to take her place.

I frowned as I sat up. I threw my legs over the side of the bed and instantly regretted not sleeping with socks on. The floor was as cold as ice. I yawned as the baby's wails got louder. I looked behind me and almost jumped out of my skin. Javon's eyes were planted right on me.

"Jesus Christ," I whispered, laying a hand on my chest. "I thought you were sleeping."

He grunted. Yawned. Scratched at his nuts. "I was until that baby started wailing." His voice was low and guttural and told of how tired he was.

I'd found out I was three months pregnant shortly after finding out one of our foster sisters, Melissa, had been the one to set Mama Claudette up to be killed.

"I don't know why she's crying," I said. "I fed her and changed her—"

"That's not our kid," he said.

I furrowed my brows in confusion. I was still halfway asleep, so I didn't readily get what he was saying.

"Huh?"

"That's not Honor crying," he said as he slowly sat up.

I watched the muscles in his back as he stood from the bed. He looked tense as he rolled his shoulders and lolled his head from side to side. The sinewy muscles in his back rolled and coiled. His ass was tight with muscles. Thighs flexed powerfully with each stride. He walked over to my rocker and snatched up his linen pajamas.

"That's Justice," he sighed.

I flipped the light switch on and got my senses about me. As I listened, I realized it was our niece wailing at the top of her lungs and not our daughter. Javon turned to look at me. I looked at the clock. It was 3:00 a.m., and most of us who had chosen to keep living in Mama Claudette's house had things to do later that Monday morning. A crying baby ruined everyone's sleep.

"You know that means that in about five minutes we're about to hear Jojo and Dani arguing," he said.

I nodded. It was a sad situation to see my little brother end up with a girl—I refused to call that bitch a woman—who wanted to do any and everything but be a mother. I didn't like to be one of those women who judged other women, but Dani had gotten with my brother when he was sixteen and she was grown and in college. That would forever make her *ain't shit* in my eyes.

But one year and a three-month-old baby later, she was proving to be exactly what I thought she was: a nothing-ass bitch.

"Go get her, Shanelle," Javon said.

I snapped my head back around to look at him like he'd lost his mind. My upper lip twitched. "Say what?" I asked.

"Go get her. If they're about to start their bullshit, Justice doesn't need to be in there with them," he said.

I shook my head, ready to put up a fight. This had been the routine far too many times. I had our own daughter to think of, and she would no doubt wake up soon because of the noise. "I'm not about to take on—" I started, then stopped.

Javon stood to his full height, then took a deep breath. Annoyance was in his eyes when he looked at me. He'd gotten fitter over the last year as well. He'd always taken care of himself, but over the last year he'd cut most meats from his diet. He ate a lot of raw fruits and vegetables and worked out more than ever. His chest and arms were sculpted, and his abs contracted and released with each breath he took.

"Look, I know I'm asking you to do something you don't want to do, but I don't want to hear that tonight. I'd have liked to sleep through the night, but that's not going to happen obviously. I told Jojo I'd let him handle his own business with Dani, but that doesn't mean I'm going to subject Justice to their bullshit. So, will you get her for me?"

I let out a deep breath while staring my husband down. Clearly, he wasn't in the mood for any back-and-forth. I could tell by the way he quirked a brow at me and tilted his head. I wanted to cuss him out; I really did. But Javon was good to me, and I never wanted for anything materially or emotionally. So I swallowed down my annoyance and headed to Jojo's room. I did stop in the nursery to check on Honor, our baby girl, who was still on her back, fast asleep. I closed the door before knocking on Jojo's door.

He didn't tell me to come in, but since Justice was screaming at the top of her lungs, I let myself in, anyway. I was surprised the door wasn't locked. The room was messier than Dani normally kept it. Clothes were hanging from hampers. Bottles were strewn about. The smell of a dirty diaper assaulted my senses.

Dani was coming from the closet when I entered the room. In her hand was a duffel bag, and she was dressed in an Adidas tracksuit. Her curly hair sat unruly on her head. She stopped abruptly when she saw me, then ran a hand through her hair nervously. I looked toward the window, where Jojo was sitting in a rocking chair with Justice. His back was to me as the chair moved backward and forward slowly.

"What's going on?" I asked no one in particular.

"Um . . . I'm leaving," Dani said.

"Where are you going at three in the morning?"

"I don't know. I'll figure it out," she said. "I just need to get away from here."

I looked down at the duffel bag, then around the room, and noticed she hadn't packed any of Justice's things. When I looked back at her, she had a defiant look in her eyes. My eyes narrowed, and I had to count to keep my temper in check.

"Don't even start, Shanelle. Since I been here, you been shitty toward me. You ain't want me here no way. So, you should be happy I'm leaving," she said.

I kept my voice as calm as I could when I asked, "What about your daughter?"

Dani glanced around, switched her weight from one foot to the other. "She gon' be all right. Jojo got her. I mean, at least until I get myself together."

"He's eighteen, Dani. He's in school. He's working. You can't leave him here to take care of a baby by himself," I said coolly.

"Well, I got shit to do too. And I'm sick of fighting with him and sick of that baby crying. I need a break. I need some time to myself," she said, agitation in her tone.

"You didn't think about before—"

"Let her go, Shanelle." Jojo's voice came out low and even, but there was no life in his tone. He sounded defeated.

It damn near broke my heart. I couldn't see his face, but the fact that it sounded as if he had resigned himself to his fate told me this had been a long time coming. My little brother knew me well, because I didn't have any intentions of letting Dani walk out of here so easily.

I wanted to shove that bitch's face into a wall, and she knew it. That was why she stayed a few feet away from me.

"Will you move so I can leave?" Dani asked loudly.

I knew she was being loud so either Uncle Snap or Javon would come in. They were the only two who could stop me from beating her ass. The nerves in my hands ticked, I wanted to punch Dani so badly. And I probably would have punched her, but something told me the last thing Jojo needed was for her and me to fight right now. I stepped to the side just as I heard Uncle Snap's bedroom door open.

Dani eased past me like she was walking through a field of land mines. She got to the threshold, then looked back at Jojo. "I'll be back . . . one day. I just need some time to think and clear my head," she said.

"What's going on?" Uncle Snap asked, his voice groggy, as he rounded the corner.

I glanced up to see he was in cotton pajamas and was pulling a T-shirt over his head.

"Bye, Dani," Jojo drawled. "I love you."

Dani rolled her shoulders. Her brows furrowed, and she chewed on her bottom lip. For a moment, her eyes darted back and forth like she wasn't sure if she wanted to leave or stay. Then she snatched up the car keys that were lying on the dresser and quickly made her way downstairs.

"What the fuck is going on?" Uncle Snap snapped, his voice louder and clearer than before.

I walked over to Jojo. My baby brother was staring straight ahead, tears rolling down his face, but there was not one bit of emotion in his eyes. He looked as if he was somewhere else. Justice had stopped crying. Her small hand was on Jojo's tearstained cheek, and she gazed up at him like she knew he needed her to chill in that moment. I reached down to take her from his arms. For a minute he stiffened; then, once realizing it was me, he loosened his grip. I signaled for Uncle Snap to go back into the hall; then I left the room and closed the door behind me.

"I don't know what's going on," I said to him. "But Dani just made my little brother a single father."

Uncle Snap scratched his head, then frowned. Downstairs, I heard Javon. Now, to a normal person, Javon being downstairs would be confusing, since I'd left him in the bedroom, but with all the secret passages we'd found in Mama Claudette's home, it was safe to assume he had used the closet in our bedroom to get downstairs.

"Leave the keys," Javon said to Dani.

"Why? It's my car, and I wanna leave," she whined.

"It's Jojo's car, which we allowed you to use since you're Justice's mother, but if you're about to run off on your responsibilities, it won't be in a ride this family funded," Javon told her.

"You have to be fucking kidding me! So, because I don't want that nigga anymore—"

I heard the front door open, and then Javon said, "You were leaving, right?" cutting off her tirade.

There was silence. I heard a car zoom by. Loud music rattled the windows of the house.

Dani tried to explain again. "I just need—"

Javon cut her off again. "The keys, Dani. I need the keys, and then you can be on your way."

I could tell by the no-nonsense tone in Javon's voice that he had very little patience. That must have shocked Dani. Javon had always been the nice one. I smirked. While I was pissed off she had hurt my little brother, she would get the perks of being attached to a McPhearson no longer.

I walked downstairs with Justice cradled in my arms. Javon shoved the door closed behind Dani. He cast his eyes in my direction before looking at Justice.

"She's going to need you more now than ever," he said.

Uncle Snap came down behind me, then sighed. "I knew that gal was fickle, but I didn't think she'd run off and leave her baby," he said.

Javon asked me, "Jojo cool?"

Justice cooed in my arms. "I'm not sure. He was staring straight ahead, looking out the window, with tears running down his face," I answered. "Maybe he's in shock."

I replayed the exchange between me and Dani for them, then told them how detached Jojo had been.

"I saw it coming," Javon said. "She hasn't been behaving very motherly. She does the least for Justice when left alone with her. When Jojo comes home, she pushes the baby off on him before hitting the streets. I just felt something in the air tonight, and I was right."

I shook my head. It finally clicked for me that once again Javon had picked up on something between them that I hadn't. I mean, I knew they were having problems. They had been since the girl moved in here, but I in no way had thought she would abandon them.

I left Uncle Snap and Javon to talk about how they would help Jojo. I headed upstairs to get Justice back to sleep. It didn't take long once she had been fed and changed. I put her next to Honor and smiled. I wouldn't have thought a year ago that I'd be a wife or a mother, but there I was.

Honor slept peacefully in a red onesie, while Justice wore purple. They were beautiful brown babies with masses of curly hair, and I'd do anything to keep them safe. As soon as that thought crossed my mind, the phone rang. My spine stiffened, because it wasn't my phone or Javon's phone. It was the private line, which meant it was Syndicate business. I guess I wouldn't have been so concerned about it if it weren't at that time of the night. Someone ringing that line now meant there was an emergency.

I closed the nursery door, then headed to the bedroom just as Javon was entering it.

"Talk," he barked into the phone. I watched quietly as his facial expression moved from anger to shock. "What?" he asked. "When?"

He turned to look at me with something akin to panic in his eyes. "I'll be there," he said. He hung up the phone.

"What's going on?" I asked.

"Yo, Uncle Snap?" Javon called out the door, ignoring me for the moment. Then he rushed into the closet, popped the light on, then started tossing clothes onto the bed.

"Javon, baby, what's going on?" I asked again.

"What up, nephew?" Uncle Snap asked, sticking his head in the door.

Javon glanced at me, then at Uncle Snap. "Get dressed. We need to head to New York. It's an emergency." Then to me, he said, "Someone killed Cavriel, and the old man was shot. Lucky says it was a hit on Cavriel, and they think it was a botched hit on Luci. Absolan is missing."

Cavriel, Absolan, and the old man, Luciano, were the heads of the Commission, which was the governing body of the mob back in New York. I'd given them a seat at the table of the Syndicate in exchange for their connections and the protection they could bring us.

"Oh, shit," Uncle Snap said. He left our room quickly.

I asked Javon. "What does this mean?"

"I don't know," Javon said as he pulled on a pair of jeans. "I won't know much of shit until I get to New York."

My heart raced, slammed into my chest. I thought about our daughter, our family. For a year now, Javon had managed to come out alive after every attempt to dismantle the Syndicate. However, if someone was aiming for the Commission, that was something else altogether.

Chapter 2

Claudette

"Mama?" Young Snap stood holding open the screen door for me.

Hotter than a hooker walking past a church, I swatted at a lone mosquito, then whipped my brow. It took me a moment to realize that he was watching with a curious look in his brown gaze. But once I did, I brushed off the rise of emotions in my spirit. I defiantly tilted my chin up. My whole body language was coded in a big "You hurt me, bitch," that only the figure behind the screen understood. Snap or Miss Jenkins, they'd see me only as being icy and posturing.

"Thank you, Ralph," I said in a manner that only he could hear, then walked up the cement steps that led into the screened porch.

Once in front of eyes that matched my own, eyes set in a diamond-shaped face that was common to the people in my family, I carefully removed my lace gloves, then moved for Snap, who now had our bags in his hand.

"Deedee," I said with disdain.

"Sista," she returned in a reserved tone.

Everything in me said to slap the taste from her mouth. Because this was my eldest sister, the desire to hit her with the side of my pistol was an automatic no-no, but there was another fact going on. As the sun poured into the porch, I could see my elder sister for the *first time in almost eight years. The fact that she was still as glamorous as she had been when I last saw her didn't surprise me.*

Deedee was three years my senior and known in the family as the carefree one. So much so that she had hopped on the first train ride outta Creek Town to see the world, ending up in Europe and breaking her promise to me by leaving me behind. My sista never used to think of herself until that day. As I looked up at where she stood on the porch, the corners of my lips dropped into a deep scowl.

Deedee's black hair was in a mess of teased curls that had been pulled up in a side ponytail, which made the curls fall like waves over her shoulders. Her makeup was done in a neutral, fresh face look, while the hands that rested on her wide hips were accented with sharp pink nails. Again, nothing in how she looked surprised me; however, what did surprise me was the slight roundness to her stomach, one that indicated not that she had gained weight but that she was carrying life.

When my gaze ripped from her stomach, then up to her face, white-hot anger could be seen in my eyes.

"You let him knock you up?" I all but yelled.

Deedee gave a light chuckle, not answering my question. My bitch of a big sister turned her back on me, then disappeared inside of the family house. On her arms, I saw bruises and the half-moon marks of fingernails that had dug into flesh. Deedee made no damned sense to me. Accepting a beat down by a lowlife of a nigga was not something Big Papa Haynes had raised us to accept. Yet here I was, staring at marks on my sister, along with a swollen belly.

"Don't walk away from me." The rage in my voice made Snap briefly look my way. When I realized that he was still there, I gave a sharp sigh and pointed inside.

"*Gawn inside. My room is the last one near the kitchen. Unless that fat cow changed it.*"

"*Yes, ma'am,*" Snap gently said, looking my way. "*Can I help ya in any way?*"

"*Just put my bags up, go to the kitchen, get chu one of them mason glasses, and pour yaself some sweet tea. I need to have a private moment, a'ight?*"

There was something hidden in the way Snap looked at me. It made nerves spark up in my stomach, something that I did my damnedest to push back, because I didn't want to confront what they could possibly mean. Or confront the way Snap sometimes watched me.

When he said, "*Yes ma'am,*" and nothing else, I gave a sigh of relief.

Once Snap went inside, I rolled my shoulders, then walked into the house our great-grandfather had built. Inside was the same as it had always been when I was but a child. Fresh smelling, except for the scent of cooked bacon, with a welcoming, warm feeling. Over the mantel was our grandmother's old shotgun. Above that, was the porter hat that belonged to our grandfather. Hanging on a brick wall near the white bookshelf and record player corner was a picture of black Jesus and a fading family photo.

Mama's rocking chair was still by the fireplace. Daddy's smoke pipe still sat on the side table, as if he was about to pick it up and give it a nice puff. Memories played in my mind. The echoes of children laughing back when I was innocent, and not the killer I would become, made me take in the tiny house until reality settled back in and had my anger blazing.

"*Deedee,*" I shouted.

"*Girl, if you don't calm all that mess.*"

I spun around to see Deedee sitting on the couch, staring at the occasionally jumpy reception on the TV. From what I could see, she was watching Soul Train.

"I woulda told ya on the phone, but you hung up on me."

Annoyed, I walked up to her and dropped my purse on the coffee table. "Of course, I did. You had just told me your monkey-ass, piece-of-trash nigga had raped our goddaughter. Yet you sit here, swollen with his child?"

"You jealous?" Deedee looked up with a smirk.

Pain was reflected in my eyes. It made me freeze where I stood, as if the wind had been knocked from my gut. Then everything happened fast. My hand whipped out on its own and landed against the side of my sister's face.

"Bitch, I might not be able to whup ya ass because of that baby, but I'll for damn sure beat the breaks off your face." My nails scraped at my sister's face.

The instinct in me made me pull out my gun from my waist, then remove the safety and point it at Deedee. "Ain't nothing in me ever jealous about what you got with that sick bastard of a nigga you call husband, you hear me?"

"Get off me, Cece! You ain't gawn shoot a damn thang in here. Mama and Daddy would rise up from the grave if you did."

She was right, but I wasn't going to admit that to her trifling ass. Which was why, when she smoothly flipped the script and took the gun from me, causing us to struggle against each other, I didn't press her and try to get it back. No, instead, we fell sideways on the couch, and I used that opening to slap her again.

"You know what happened, and you got the damned nerve to say that shit to me and smile, huh?" I said in between hits. "But call me down hea' to handle shit you stupidly got yaself into on ya own? You knew what typa demon he was, and yet you still married him."

By this time, I was straddling my sister on the couch, slapping her and pulling at her hair. My anger was so palpable that I didn't even notice that Snap had rushed back into the living room. The pounding of his shoes, which shook the house, didn't stop me.

"Get. Off. Me." When Deedee hit me, her forearm slamming into my nose and causing blood to flow, tears slid down my face and mixed with the blood that stained my white top, but this couldn't stop my rage.

Pulling at my hair, then pushing me back with her foot, Deedee worked her way up from the couch. When she moved to swing at me, Snap did something like a floor slide, where he managed to cover me and wrap me in his hold to pick me up.

Tears fell, and I buried my face in his chest. He made me wish that Kingston was here. He made me come close to realizing something else that I wasn't ready for.

"Aye, ya two wild chickens, calm down, before y'all destroy the house," Snap ordered. He held me behind his back with his large hand and looked between us with a taut jaw.

"This cow just doesn't care that she ruined everything by messing with that nasty old bastard," I yelled at my sister, pointing and trying to get at her.

I could see tears sliding down my sister's face. Her hair had her looking like a rooster. I knew my makeup was dripping down my face. We both looked a hot country mess but didn't care.

"An' you don't get it. I had to," Deedee sputtered. Her arms wrapped around her belly; then she looked at me directly.

It was her following confession, delivered with her broken voice, that made me stop my fighting and almost faint. "Baby sista, I had to. The baby ain't his. It's Luci's."

Chapter 3

Javon

When I was a kid, I used to have this thing where I'd stare up at the sky as long as I could, just to imagine what it was like to live free. No restrictions. No running in the street from the bullshit of being hungry, dirty, and looked at as a beating bag. In those brief seconds, I knew what serenity was, and it helped me get through whatever I had to.

Even when I lived with Mama, I'd find myself gazing off to study the sky.

Mama would say, "Sometimes even the sky gotta get mad. Otherwise, we little folk and the land can't get nourished or can't start anew."

Mama always had a way with words in getting us kids together, even when we didn't want to hear it. I missed her every day, every hour, every minute and wished she was still with us. The day of her funeral had caused the skies to rage, and with it had come a change that made our family start anew. It was wild, and during that ride, I felt as if we all were going to drown if I couldn't pull this shit off and get ahead of the storm. But I'd done it.

We'd all done it and survived. Mama had made us eight hood brats—me, Cory, Shanelle, Inez, Monty, Navy, Jojo, and, before her betrayal, even Melissa—stronger. I'd forever be hurt about Mama being taken from us and dropping us in this wicked world. But at the same time,

I was grateful that she hadn't abandoned us in her own way.

Her legacy was mine, and in the end, through all the blood loss and tears with keeping it going, I had earned my right to it.

"Nephew, you up?"

I sat on a private plane, staring out the window at the early morning darkness. It was beautiful watching the clouds shift to reveal different colors of the sky, a range of midnight to light, as the day awakened to the rising sun. Made me think of my life. Made me think of the moves I had made for my family. For my wife, for my baby girl, and yes, even for my niece.

"What we're stepping into is dangerous, Uncle," I said as my answer to let him know that I was awake.

The sound of Uncle Snap shifting in his seat drew my attention toward him. He sat with his tobacco hat resting on his lap, opposite me and next to a sleeping Cory. My brotha sat with the side of his face plastered to the cozy plane seat, his mouth half open, but with his hands fisted. It was a look and a posture that I was used to with him. It meant he wasn't deeply sleeping.

"Indeed, it is, Von," Uncle Snap said, stretching to rub his palms against his thighs. "But we all know that. What you really askin'?"

My tongue ran against my lower lip. I glanced at Cory, then back to Uncle Snap. "How'd Mama compartmentalize her normal life as a mother with being who she really was and with the losses?"

"Ah. Been waiting fa' ya to ask me that part of all this change in ya life."

Sometimes, I still chuckled when Unc's country accent jumped out. A part of me didn't want to come off as weak in Uncle Snap's eyes, but the reality of the game was, he'd been there through my growth and falls, so this was nothing.

"How'd she do it?" I asked again. "I have us, my siblings, to look after. Yeah, we're all adults, but still, two of our clan are still in that middle, between being kids and adults. Jojo just was hit with the hardest adult shit ever." I nodded to Cory, and as I did so, he shifted his head and looked at me.

"Inez and I will be all right," he said groggily. "Shit, I mean, the rehabilitation, the doctor visits, it's pushing at our addictions, but I promised her, myself, and the family that we'd not go down that type of slope ever again. So care for us, but don't put us on that weight you've been carrying, *kuya*."

Kuya was Tagalog for "brother."

"You know how I am," I said quietly.

The weight of being an elder sibling could be hard, let alone the weight of being a leader. The past year had taught me that. Starting my own financial analyst security firm, J.M. & Co., by staging a walkout with my old employees, whom I had trained, had taught me that. Since I was now a husband and a father to a beautiful baby girl, the weight of my choices and the demands of my work as a part of the Syndicate had me questioning again whether it was worth it.

"I'm glad you're asking all the important questions, nephew. That's why I'm here. Why I promised Mama that I'd look out for you all." Shifting forward, Uncle opened the front of his button-down coat— it was cold and snowing in NYC—and pulled out something that looked like a cloth-wrapped book. Inside were letters tied together with string.

"It's time that you had this," Uncle Snap said. "I was supposed to give this to you the moment you succeeded in taking over Mama's chair. With everything that happened, there just wasn't any time, and when Mama's anniversary passed . . . it became hard to hand over something connected to her. But it's time."

Mama's journal was back at the house, protected by
Shanelle. I had long since had everyone in the fam read
the most important parts of it. Shanelle had even made
me a copy of a page of Mama's journal to keep with me
whenever I left to do Syndicate work. Now it looked like
Uncle had another journal, and I was silently bugging out.

"Another journal from Mama?" I asked.

"Naw. Right here is grown-man business." Uncle Snap
glanced between me and Cory. "See, it takes a strong man
to love a woman like Mama. That woman had a heart like
no other. It was so big, so connecting, it was hard not to
become part of that woman's spiritual flesh. That's how
it was with her and boss man King. It was how it was
between me and her later in life. Mama had enough room
for only you kids and that brotha, along with myself."
Something in Uncle Snap's eyes changed briefly as he
said, "And one other, as yawl know."

What wasn't being said was what I had learned in
Mama's journal: her brief time with the Commission
head himself, Luciano Acardi.

Uncle Snap reached over and handed me the bundle.
His hand patted the surface of it in respect. "So, that
there are the recordings of a mind that learned a few
things from Mama while schooling her as well. My
former mentor. The man who put me in Mama's life,
Kingston McPhearson."

I looked at the bundle, then carefully tucked it in my
black blazer-style coat. I had mad respect for my uncle. It
had to have been hard to love Mama how he had in secret.
"Thank you, Uncle."

The OG gave a gentle sigh as he looked out the window.
"Ain't nothin' but what was the time to do. There's gonna
be some thangs in those letters and that journal that you
both are gonna need to know. Especially when we land in
New York again."

"What do you mean?" Cory asked before I could.

Stretching his legs out, Uncle Snap gave a slight chuckle. He looked at his watch, then at the two of us. "Gawn and pull out that bundle again, Von, and read the letters. Those are from Mama to King."

I did as he asked, and then gently put the journal back in my coat. I then pulled out the first letter I saw and opened it. "Dear King, I wish you were here with me, but I know a leader has to do what he's destined for, like you taught me," I said, reading aloud. I paused and looked at Uncle Snap.

"I'm all right, nephew. Read on and let me tell yawl the rest of the story of why Mama went down to ole Creek Town to protect ya mama, Toya, after her assault."

Both Cory and I blinked in confusion and said in unison, "There's more?"

"Mm-hmm . . ." Uncle Snap ran his hand over his cap and looked at us with sadness and happiness behind his moist eyes. "That it is. Sometimes, as yawl learned, people can do the most damaging thangs, to the point that sometimes you gotta cut family from ya life and act like they never existed."

Turbulence in the plane made us shake. We waited it out until the ride became smooth again, and then Uncle Snap pointed toward the letter.

"That's what Mama had to do to get through her life in the Syndicate. That's what she did when she became a foster mama as well. Family was everything to her, but when family breaks you, you sometimes gotta do what's best for your heart. That was . . . until the day she got a call. Gawn and read that first letter before we land."

I glanced at Cory. If what Uncle Snap had said was in the letters was really there, then Mama and I had more in common than I knew. I licked my lips again and began to read, and I kept reading until we finally landed New York.

***

"Ain't no fucking way," Cory said in a low voice as he sat by my side. "This shit is wild, my nigga. What do we tell Lucky? Shit . . . Do we even tell him? is the real question."

I was on my cell, texting Shanelle in code that we had landed, telling her to send me pics of her and our baby girl. Because, mentally, I had just been fucked up by Mama's secrets, as my brother was so eloquently saying by my side. I then sent a text to Monty to remind him to protect the family house with the Thieves, who were the family's personal bodyguards, and especially to keep an eye on Jojo. After that, I quickly stashed my cell, looked at Uncle Snap, and then rubbed the waves on my head.

I said, "We don't say shit until—"

"Until we handle this business, nephew, and until we come face-to-face with his mother," Uncle Snap interrupted. "Those letters have been copied, with a second one written just for her sister. I know Jai sent them on Mama's behalf, but as you see, the woman ain't reached out to me about it. So, we keep our mouths shut until we—I—am in her face. Understood, nephews?"

This was the time that we had to step back and let Uncle Snap control the game. And honestly, I was thankful, because I didn't know what to do with this shit.

Cory said, "But, all this time, Mama had a sister and ain't said shit. Why?"

"Right. I met her. . . . I knew I wasn't tripping when I saw her. She looks like Mama, but different. Like unless you knew Mama, you'd just say that they had a passing similarity. But fuck, that woman is her mirror, just older and Lucky's mother."

Uncle Snap rubbed the back of his neck, with a frown. "Yes, and she is a hellion. And yawl both know a bit about secrets and not revealing identities, remember?"

Cory thumbed his nose. I could tell the wheels in his head were turning while we were exiting the plane. "A'ight. At first it was because they were mad at each other. But after, it was what?"

"Protection within the Commission itself. Something the Syndicate, at that time, didn't need to know. That's it," replied Uncle Snap. "Some shit is just for family, ya feel me? But yawl will find that out in the rest of the letters."

"This is crazy," I quietly said to myself.

The little bit that I had read, I knew that I wanted to send to Shanelle. I needed her thoughts on this too, because sometimes it took a woman who'd been through shit to understand another woman's plight. So I planned to send a sealed copy back with one of the "Forty Thieves."

"We'll be chill and play it as is. For now, we need to find out who's offing the Commission," Cory said.

"Agreed," I said, glancing around the airport.

Several holding buildings for various planes flanked us, as well as the private jet behind us. The chill in the air, mixed with the snow on the landing strip, had all our teeth slightly chattering. Occasional flashing lights could be seen in the distant morning sky. We had arrived in New York City at seven in the morning. Two slick black armored Escalade SUVs with reinforced wheels pulled up. From the sound of the engines, I knew that they were tricked out for speed.

Two men stepped out of the rides, both in black suits and black leather, with driver's gloves and hats. Cory gave a nod, and four of the Forty Thieves who were with us moved in to inspect the cars and the drivers. Once everything was cleared, the drivers included, we all entered one of the rides, while our Thieves got in the second SUV.

I gave a sidelong glance at one of the drivers, then chuckled to myself. The inside of the SUV had been

redesigned for luxury. There were four rows of espres-
so-toned leather seats, with the Acardi moniker on the
headrests. On the ceiling were folded-up screens, while
the back of each seat had a compartment for a laptop and
a keyboard. A mini fridge had also been incorporated
into the design.

"Very nice," Cory said as he relaxed.

"It should be. Cost a mint, *capish*?" said our driver.

"A'ight, Lucky. What's going on for you to be dressed
like the help, my dude?" I asked the back of his cap-wear-
ing head.

I wanted to talk to the brother about everything. I
was now studying him, just to see if he had any traces of
Mama's family traits. Lucky pulled off smoothly, leaving
the lot behind us. It was the morning rush hour, and the
roads were thick, especially the highway that we were
now entering.

"So, what's up with the look?" I asked.

An anxiousness in my spirit had me checking our surroundings. I saw Cory, who sat in the front with Lucky,
do the same thing. Everything looked normal. There
were some old jalopies, luxury rides, everyday new rides,
some trucks, some hybrids, a few service rides, vans, and
more.

I asked, "Is it really that bad that you gotta meet us
incog-negro?"

Lucky's leather-gloved hands gripped the steering
wheel to the point that they strained under his hold.
Lucky then looked left over his shoulder before quickly
swerving the car through incoming traffic.

"Someone tried to kill my uncle. Shot him clear above
his heart and into his shoulder," Lucky said grimly.
"Someone broke into Cavriel's home, the place he felt
was his sanctuary, and desecrated it by shooting him
point-blank in the head while he was in the middle of his
Shabbat. Now Absolan is gone. His church ransacked."

There was a moment of silence, until I heard a beeping.

"You made the right choice in reaching out to us. We got you," I assured him.

Make no mistake, everything Lucky had stated made me think that the war that was coming to the Commission was a well-planned hit. Because the old heads were out of commission, it was up to us in the new generation to protect the foundation.

Lucky gave me a quick look, then nodded. "Good, because we have a problem. That's my alert that we have trouble." He glanced in his mirror, then said, "We're being followed."

Immediately, I turned to consider the clusterfuck of cars on the highway. "Cory," I simply stated while I moved to pull out my Glock.

"Already checking our eyes," Cory responded, clicking on his cell, then raising it to his ear. "What's the rundown?" Cory made some "mm-hmms," then said, "There . . . white van on our right. Two lanes over, at our three-thirty. The windows are tinted, so they can't make out who it is."

Thumbing my nose, I scowled. "Lucky, what are you thinking?"

"I'm thinking that I was trailed. They had to have been parked somewhere near the airport," he answered.

"So, what are you going to do?" I asked, studying the brother.

Lucky watched our back, then hit his Bluetooth to make a call.

"Waiting on orders, boss," the voice said on the other end.

"I know you all see that van," Lucky said. "It is trailing us. Go ahead and let it ride us. Cloak the license plates, and then push them off the road."

"Yes, sir." With a click, the call was ended.

"Ante up, my friends," Lucky said. "I'm about to hit this gas. If you got silencers, use those."

We all nodded, ready for the bullshit. Ready to do what we did best and take out some motherfuckers. As we went in our pockets for our silencer pieces, Lucky hit the switches for the automatic windows to open them. Cory reached in his black cardigan coat and pulled up a black mouth mask. His long crinkled locs were pulled back so that he wouldn't get them in his face. So, he was good on that. Cory positioned himself and glared, reminding me of some Method Man look back in the day.

Cory asked, "Ready?"

Pulling up my own mask, I gave a nod and looked at Uncle Snap. "Ready."

Uncle Snap tilted his head low, then took the winter scarf on his coat and wrapped it around his body. He reached by his seat and pulled out a suitcase. After popping it open, he reached in and removed two disks. When he squeezed the sides, lights lit up on them, and then we swapped weapons. He then began putting together a long shotgun.

"Go," was all he said.

Lucky hit the brakes, then maneuvered the car to where we were in a clear lane. Our guards behind us whipped their SUV in a way that forced the van to the side railing, which allowed us to coast up along the side of the van. We all turned to look at the van. When the sliding door of that bitch opened, we knew that this was no accident.

"Take 'em down," I yelled. I threw the disks in the van. Uncle Snap tossed me my gun and at once started taking out some niggas.

Inside the van, I could see that they were all white dudes, which I made a note of, with a female driver. Cory leaned over to hold the steering wheel and gave Lucky his Glock. More rounds were pumped off. Most of the cars around us saw only that we were speeding. Some honked their horn and moved out of our way. Only a few realized that we were in the middle of gunplay.

"Get them off the road," someone shouted from the van.

Big mistake. These stereotypical guido-looking moth-erfuckers aimed their weapons at us, then emptied all they had. The force of their guns caused the armored car to shake. The noise was so loud that we couldn't hide our actions anymore. Lucky stopped his shooting to take over the wheel. We all did our best to shield ourselves.

Cory let off some rounds. I did the same, but it was Lucky's quick thinking that got us out of there. Working the car like it was a part of him, he shifted, then made our ride jet forward so that our guards behind us took our place. Everyone else in the car who wasn't driving watched them take over our stalkers.

"Ahead is an exit, and the cops are coming. I'm getting us to the family high-rise, so bear with me, fam," Lucky announced. Because of his quick driving, Lucky had managed to trip up our own guards, to the point that our cell phones began going off. When he guided us back on the highway in the opposite direction in order to take a roundabout way, I couldn't help but chuckle to myself. There had been several accidents on the highway because of us, and one involved the van that had trailed us.

Somehow that bitch was upside down, and our security was nowhere to be found.

We all put our weapons away and sent messages to our security team that we were good. This fast-paced mofo named Lucky then took us through back ways until we ended up coming up on an unassuming garage. Like a drift car expert, Lucky whipped the car around to back us up. Lucky parked, looked at us, and sighed.

"Y'all have a floor to yourselves, with staff like before," he said as our guards opened the car doors. "Welcome back to NYC. We always got something to throw at cha."

"So tomorrow, after breakfast, we all do this again?" I said jokingly, causing everyone to laugh.

In the end, we had lived for another day. That shit with Lucky made me think of Mama and what I knew. Telling him was still up in the air. However, saving the Commission was our priority. We just now had to find out who those niggas were. What the hell had we just stepped into?

Chapter 4

Uncle Snap

It had been three hours since we'd touched down in New York. Despite Lucky wanting us to get to the safe-house location where the Old Italian was being doctored, Javon wanted to lay low for a few hours. So, Lucky had left to make sure everything was still in order with his uncle.

"We need to reassess how we move here. I didn't think we would get off the plane and step right into the Wild West," he'd said.

I agreed with my nephew there.

"Shit was crazy," Cory said. "Whoever is after these old heads is trying to take out every and anyone close to them too."

"A king's descent," I said as I poured some moonshine into my favorite mason jar.

"A what?" Cory asked.

"A king's descent," I repeated.

"It's something like a queen's gambit," Javon said, causing me to nod. "Only with a descent, they're not aiming to take out one leader. They're aiming for the heads of the entire organization."

I took a sip of my moonshine, then wiped my mouth. "Right, right. They start with the most powerful and work their way down the bloodlines, trying to make it so no new blood can step in and claim the empty seat," I said.

"Just so we're clear," Cory added, "this shit has nothing to do with the Syndicate, but everything to do with the Commission?"

Javon nodded. "As far as we know, right now, yeah."

I looked around the luxury high-rise. I had to say one thing—the Acardi men knew how to live in style. They'd spared no expense with this place. There was little doubt in my mind that the doorknobs were real gold. And since Lucky had jokingly bragged about the Italian marble on the floor being Botticino, I knew that was just as good as walking on gold. The curtains and shades had been hand sewn by the best. I was sure the cows used for the leather sofas had been handpicked by Luci himself.

For some reason, that shit annoyed me. Everything annoyed me. I'd given Javon King's journal. It had taken me years to get through it myself. There was one thing in it that had always bothered me. One thing that was going to make Javon see me in a different light, and I wasn't ready for that.

"Hey, Unc, you cool?"

I snapped my head around to stare at Cory. I saw him, but I didn't see him. It was as if I was looking right through him, seeing another time and place.

I frowned. "I didn't mean it," I said.

"You didn't mean what, Unc?" he asked, dipping his head to get a better look in my eyes.

I glanced around the room. I knew Javon was looking at me, but I focused my eyes everywhere but on him.

I slapped a hand on Cory's shoulder. "Nothing, nephew. Nothing. Was thinking on some old shit. Got caught up in memories and shit."

I gave his back a pat, then moved out of Javon's line of vision. While Cory and I were close, Javon and I were closer. He was able to read me and call me on my shit quicker than Cory was.

"What time did Lucky say he was coming back?" I asked while walking into the kitchen.

"Should be back in here in a minute," Cory answered.

The fact that Javon hadn't spoken up yet wasn't lost on me. It meant that nigga was inside of his head, thinking shit. Trying to piece shit together. I didn't need that. I needed to keep him from that part of the truth for as long as I could. Some shit not even Mama needed to know. It had been for her own safety. But I was sure nephew would have seen it as a betrayal. It was just the way he viewed things. I grabbed a glass of ice, then got some paper towels to wipe the sweat from my forehead. I walked back to where I'd set up shop next to the window. I poured some moonshine over the ice, then took a sip.

"Yo, Unc, you behaving mad weird right now," Cory said. "You drinking ya shine out of a tumbler with ice and shit, my nigga."

"Yeah, I know, nephew. Being up here got me anxious. Some shit just don't feel right, is all. Forgive me."

I glanced at Javon, and nephew had a gaze fixed on me that told me he had peeped game. Cory laughed and said something about me needing to chill out, because I was making him nervous. I didn't really pay attention to what he was saying. My heart rate sped up. Javon stood across the room, next to the expensive piano, arms folded across his chest, feet planted wide.

"How far you done got in King's journal, Javon?" I asked him.

"I haven't," he responded, his tone on the verge of being cold.

I took another sip of the moonshine on the rocks. "You gone probably want to go ahead—"

Before I could finish what I wanted to say, the locks turned on the door. All three of us drew our weapons and aimed them at the door. Luckily for Lucky, we weren't paranoid and trigger happy. Otherwise, he'd have been a dead man.

Dressed in the same driver's attire that he had been in earlier, Lucky told us it was safer to move now.

By the time we made it to the undisclosed location where the Old Italian was, my nerves had somewhat calmed down, as we had other shit to worry about at the moment, and I needed to be on my Ps and Qs when watching Javon's back while we were out.

Lucky pulled up to a building that looked like an abandoned hospital. It had no more than seven or eight floors. Many windows were broken. Some were boarded up. The front doors hung from their hinges. It really didn't look like a safe space to be hiding anybody, but knowing what I knew, it was safe to bet that there was more to the building than met the eye.

I knew we were in upstate New York, but since Lucky had driven in a maze pattern, I couldn't readily say where exactly.

"Y'all got the old head up in this quarantine-type-looking joint?" Cory asked as we exited the truck. "Looks like we about to step into a zombie apocalypse or some shit."

"Looks can be deceiving," Lucky said. "Follow me."

The inside of the building was just as shabby as the outside. It looked as if we had just stepped into an area from a disaster movie. Tables were strewn about. Heart monitors that no longer worked were turned over on the floor. Old hospital beds and gurneys looked as if they'd been pushed aside in a rush and just left wherever they rolled. The smell was rancid. I was half scared that the syringes we were stepping on would pierce the bottom of the expensive-ass shoes we were wearing.

"Nigga, you should've gave us hazmat suits or some shit. It's a fucking mess in here," Cory said. "Y'all can't be trying to save that old nigga in all this filth. I'm sure that nigga can die from the germs in this bitch alone."

Lucky chuckled. Javon and I walked in silence. Lucky led us down several flights of stairs until we made it to a set of double doors that stood out in stark contrast to the rest of the building. The brass doors had a security panel, which Lucky waved his hand in front of. Locks and latches could be heard whirring and ticking, and then a loud buzz caused the door to open. As soon as it did, heavily armed men and women dressed in all black greeted us.

"At ease," Lucky said. "It's me."

The lights were bright. The hall was clean, and it looked more like the hospital it was supposed to be. We walked past several rooms before Lucky finally stopped in front of one. He pulled off the chauffeur's hat he'd been wearing, then took a deep breath. It was only then that I was able to see the stress on the boy's shoulders.

"The old man may not be lucid when we get in here," he said, glancing at all of us before looking at Javon. "There is something I didn't tell you before."

I took a step back, then looked at Javon. His face was stoic when he responded. "I'm listening."

"I told you how Cavriel was killed, but it was where he was killed that gives me pause. Same as where my uncle was shot. They were in their homes. If you know anything about these old heads, then you know they are very particular about who they let in their homes."

Javon nodded. "So you're thinking this is internal."

Lucky frowned. "That would be the logical thing to think, right? But it's just too obvious. Feels like some shit is missing or that the killer or killers would want us to think that, right?"

"Have you talked to the other families?" Javon asked him.

"That's the plan once we leave here. Uncle Luci specifically asked for you to be brought in. This wasn't my call."

"What was his reason?" Javon asked.

"He said you owe him one."

"That old man knows that's not how our relationship works. I made that clear to him last time I was here," Javon said.

"Well, you're going to need to get over whatever loyalties you have to Claudette and her ever-present dope boy— you know him as Snap—and come to terms with the fact you do owe Luci a favor."

My eye twitched and my soul turned to frost when I heard the voice of the woman I detested more than life itself. I turned my head to look at her, and my soul broke into a million little pieces. She looked like my woman so much that for a second I was drunk enough to want to grab her and hold her. Tell her how much I missed her . . . But she wasn't. She could never be, no matter how many times or how many ways she tried to be.

She was even dressed like my woman. From her long pressed hair, which was parted down the middle to curtain her diamond-shaped face, to the way she was dressed in a form-fitting black dress. Her body was shaped like an hourglass . . . just like my woman's. And she had breasts and hips that made any man take notice, no matter his race or sexuality.

I remembered the pain she'd caused my woman over the years. Remembered Mama's tears and her angry rants about why and how her own flesh and blood could turn into such a cruel and evil-intentioned human being at times. Even after all the shit Mama had tried to do to ease the waters.

"Shut up, bitch," I shouted before my sense of decorum could catch up to me.

My voice didn't even sound like my own to me, so it wasn't a surprise to me that Cory and Javon looked at me as if I'd grown two heads.

Lucky tilted his head, then scowled at me. I shot him a look that mirrored the one I'd given his nothing-ass mama.

"I'm going to need you to never in your life disrespect my mother like that again, or it will be the last thing you do," he threatened.

"Nigga . . . fuck you and yo' gutter-ass mama," I replied, slurring my words.

And just like that, a line had been drawn in the sand. Javon and Cory drew down on Lucky just as he pulled his piece on me. My gun was in my hand, but I had mine aimed at his mother.

"Okay, now I need everyone to calm down," Javon said, his voice calm—too calm. "Lucky, you know I've always come into their space with absolute respect."

"Then you forgot to give that nigga the memo," Lucky spat.

"Uncle Snap," Javon called out to me.

My eyes never left my woman's blood-related doppelgänger, and neither did the aim of my gun.

"You're feeling guilty, huh, Ralph?" she taunted me. "Your demons coming back to haunt you now? I told her she was too good for you. She could have had everything—"

"She *did* have everything," I yelled through clenched teeth.

"But she chose to live in the slums with you and these vagabonds she called her children."

"Vagabonds," Cory repeated. The tone in his voice said he was offended.

"Shut up, Deedee," I snapped.

"Lucky," Javon said, "I'm going to put my gun away, and then I'm going to instruct Uncle Snap and Cory to do the same. Once that's done, and after we go in to see the old man, we can sit down and discuss some things that would better explain what just happened and why it happened. You know I'm a man of my word. Give me that."

For a few tense seconds, nobody moved. But like always, I felt Mama somewhere close to me. So, I dropped my hand, then tucked my gun away.

"Sorry, nephew," I said to Javon.

"I know, Uncle Snap."

Chapter 5

Javon

"Who is Deedee?" I heard Lucky ask while I headed to Luci's room.

"I don't know what a Deedee is, sweetheart, but my designation is Giovanna Acardi, and that tacky vagrant will address me respectfully."

A harsh laugh came from Uncle Snap as he said, "You dress a backwater pygmy rattlesnake up in Versace and gaudy diamonds with pearls, and she forget she got the same dirty moonshine in her blood as I do."

Clearly, we all were in a stressful situation, and it had those of us with a more restrained mind-set chilling, while others, like Uncle Snap, were flipping the hell out. On some real shit, it didn't surprise me. He was grieving still, so this made a helluva lot of sense. I just needed him not to be sipping on that Devil's piss and to be reining in the chaos for a bit. We had shit to do, and I already was on edge about being shot at and chased, along with finding out more of Mama's secrets.

So, with an inward sigh, I added Uncle Snap to my mental list of people to watch. Before that, it was Cory's wild ass, but now it was the old man. Especially, since our "aunt" had hit us with some bougie-ass code word for "thug."

When I walked past him—after he apologized to me—I let him know that I understood where he was coming from. Grief was hard to move past, especially when it was wearing the face of the one we lost and talking like she was better than the sun and the moon.

Inwardly, keeping my thoughts in check, I glanced at Cory and said, "Keep them cool, bro. Mainly Uncle here."

"Got you," he said as he walked up on Uncle Snap and wrapped an arm around him. "So, she really called us vagabonds, huh?"

"Don't start it again, man, please," I said behind me.

When I walked toward the room, I heard Uncle Snap say, "Bitch gotta new name and some rocks on her fangas, and she think she's a black Sophia Loren."

"*Shit!*" I heard Cory add, which had me shaking my head.

I had chosen the wrong one to keep an eye on the OG. Damn, I hoped they didn't turn the place out. As I moved down the pristine, clean ward, I heard the sound of an air pump churning. Luci's people made every effort to make this area sterile, and that meant sending in clean, sterile air, keeping the place clean, and then some. An abandoned, creepy, and disgusting hospital was above, but under it was a high-tech ward worthy of a government operation.

Once outside of Luci's room, I rolled my shoulders, then walked in. The room was cozy but hygienic. On a small table next to a window sat a family portrait of a younger Luciano, his father, and siblings. Beeping from the monitor made me anxious. It put me in a place that had me reflecting on Mama Claudette. Another elder was on the cusp of death, and the shit was unnerving. I could hear Luci sucking up air. When I walked to his bed, which was next to a recliner chair, the scene made me turn my back on him for a moment.

The old man had a breathing mask on his face. His chest slowly rose up and down with each breath that he took. It was clean shaven and covered in bandages. I could see where he had been shot. I could see the bruises, and it fucked with me. Mama had been left on the concrete in the alley where she had been shot to bleed out and eventually be taken to the hospital.

By then it had been too late. By then, there was nothing in her dead shell that could be saved—nothing. All light had been snuffed out. Any hope and chances gone.

I fisted my hands, and the sudden hate that I had for Melissa made me clench my jaw. A nerve on the side of my face began to twitch. Cords and tubes connected to the machines and IVs branched out from the old man. A thermal cover and sheet kept his body temperature in check, while his haggard face was covered in a five o' clock shadow.

"Javon?"

I turned at the sound of the old man's exhausted voice. "Yes, sir. It's me."

Luci clicked a button on the side of his bed that made it rise. His other hand was holding the oxygen mask, and he moved it.

"Come sit, son," he grunted, then looked toward the chair.

As I moved to sit, he coughed, then spoke again. "Thank you for coming here. I know this is a difficult moment, for us all."

Liquid involuntarily spilled from the corners of his bloodshot eyes. He looked dehydrated. His lips were cracked, and it annoyed me. Motherfuckers couldn't do the smallest thing like get the old man some *grease de la shards of glass*, aka Carmex?

After undoing the button of my blazer, I sat and ran my palms against my thighs. "Of course, when one of our own need help, then that's what we do. We come to help."

"Yes, that's what I was counting on. . . ." Luci took a deep breath. "But my main thing is that I was hoping family can help each other above all other things."

I sat quietly. I wasn't sure why he'd say that to me. There was no way that I had revealed my knowledge about Lucky's true parentage, so I kept my poker face on and just sat back. But a moment later, I told him, "You said that we owe you." I couldn't help myself. That shit still sat in the corners of my mind and bothered me. "Per my last visit, all debts had been voided."

"Yes." Luci took a deep breath. "However, sometimes there's addendums that cancel that out."

"We were already on our way in good faith and as allies to you, Luciano." I shifted to lean against my knees while looking him in his eyes. My voice stayed at a mellow level out of respect. "You didn't have to go there to get me here."

"Think of it as you and Lucky's final lesson. I need your complete help in sniffing out the truth and finding Absolan. Whoever did this was several steps ahead of all of us on the Commission and close enough to us that it is almost as if we were bedfellows." Luci coughed, took a breath, then closed his eyes. "It is as if this person went into the old codebook of the past. This is a classic underground hit, and in order for you new generations to effectively carry on for us older goons, you must take a walk in the past. If you recall our conversation about honoring the elders . . ."

A flash of our very first meeting, and me eventually taking over the Syndicate, came to mind. I gave a quiet nod. "I recall, and you have my word that we'll find out what's real and what's not."

"Good." There was a sickly silence. One that was sucked up by the sound of monitors beeping and the oxygen machine whirling. "It's time for the truth to come to light. That was Claudette's favorite phrase. Loving two women at once is not something I was expecting, but it happened.

If it is my time, I only hope that Claudette finds her way to me again."

Quietly, I stood. Mama was loved deeply, and she loved deeply. "How Mama's heart was, I'm sure she'll greet you in stride, old man. But for now, how about we hold that off for some years, okay? You should share that past stuff with Lucky, though, before he shoots my uncle for disrespecting his mother."

A wheezing laugh came from Luci; he then grabbed my wrist and looked me. "Maybe I will . . . maybe I will."

I gave him a look, studying the old man while feeling a little annoyed at him for being laid up like this.

"Until then, remove my enemy's ears and fingers. Save their tongues for their confession. Then slice their throats for the disrespect they reaped." Luci dropped his hold, the little bit of strength that he had now gone.

"I'll do that and more. I am a child of Claudette," I reassured him, then headed out.

I really didn't have a straightforward plan for finding out who had strategically taken down the Commission, but I knew being at the hospital wasn't going to kick this off. As I walked out into the pool of tension outside Luci's room, I paused to address everyone, including the diva, Giovanna Acardi. Cory was leaning against a wall, with his arms crossed, by our uncle. Uncle Snap sat mean mugging Lucky's mother with a glass against his palms, while Lucky stood pacing in front of her.

"All right. We need to calm this episode of *Family Feud* and go handle business. The old man is resting. Bella donna Giovanna, he's asking for you." I lied about that last part. She looked like Lynn Whitfield did when playing a rude-ass, angry-ass woman, and I just needed her outta the room.

Lucky said, "There is no feud if the OG chills on my mother. I don't know who he thinks she is—"

"Don't, sweetheart. Just leave it alone," Giovanna said quickly. "He's just a drunk who is still mourning a ghost who never wanted him."

A quick flash of confusion hit Lucky's face. His narrowed gaze focused on his mother as he tilted his head but didn't say a thing. We all could tell that he was wondering how the hell she knew him that well even to say that.

"Always a slick-talking gutta bitch and always thinkin' 'bout cha self before ya own."

"Uncle Snap. Let's dial this back," Cory interjected. "The old man in the back is waiting."

Giovanna reached up and patted her son's face. She then left without a word, strong eyeing us on the way out.

It was clear that the woman formally known as Deedee was problematic as fuck. I thumbed my nose, then looked at my watch. "Yeah . . . anyway. We have a little time here. Lucky, take us to Cavriel's home."

"There's nothing there to see. We went through—"

I held a hand up, stopping Lucky in midsentence. Cory strolled up on my left, and uncle followed.

"Sometimes, you just want to see if niggas are watching, and sometimes you just want to draw them motherfuckers out and have a nice conversation."

Quirking an eyebrow, I glanced at Lucky.

"Can we all just talk to some niggas, homie?" Cory said, finishing for me with a chuckle.

Lucky scowled, then gave a nod. "Guess it's game time, then. Let's go have that conversation."

We exited the ward, passing nurses who were caring for a few of Carviel's surviving family and for bodyguards loyal to the Commission. Once we made it to the car, Lucky did his thing as a driver and whipped the car back through the streets of New York City. Cars peddled past us. Pedestrians did their walk, and we prepared ourselves for the shit war that was going to go down.

***

Before us was an old forty-foot-tall limestone building. I listened as Lucky explained its history.

"Cavriel bought this home to be near his community and to protect it. The building was built in nineteen fifteen. There's tunnels that run through the place. They were built during Prohibition," Lucky explained.

The brotha was leaning with his driver's hat tilted to obscure his face. One arm was stretched out, pointing ahead of us, while one of his black gloved hands dangled over the steering wheel.

"Since then, Cavriel reinforced the walls of all the tunnels and the secret passage. Security was put in by his hand, so that no one would know where the cameras were except him. His private monitor room was found by us, though."

"The building connected to his home?" I asked, taking in the four-story beauty, with its French-style front, wooden door, balcony front, and slanted roof.

"He owned it. Turned it into a storage area for himself and a museum for the Jewish community called Shabbat. It's also heavily secured," Lucky explained.

"As we learned, secure don't mean shit," Cory explained. "There's access from the roof. The front, the side that's connected to the building. Since you know about the tunnels, whoever went at Cavriel more than likely knew about them too. Or not."

Cory shifted in his seat. "Anyone could scope the place, as we are, by hiding in the several buildings surrounding Cavriel. Did he own them?"

"He owns the whole block and the surrounding area," Lucky said with a chuckle. "His crew takes up residence in the Jewish deli on the corner. Some in the barbershop over there."

"And if you know the schematics, so did whoever was able to break in, point being this shit feels in-house, and we know a lot about how your own can turn on you." Cory shifted to undo his seat belt. "My suggestion here is, snap up that nigga who keeps circling the block as he walks. Take out that black van near the fenced tree and get in Cavriel's crib."

"Take the ears and fingers and tongues—" I began.

"For confession. And then slice their throats. That's the way of the Commission," Lucky interrupted.

Uncle Snap gave a grunt, then exited the car. He pulled out his Glock, then removed the safety. "And put two to the skull. That's Snap's way."

I watched Uncle Snap walk off. "Cory," I said.

"All ready covering his back, bro." Cory pulled his crinkled locs into a knot, then pulled on his hoodie as he followed our uncle.

"Ride around the back, Lucky," I said while checking my coat.

Lucky gave me a nod. "They'll be waiting, so move fast."

I gave a chuckle, ready to end some lives. "No doubt."

As soon as Lucky drove up, he flashed the headlights to his ride on the goons who were hiding in plain sight. None of them were Commission folk. Lucky quickly removed his coat, revealing his Kevlar vest. He tossed his hat to the side, then pulled out his Glock.

"What you got on you, Von?"

"Several knives and my Glocks. That's it."

After hitting the glove compartment, he reached in and tossed me some things. "Now you have a little bit more. Let's go."

"Hey. Take them down!" shouted one of the goons outside the car. Bullets rained down and bounced off the armored car.

We dipped our heads and partially rolled down the windows. I popped my hand up and squeezed off my rounds. Lucky swiftly moved out of the car. From the corner of my eye, I saw him pull out two hand knives. He snapped them out so that they were longer, then gripped them and gave a one-two punch toward the goon who rushed him. Dude drew his hands up like a boxer, dropped his gait low to send punches against his foe's ribs. He then used that moment to run his blade against the man's side, stabbing him.

I used that moment to rush into the house. I was greeted by two dudes dressed in black. I took my gun and pumped out more bullets. One to the head, one to the chest, one in the leg. Because we were loud, more dudes came out.

"Who the fuck are y'all, huh?" I yelled.

Sweat dripped in my eyes. I ran forward, sent my fist into the jaw of one of the goons. I followed that by grabbing the nigga and slamming him to the floor, with me following. Shit hurt and knocked the wind out of me.

I rolled to the side and tried to move up but was met with a foot in my side. I bared my teeth and rolled over, letting rounds out. When the body dropped, I was met by more bullets, which flew at me. I finessed and slid across the marble floor, trying to escape them, and made it behind a pillar.

"Nephew, stay down," someone shouted at me. It was Uncle Snap.

"We have you covered," Cory hollered.

"Great," I hollered back. "What went down, and what's my best options here?"

I could hear feet moving around. Pristine vases shattered. Flowers went flying in the air. This shit was like some sort of movie. When I moved, more bullets followed.

I didn't see Lucky, and that bothered me. We didn't need him killed.

"Stairs clear!" Cory shouted.

Relieved, I hopped, looked left and right, and then ran by the stairs straight to a hall.

"Behind you, nephew," I heard Uncle Snap say. He moved to my side, and we made sure to stay near the walls.

"We were about to check out the building but saw you two ride up on a handful of bastards," Uncle Snap told me. "Shit was lookin' like a cock fest. So, we busted in through the building connected to the house. Found a passage leading directly into this bitch."

"You see anything inside?" I said, looking around the corner.

"Naw, but I did find shell casings," he said.

"That's damn good." I got ready to move around the corner, and when I did, Lucky was in front of us.

Sweat ran down his face as well. He was panting hard and shaking his head. "I don't know who these bitches are, but they are making it hard to kill them. I got it clear in the back."

"We have it clear upstairs," Uncle Snap said, pointing his gun down.

"Then . . ." I paused and gave a sharp whistle.

When it was returned in a two-beat rhythm, I exhaled. "Cory has it cleared behind us. Let's be quick in checking out the passage you two found, Uncle, and then let's get out of here."

I looked at Lucky and gave him a reassuring nod. "They found shell casings."

"Where?" Lucky asked, with a surprised glance.

Uncle Snap explained, and Lucky shook his head. "I'm impressed. Glad I made that call."

Once Cory was in front of us, we all then went to inspect the bodies. Afterward, we called in the cleaning crew, exited the premises, then went to our private apartment to rest. This shit was by no means an amateur moment. Ambush, surprise, and take down as fast as you could were the steps taken in this type of war. Whatever goods that could be found were going to do nothing but further our investigation.

Chapter 6

Claudette

It felt like the rug had been pulled out from under my feet. Everything in the room began spinning, and I found myself backing away from the couch to find a seat. The baby was Luciano's? Something in my heart began to hurt. I knew it shouldn't hurt, but it did. My big sister had effectively gutted me again.

"Right here, Mama," I heard Snap say to me.

His hand was out, and I took it. It was warm and large. Gave me a bit of stability in the moment as the light creaking of my mama's favorite chair kept me halfway in the reality I was in.

"Thank you, Raphael," I muttered, keeping my eyes on my sister. "I . . . I need you to explain to me when you both became reacquainted."

Deedee stayed standing, pressed against the wall, as she recollected her time with Luciano. "I ran into him last year in Italy. You know how I love paintings, and he happened to be there and saw me. Thought I was you from afar. We talked. Ate. Drank. Danced. Reminisced about the time you introduced us when I went with you and King to his private event at the Shabbat Museum."

"Then you two decided to screw?" I heard myself say in a strange hurt tone.

"Sis," Deedee scoffed. "It ain't like it's something we hadn't done already, and you know that. The man is fine,

always smells good, and besides, he was still heartbro-
ken over you choosing Kingston over him. So, why not
reap the benefits of a good fun time with him again? If I
can help him and receive a little money because he sees
you in me, then so what?"

My mouth dropped at the disrespect. How could she
treat that man like that? How could she treat me like
this? All I had ever done was love her while we were
growing up, but the older I'd become, the more I could
see just how selfish she really was.

"See . . . this is why we have our problems, and I just
don't understand it." I slapped my hands on the arms of
my chair. "When I kicked your low-life ass the first time
you tried Kingston, I thought you'd get it in your head to
stop trying me, but, bitch, I see you still got a lot of nerve
in you."

"Girl, get over yourself. I was drunk then." Deedee
flipped her hand in the air. "Don't make this out to be a
quarrel over some men, gal. Because this ain't what that
is. I really do care about Luciano."

As I pushed up from my chair, my face contorted into
a scowl. "Then why isn't your ignorant ass there with
him now, huh? Why run? Why hide and marry the town
pedophile?"

"He was offer'n' is why, and . . . I didn't want Luciano
to know. He still loves you, and I ain't blind to that shit.
Fun sex with him is one thing, but being locked in a
marriage with a man that loves my sister . . ."

"Please. Now you get over yaself. Luciano is an honor-
able man. He may or may not love me, but I rememba
him speaking about cha. Lovin' that ya are an artist.
Lovin' that ya were carefree . . ." My heart ached to say
these things, but they were true. Kingston was too deep
in my heart for me ever to think about leaving him for
Luciano. I had a problem with my heart. I wanted too

much. *Maybe that's why my sister left me in this town so long ago. I was greedy.*

"Hmm. Yet here you are, jealous 'bout me pulling that wealthy, sexy man." Deedee laughed. "Or are ya worried 'cus he's a big kingpin and you still want me away from that life?"

"Kiss my entire ass, Delores. All *of it,*" I spat out. "You never understood me. You left me here after lyin' 'bout brangin' me with ya, and then you turn into this otha person, hell-bent on hurting me. If you eva in your low-life life eva throw in ma face about you being pregnant, I swear on our dead daddy's and mama's graves that I'll bury you right next to them."

I was breathing so hard that I looked like a dragon. I saw red. The heat in the house due to the weather, along with my anger, had me sweating. All I wanted to do was wrap my hands around Deedee's throat right now. This wasn't how she should be treating me, but here she was, being a crass-ass piece of trash.

"Did you call me down here just to gloat, Delores?" *I needed to know. I wiped my brow. Snap still stood in between us as a buffer.*

My sister pushed away from the wall and moved toward the kitchen. "You're the only one left in the family who I knew could do what needs to be done. Lonnie is disgusting. He knew this baby wasn't his, and he married me, anyway. Said he always wanted a Haynes girl."

I felt sick. "Why, Deedee? This doesn't make any sense," *I muttered.*

"If Luciano's enemies knew that he was about to be a father, we . . ." *Deedee paused and laid a hand on her belly.* "We'd become a liability. This was the best way that I could protect us, and that's the full truth, Cece. I came back and hid. I thought I could keep Lonnie away *from the girls since everyone here was too afraid to kill him, but I was being stupid. It was about hiding, nothing else, until he put his hands on our goddaughter. I couldn't let that go."*

Tears of anger slipped down my face. My life felt flipped. I had always been the one to protect Deedee, as if I were the elder sister. Now her choices were causing problems, and I had to clean it up.

"Where he at?" I muttered low.

Deedee quietly walked to the kitchen, then came back with a cold beer, two glasses, and a pitcher of ice water. I watched her pour the clear liquid in the glasses.

"He probably knows y'all in town. Probably relieved it ain't Kingston. So, he's hiding at the bar."

I glanced at Snap, then wrapped my arms around myself. "We'll let him stew, and tomorrow he'll be handled. Then we'll go. But before that, you need to reach out to Luciano. He'll never forgive either of us if we hid his child. That man will protect you come hell or high water, and you know that I will."

"Why? Because you love him?" Deedee just had to throw digs at me.

"No. Because I'm not selfish like you." With that, I knocked over one of the glasses and walked past my sister. Stopping, I gave her a glare. "Don't bother me. I need to think."

After that, I stood in my old room, talking to Snap. "I want ya to rememba all of this, Snap. I loved my sister, but she's always been the type to reach fa the stars an' stand on whoever can get her there. It took me a long time to understand that in her an' accept it."

"Yes, ma'am, I will." Snap sat my bags down, then took his hat off and held it in his hands. "Sometimes family can be broken so bad that all ya can do is let them be how they be. Ain't nothing ya can do 'bout that."

Staring at Snap, I sighed. "My heart has always been only for Kingston. He knows everything about Luciano . . . knows I had my trysts."

"Mama . . . if you don't mind, but don't let your sista twist ya mind. That's all I'm gonna say 'bout that. The rest ain't my business. I'm just here to protect ya."

For a moment, I swore there was a flash of jealousy in his eyes. I stepped forward and laid a hand against the front of his shoulder. "And I respect that with all of me. Thank ya for being here. For a second, you were Kingston fa me. I needed someone to talk to. I'm sorry about that. You can go ahead to your room now. I know ya have ta report to King."

Snap looked down at me, then at my hand. He reached up and smoothed back some of the flyaway strands of hair around my face. "Yes, ma'am, I do." He paused, then said, "I know Boss King would want me to tell ya not to eva worry 'bout talking to me. I'll always listen to ya, Mama, always."

Snap then stepped back and went to the door. "You rest well, Mama."

"You too, Snap. Thank you again," I said, then watched him quietly close the door as I sat on the edge of the bed, tired of fighting my sister and missing my Kingston.

Chapter 7

Kingston

Something strange was going on. I couldn't put my finger on it, but the hairs standing on the back of my neck told me this meeting would be different. I, by any other words, was a made man. Born on March 20, 1945, in Mississippi, ten years after my father could no longer make a profit in sharecropping, I had learned early on that the world was no place for a person with black skin.

However, just like my father hadn't let Prohibition stop him from bootlegging, I rarely let anything stop me. When white folk hadn't wanted to give my father legal work, King Sr. had found a way around it. Daddy had been the only colored man whom the real Godfather had done business with during Prohibition.

My parents had been well connected to the Harlem underworld. I'd heard all the stories about how they had dined with the likes of St. Clair and Holstein, Harlem's top numbers racket bosses. It was as if I had been destined to be who I was. It was in my blood.

My father had been respected by the Italians, Jews, and Irish alike, something that was rare for a colored man back then. He had also passed all that knowledge down to me. While my father had been as black as the night was long, I was fair-skinned and my hair was wavy, and depending on the day, I could probably pass for Italian if my skin was pale enough. However, when I opened my mouth, everyone around knew I was a black man. The thick lips, height, build, and broad nose might have given that away, too.

My father had taught me always to carry myself like my namesake and always to take pride in my appearance.

"These white men don't respect no nigga as is, but when you do business with they kind, make sure you step into that room in ya best. Let 'em know that ya all bleed the same red blood, son. And ain't no man got no right to make another feel less than based on the color of the skin he wearing. This family done worked hard for where we are," I remembered my father saying. "And the only way we give up our claim is in a body bag. And they knows it. They won't touch us, though. We too connected. Got our hands tied to too many uppity folk."

It was that night that my father had taken me to meet James Haynes. While Daddy dealt in moonshine, rum, and hooch for mobsters like the real Godfather and Lucky Luciano, Haynes was known for his dealings with drugs. He had been moving marijuana since the thirties, supplying all the tea pads from New York to Mississippi.

That was neither here nor there. I had other things on my mind. The Commission had called a meeting with me, which was odd, considering I'd just met them during the earlier part of the month. It was rare they met so soon after another meeting. It was too risky, and I knew that. But when the Commission called, I answered. It was a part of our working relationship.

The Syndicate was my brainchild. I hadn't thought it would work at first. It had taken years of well-thought-out plans and power moves to make it work. It had started out as just an idea of mine. I had pull behind my name because of who my father had been and who we knew. It wasn't until after I met my wife and took a trip to Vegas that it all came to be.

I looked outside my office window at the kids lining up at the door. Summertime meant the end of school, and all the kids who had passed, whether it was with honors or not, knew I paid good money to see their report cards. That was the way we rolled in our community, Claudette and I. We were a staple. We made sure to put out ten times as much good as we did the bad.

We kept our heads low and our pockets fat. We did our dirt, and we made sure it never followed us home. I smiled as I watched as many as fifty kids line up outside my door. Elementary, middle school, and high school kids alike were out there. Kids of all ethnicities. Made me think about the miscarriage my wife had had a few weeks back.

It seemed that the universe didn't want me to leave a legacy behind. Sometimes it bothered me. I wanted a child, a son or a daughter. I'd give anything to have one. However, I guessed God was punishing us, me specifically. He wouldn't let my wife carry my child full term. He'd give us six to eight weeks, and then he'd rip my child right from her womb. Motherfucker.

God and I had always had a tricky relationship. If the sun was shining and I was enjoying it, the minute God knew I was enjoying it, He'd send in rain and clouds. I guess that was my penance for the dirt I'd done in my lifetime. And at forty, I'd done some shit that would offend Lucifer Morningstar himself.

I stood, then peeped out my blinds. The neighborhood was rife with life. Atlanta was a black city. We black people had made this city what it was. The sun was shining. Music blasted from someone's car. I heard an ice cream truck in the distance and knew the kids would be anxious to get their money to get to it.

The grass was green and lush. Beautiful pink, white, red, and yellow flowers had bloomed on some of the

*trees. Old man Charlie was mowing the lawn of a house
across the tracks. I pulled the timepiece from my pocket.
It was one Claudette had bought for me. I caught a
glimpse of myself in the window's reflection. My dress
slacks had been tailored to fit my tall, athletic frame.
Black suspenders lay against my white dress shirt,
the sleeves of which had been rolled up to my elbows.
Italian leather wing-tipped shoes that Claudette had
hand-stitched in Italy were on my feet. That woman
loved to dress me, and I loved to undress her. I chuckled.
Opposites attract, right?*

*Nevertheless, she hadn't called me yet, which meant
Deedee had stressed her out. I'd sent Snap with her in
hopes she wouldn't have to get her hands too dirty, but
knowing my woman the way I did, she would more than
likely get hands on. You didn't fuck with her family.*

"Shut cho black ass up," whipped me from my thoughts.

*I looked out the window and frowned. The kids all
stood in their uniforms: white collared shirts, blue skirts
for the girls, slacks for the boys, and blazers with the
school crest on them.*

*"Manuel, if you call me out my name again, I'm going
take my foot and slide it in the crack of your dusty yellow ass. You don't get to call me black like it's an insult
because you're light, bright, and damn near white."*

*"Why she always talkin' like she a white girl or sum-
min'?" I heard one of the other kids whisper.*

*Ella was a ninth-grade girl whom most young boys
didn't know what to make of. She was dark skinned and
slim, and she had long hair and light eyes, which they
had never seen on a dark-skinned girl before. She was
an anomaly to them. Manuel, a Seminole kid whose
folks lived on a nearby rez, was shooting daggers at her
like she had said something to offend him.*

"I ain't white, and you know it," he snapped at her. "And stop calling me Manuel. My father said my name is Nighthawk."

Some kids laughed, those who weren't scared to laugh. At fourteen, Manuel was as big as an ox, and he had hands the size of baseball mittens.

Ella laughed. "Ha. I'll call you Manuel until you can stop calling me black," she snapped, stepping out of line, rolling her neck.

"You black, ain't you?" he shot back.

"Yes, I am black, but you're not going to be calling me black because of my skin tone is what I mean, like it's an insult."

"Then stop telling lies."

"What lie did I tell?"

"Yo' ass ain't got no Indian in you. You black as hell."

Ella's eyes narrowed as she stepped farther out of line. She plopped her hands on her slim hips. "I've got Indian in me, and you're just going to have to accept that, Manuel," she said, slowly enunciating his name just to piss him off, I assumed.

Manuel's upper lip twitched. "You don't look like no Indian I done ever saw. The only Indian you probably done had in you has a dick attached to the end."

The kids in the line fell out laughing. Ella was embarrassed. It didn't take long for that embarrassment to turn to anger, as her eyes narrowed and her fists dropped down by her side, and rightfully so. I tilted my head to the side, my frown deepening. I was disappointed in Manuel. I expected the kind of behavior he was exhibiting from other young males, but not from one on my payroll.

"Why, you ole half-breed nigger. You think you a better Indian than me because you got damn near white skin and a mixed-ass-mutt white mama? I hate to hurt ya

feelings, brown boy, but ya pappy is a black Seminole,"
she spat. "And they probably came from Florida, where
most of the black Seminoles from the South came from.
Ya ancestors was probably slaves just like mine. I can
prove my native blood because I got descendants on
the Dawes Rolls, and my granny got her Certificate of
Degree of Indian Blood. Bet ya mutt-ass mama ain't got
that. So, if ya daddy didn't come around claiming ya,
you'd be just another mixed nigger."

It was so venomous that it made my flesh crawl.
She had spat each word through clenched teeth, and
that proper way she always spoke went right out the
window. It was kind of funny. She reminded me of my
woman when I'd first met her back in the day.

"Furthermore," Ella continued, "my Indian blood is
Cherokee and Taino. So, we royalty round these parts.
If anybody betwixt us is more Indian than the next, it
would be my black ass, freedman."

"Betwixt," another kid repeated, looking around,
confused.

Another kid asked, "Does she mean Twix?"

"Like the candy?" someone else shouted.

"Shut up," Manuel warned as he stepped closer to her.

"Who gon' make me?" Ella said, taking a step closer to
him.

I noticed her sleight of hand, too. She had gone into
her carrying bag and had come back out with a switch-
blade. She whipped that motherfucker so beautifully
that it swooshed and clinged in the air, making music
as she readied for war. I laughed to myself. I knew
my woman's soldiers when I saw them. That was all
Claudette's training right there.

By now, the whole neighborhood was looking on.
Some of my men were leaning against cars, laughing,
while others in the town were either shaking their heads
or outright trying to egg them on.

Manuel growled out, "You shut cho' lying ass up before I cave ya mouth in."

He made the mistake of getting too close to the girl, and for his mistake, she whipped the knife back and forth like she was Zorro, causing the other kids to scatter.

Manuel stopped, faked left, and tried to move right, but Ella stayed right with him.

"I ain't scared of you, Manuel. I'll slice your throat, so the only way you can breathe is out ya asshole, nigga," Ella threatened. "I ain't one of these little boys you can beat down. Run up."

A chorus of "Oh shit" rang out.

My back door opened, and one of my men came running in. "Ah, boss, you see this?" Cleophus asked.

"I see it," I said without turning to look at him.

"You want us to stop it?"

I didn't answer him. Was too busy watching Manuel fake left again. Only this time, when Ella thought he was coming from the right, he stayed left and smacked the girl so hard, the crowd gasped.

"I said shut up, bitch," Manuel yelled.

He'd been hanging around his father too much. That drunk-ass Indian was teaching his son all the wrong shit. I'd have to reprogram one of my best fighters once again. Ella went down to the ground, but she hopped right back up. She removed the strap of her carrying bag from around her neck and shoulders, then dropped the bag to the ground. Her schoolbooks came sliding out.

She kicked off her shoes, then touched her mouth. She was bleeding. Manuel had made the mistake of thinking Ella was one of the regular neighborhood girls. Just like Ella didn't know Manuel worked for me, Manuel didn't know Ella worked for Claudette.

Tears flowed down her dark cheeks. Her hair blew in the wind as she balled one fist. It was her turn to *fake left, only when she did it, she took a running leap to the left and ended up to the right, with her fist in the air. Manuel was watching the knife in her right hand, totally missing the blade in the left. She sliced him across his face good.*

"Holy shit," Cleophus said behind me.

I'd seen enough. I raised the blinds so all the kids could finally see me. I nodded for my men to move in just as Ella was about to try to make good on her threat of slicing the boy's throat. I didn't think Manuel had taken the girl serious. She'd come from a bad home. I remembered her telling Claudette that before she allowed another man to lay hands on her in such a way, she'd kill him. At such a young age, no young girl should have had to think that way.

Once the kids saw me, all their cheering and boisterous laughter stopped. They each stood up to their full height and got back to their best behavior.

About five of my men were trying to hold back fourteen-year-old Manuel—who was just as big as they were—while three more were trying to get ahold of Ella and her knives.

"I will kill you, nigga!" *she yelled, spittle and blood flying from her lips.*

Her eyes were wild, and sweat made strings of her hair stick to her face. She looked like a madwoman. I slapped the window once, and they both turned to look at me. Instantly, their madness stopped. Manuel took a deep breath and yanked away from my men, getting himself together. Ella's eyes widened, and she stopped struggling. She let Denton, another one of my men, take her knives as she righted herself and stood still.

I moved from the window to open the door. I stepped out onto the porch, and my eyes landed on Manuel first. The noise and the ruckus that had been going on before were no more. It was as quiet as it was hot, and it was hotter than fish grease in hell.

"What in hell is wrong with you?" I asked, my question directed at Manuel.

He frowned, then dropped his head before looking back at me. Blood was leaking down the side of his face. I turned to Ella.

"And I'm sure Claudette would be real proud," I said to her.

Her shoulders slumped, and she turned into the little girl she was as she twiddled her thumbs.

"You two, in my office, now," I ordered.

Ella hurriedly snatched up her bag and shoes, then rushed by me into my office. Manuel followed. Once they were inside, I gave all the other children stern glares, which they knew showed my disappointment at the way they'd decided to act as well. Still, I took the time to look at each and every report card and to reward them accordingly. I'd never seen a bunch of happier children. That made my heart smile.

Once back in my office, I handed Manuel a bucket of cleaning supplies. He looked peeved.

"I'm tempted to cancel your fight next week," I said to him. "Behaving like a common thug isn't how I like the young men on my payroll to represent me."

Manuel's face went slack; then his jaw became set in stone. Disappointment was etched all across his features. The boy liked to fight. It was all in his DNA. I'd seen Manuel, at fourteen, put a full-grown man on his ass. So, in order to keep him out of trouble, I put him in the ring. He hadn't lost me a fight since I'd been sponsoring him.

"I'm sorry, King, but she—"

"A man should never do what?"

"Pick on a defenseless woman, but she wasn't defen—"

"The merit of a man is his ability to do what, Nighthawk?"

"The merit of a man is his ability to take ownership of his own bullshit, sir," he said in a low voice.

"So, that means what?"

"Not making excuses for my deplorable actions, sir."

"After you clean yourself up, I expect the basement to be spick and span by the end of the night."

Manuel looked at me with pleading eyes. I knew that plea was for me not to cancel his fight. He'd been training hard for it for the past four months. A boy out of New York wanted to fight him. The purse was already set at seventy grand. He turned to head to the bathroom.

"Manuel," I called out.

He stopped, then turned. "Yessir?"

"You forgetting something?"

He turned to Ella, then said, "I'm sorry for putting my hands on you. A man should never hit a woman unless he has no choice but to defend himself as such."

"And you make sure to bring something out of that bathroom to help her clean her lip up too," I said to him as he walked away.

I turned to Ella and found her smirking at Manuel.

"And Claudette taught you to behave as a wild banshee?" I asked.

"N-no, sir," she said.

"She teach you to be slanging that damn blade like you a samurai?"

"Well, sir, if the time calls for it, yes, she did," Ella answered honestly.

"And the time called for it?"

"That big nigga was after me. I'd say so, sir."

"The merit of a woman is her ability to do what, Ella?"

Her shoulders slumped. She wasn't so confident now. "The merit of a woman is her ability to walk away from conflict, sir."

"So, you mean to tell me you couldn't have walked away from that conflict long before it became an all-out war?"

"I could have, but he—"

"A woman," I said, gazing at Ella, knowing she knew what I was about to say.

She finished my sentence for me. "Never makes excuses for her bad behavior. She accepts the consequences of her actions all the while mentally pledging to do better next time, if there is to be a next time."

"I expect you and Manuel to work together to get that basement cleaned, and you will allow him to patch up your lip. Are we clear?"

Ella's lips pressed into a thin line. Her eyes narrowed as she crossed her arms across her chest. Her annoyance didn't move me. I sent her to the bathroom with Manuel, knowing the storm had subsided. I chuckled to myself while going to sit down.

I rolled my shoulders, trying to stave off the chills running up and down my back. The day felt odd for some reason. Something just didn't feel right. Maybe it was the fact that I still felt it peculiar that the Commission had called a meeting with me again. Maybe it was the fact that my woman was in Creek Town without me. Either way, something felt off, and I couldn't shake it.

I pulled down my ledger and double-checked my numbers. All my shipments were in check. All members of the Syndicate were accounted for. We'd just had our annual meeting, where we all sat down and talked about where we wanted to take the Syndicate next. The Irish were giving me a bit of a problem, but nothing that couldn't be handled in-house. Monies had been divvied up. Everyone's pockets were fat. Product was up; arrests were down. Pipelines were clean and clear.

Quite frankly, it had been one of the best years the Syndicate had seen. . . .

And yet there was a monkey on my back today that I just couldn't shake. I picked up the phone to dial my wife. The phone at her parents' home rang three times before someone answered.

"Hello," Deedee barked into the phone.

Being that she had an attitude, I knew shit hadn't gone smoothly.

"I'd like to speak to my wife," I said, wanting to keep the conversation with her short.

"I'd like a few million fucking dollars and a new life. We can't all get what we want," she replied sarcastically.

"Put my wife on the phone, Deedee."

"And if I don't?"

"I'm going to have my man Snap put a bullet in your asshole."

"Ugh," she spat into the phone.

Disgust had been ladled all in her response. I didn't give a shit. The woman got on my nerves, and the only reason I tolerated her was for my wife.

"Claudette, the uncouth nigga you married is on the phone," Deedee yelled.

A few seconds later, the beautiful sound of my wife's voice came through the line. "Baby. King, everything okay?" she asked.

Her voice was strained, and that alarmed me. "Don't worry about me. You okay? Do you need me to come? Because I can lock it all down and come to you."

"No, no. Don't leave your post. I'm . . . I'll be okay. Just . . . damn Deedee done brought that goddamn child-molesting pedophile into my family. And she's pregnant, King. She's pregnant."

"By that clown?"

"No." She got quiet, which told me there was something more to this story.

"By who, baby?" I asked her.

"Luciano."

It was my turn to get quiet. It was no secret that Luciano and my wife had dallied a few times before I made her my wife. The slick-tongued Italian was still after her, so the fact that he went after what he considered the next best thing didn't surprise me.

I didn't like to hear her stressed. It crushed my soul the way those folk back in Creek Town could suck the vibrancy right out of her. Her family was a pack of toxic leeches. I knew telling her about what Deedee's husband had done to Toya would send her running down there, but she loved that little girl, even when Toya, just like Deedee, would do everything in her power to spit in my queen's face.

"Well, I guess you're going to hear about it sooner or later," I said.

"Hear about what, King?" Claudette asked.

"We had an all-out war between the Cherokee/Taino and the Seminole out here today," I said, changing the subject to take Claudette's mind off the bullshit she had walked into.

"Huh? Say wha—" she said, then stopped. "Oh, sweet Mary's virgin ass, did Ella and Manuel have a fight?"

I laughed. "Indeed."

I did a rundown of what had happened and the words that had been exchanged. By the time I was done, Claudette was laughing and threatening me to keep my mannish boys from her girls at the same time.

"Oh, no, Ella didn't say that to that boy," she cried in a fit of laughter.

"Oh yeah, Mama, she said it. That gal a wildcat, cha? You need to get a handle on your girls, running around

here, slanging knives and threatening to have folk breathe through their assholes and shit."

"As soon as you get Nighthawk from around his drunk daddy on that damn rez. If that boy had respected my little queen, none of this would have happened."

"Naw. I'm of the mind she baited him in. Everyone around here know how sensitive Manuel is about his Native heritage."

"What's that got to do with hot piss on a tin roof?"

"All these little black girls with long hair claim they got Indian in their family."

"And Ella actually does."

I smiled, loving to hear that I could change my wife's mood in a split second. I had called to tell her about the meeting with the Commission, but as soon as I'd heard the stress in her voice, I'd changed my mind. Telling her about the meeting would have only set her nerves on end, like it had mine.

Her happiness was short lived, though.

In the background, I heard a ruckus, and then Snap said, "Mama, you'd better get out here."

"Why? What's happening? Why is Deedee screaming like that?" she asked him.

"Toya coming down the street. She beat up real bad," he said.

I heard when the phone hit the floor. I knew Claudette was gone before Snap picked up the phone.

"Boss," he said.

"Yeah, son?"

"Knew she was talking to you by the smile on her face."

I chuckled inwardly, then asked, "How bad is it down there?"

"We're going to need to call the police," he said.

That was code for Claudette was going to have to kill someone.

"You just make sure no harm come to my woman, Snap."

"Yes, sir."

I hung up the phone, hating that I hadn't got to tell Claudette I loved her.

Chapter 8

Uncle Snap

I looked at Javon once we had made it back to the hospital and had some alone time. He had King's journal in his hand. I ran my hand through my hair, crossed, then uncrossed my arms.

"We kinda ran through Cavriel's place real reckless, nephew. You got a reason for that?" I asked him.

"Reckless?"

"Yeah. We ran through there like Wild Bill, scraped up some shell casing, and that was that. We didn't really look around for no clues or nothing that may have pointed to who did it or even who took Absolan. Just kind of went in, shot shit up, and moved out."

Javon closed the book, crossed one leg over the other, then studied me. "So even after this whole time, even after I've proven to be an effective leader, you still doubt me, Unc?"

"Not doubting you, nephew. It's because you've proven to be effective that I'm asking the method to your madness, is all. It's not like you to be so haphazard."

"Then if you know there's always a method to my madness, you should be comfortable with what I did today."

I couldn't say anything there. He had called me on my bullshit. I was about to tell him as much until Deedee walked in. She had a girl who looked like she could be Lucky's sister in tow. Beautiful girl of mixed race. You know, typical mixed-looking chick. Nothing really special about her looks. But she had her eyes set on Javon.

"This is my daughter, Lucky's sister," Deedee said. "Giana Monroe Acardi is her name."

I rolled my fucking eyes. She was so proud of her fucking self, birthing Luciano Acardi's kids.

Javon gave me a look that told me to keep cool. Giana, in her painted-on leather tights, thigh-high boots, and thin blouse, sauntered over to Javon.

She extended her hand and said, "Hello, Javon."

Javon looked at her hand but not at her. "We've met," was all he said. He didn't take her hand, though, which surprised me. Nephew was normally about decorum.

Giana was caught off guard and clearly taken aback by his rudeness. She said, "Yes, we have. Last time you were visiting Uncle Luci."

"Good. You remember. So, let's get this little game out the way," he said, closing the journal and putting it back in the inner breast pocket of his jacket.

"I have a wife who can shoot at a ninety degree around a corner, blindfolded," he said to Giana, then looked at Deedee. "You don't want those kinds of problems on your ass, so don't come offering me your daughter. Shanelle will shoot, and she will shoot to kill. I don't want to be on the end of her wrath, so I don't have shit to offer your daughter, not even dick."

Deedee took an offended step back, then gave a slow blink. "Why, I never," she gasped.

"And neither you nor your daughter ever will," Javon said, then stood. "Let's go, Unc."

I shot daggers at Deedee with my eyes, then followed my nephew.

"You are disrespectful, just like King and Snap. How fitting she'd pick a male orphan like the husband she got killed," Deedee spat at our backs.

Javon stopped, took a deep breath, then turned around. By now, Lucky had heard his mother's loud-ass mouth and stepped outside of the Old Italian's room.

"What's going on?" Lucky asked. "Ma, you okay?"

"Why did you bring them here?" she asked her son.

"Uncle Luci asked for them, Ma. They're good men. They can help us find out who did this."

"They have no couth."

"She just tried to offer me your sister, and I have no couth?" Javon said, sarcasm in his tone.

Giana cut in. "She was introducing me to him. Nothing more."

Deedee twisted her mouth. "I should have known anything Toya bred would—"

"Why didn't you come to her funeral?" I asked.

She turned to me. "What?"

"Why didn't you come to your sister's funeral?"

Deedee opened her mouth. She looked like a damn fish as she tried to talk and nothing came out.

"Sister," Lucky repeated.

The boy looked as confused as his sister.

Deedee, looked at her children, specifically her son, then back at me. "You know she wouldn't have wanted me there," she said.

"You lying sack of shit," I spat out at her. "She still loved your conniving ass, even after all you'd done to her."

Deedee drew in a hard breath. "You've got some fucking nerve when you're the one who brought her goddamn killer in her house. *You*, Raphael, are the reason she's dead."

It was no guess how she knew that, since Lucky had been the one to help take down Elias, the man who had helped Melissa kill Mama.

"Ma, chill," Lucky said.

He, his sister, and his mother went back and forth at one another in Italian, while Javon placed himself strategically in front of me. He knew anger simmered just underneath my skin. I knew he could feel the anger and angst seething just below my surface. What Deedee had said had been eating me alive since the moment I found out it was Melissa who'd helped to orchestrate her death.

"Move outside, Uncle Snap," Javon said.

I didn't give him any lip. I was quite sure I'd embarrassed him and myself enough.

"You're letting your emotions get the better of you," he said once we were in a secluded area. "Since you handed me King's journal, you've been going through something. Whatever it is, squash it until we're back on home turf. Will you do that for me?"

I grunted my response.

Javon chuckled. I didn't know why he chuckled. I couldn't read his body language. "Did you know King had a meeting with the Commission on the day he died?" he asked me out of the blue.

I frowned "Huh? No."

I thought back to all those years ago, to the day Mama and I went to Creek Town to take care of Toya's rapist. That wouldn't have made any sense. The Commission and the Syndicate had already had their annual summit. Wouldn't make a lick of sense for them to call a meeting with the Syndicate again so soon. I told Javon as much.

"You didn't really read his journal, did you, Unc?" he asked.

"I started it but couldn't finish. Too many memories with him and Claudette. Too many memories of my old mentor. Shit got me fucking emotional," I finally confessed.

"It's right in his journal. I started from his last pages. He said the Commission called a meeting, and just like you, he was confused by it."

"That makes no fucking sense," I said.

"King's murder was never solved, right?"

"No. We knew someone did it, but even after we wreaked havoc all over the States to find out who had done it, we never did."

"Who has enough power to cover their asses so thoroughly, Unc?"

I took a step back as the reality slammed into my chest like a head-on collision. "No . . . you don't think . . .you don't think the Commission . . ."

That shit sobered me right on up. Would Luciano be so cruel as to kill Mama's husband, my mentor, just to get another shot at being with her? As far as I knew, King was in good standing with the Commission, so why would they kill him? Although, King had been a black man with a lot of power. That made the establishment nervous.

He gave King's journal in his pocket a tap. "Cavriel's murder isn't the only one I plan to solve. We find Absolan, and then we get these old heads to tell us who killed King, or I'll dismantle the Commission from the inside out."

Chapter 9

Cory

"Sir, we have activity."

I held my hand out and was immediately presented with a tablet. By my side was one of my Forty Thieves. This one was a Korean brotha with a spiked fade, and he was in all black from his boots to his gloves. On the side of his neck, curling under his ear, was a tattoo that rivaled my own. He was called Sino and was our lead bodyguard.

Moving the tablet in front of me, I scanned the video before me, swiping and tapping on the screen to change the visual perspective. My brother was a madman, and like a moth to a flame, our ambush drew out the one we were looking for—the goons who were working for whoever had gunned for the Commission.

"Just like magic," I said with a smirk. As I exited the hospital and walked toward the ride I had requested, I continued watching the video. "Kind of sloppy of them, huh?"

"Indeed, sir, but when the hired help is sloppy, it makes it easy for us to determine several things. One, whether it's a trap. Two, they want to know who had taken out their men. And three, whether it is a decoy."

An amused chuckle made me look up at the brother who was part of our team. "What you determined Luciano's men to be?"

Sino gave a shadow of a smile. "For now, they appear as loyal as ever. No stench of disloyal behaviors is kicking off, sir. However, that doesn't mean a damned thing."

"No doubt. An old lesson well learned." With a sigh, I handed the tablet back and folded my arms over my chest. "A trail has been put on them?"

"Yes, sir."

Rubbing my jaw, I continued processing. My mind was on the shell casings, but also on the need to get back to Carviel's. We had rushed out as fast as we had only because of the attention brought our way, which was purposeful, but we still needed more than what we had.

"Good. How is the search going in the empty building across the street? You all followed my report?"

Sino gave me another nod. "I have a few combing through the tunnels. So far, no footprints or anything out of order, but we are still investigating and have breached Carviel's home, per your request, sir."

This was why I was Von's shadow and part of his security. I realized the importance, the gravity of my role after almost dying. When Von needed additional hands, I'd be that, and so I was. It was part of the plan, and I intended to sniff around while others thought we were distracted.

"A'ight, keep me abreast of everything. If anything seems shifty, contact me immediately."

"Yes, sir." Sino gave the Forty Thieves a nod of respect, then left the hospital.

As for myself, I moved back to the secret bunker hospital. I had been given a time line of who all had been around Absolan before he disappeared. In the notes, it was reported that Absolan had been about his regular routine: spending time at his favorite spa, making his rounds in the community, giving prayers and seeing what was needed, and overseeing the usual confession.

The name Paulo Begetti was also on the list. From what was written, Paulo was Absolan's transport man and ran a deli in the priest's zone. He had been the one to alert

Lucky that Absolan was missing. However, there were some time inconsistencies, and from what my crew had found out from a little digging into some cameras around the way, it looked like Paulo might have some dealings with the actual kidnappers. On the camera footage, they had seen two goons, who we had killed at Cavriel's home, exiting the deli.

Something to report to Von. I quietly walked in thought, going over in my head why Absolan had been left alive but taken. Why hadn't any piece of him shown up? It wasn't sitting right with me.

"But she's your sister, Mama. You and the old man didn't feel it important enough to tell me? Especially after I put my life on the line for . . . for basically family?"

I stopped in my tracks at the sound of Lucky's voice. From where I stood, it sounded like some truths had finally come out, and since it wasn't any of my business, a nigga walked on and sought out my uncle and brother.

Finding them didn't take long. Von was on his phone, pacing back and forth. When I heard Shanelle's name, I relaxed.

"Unc Snap." I strolled up to the OG, then pulled up a chair to sit in front of him as he sat just outside the cafeteria at the hospital. Even though it was a new day, no one had gotten any real sleep after last night. "I need your help."

I figured Uncle Snap needed this distraction, because as I looked him in his eyes, I could tell that his mind was far away.

"What you need, nephew?"

Damn, his voice was groggy.

"Since the castings are being analyzed, you know I'm having the Forty T sweep all the houses except Absolan's residence."

"And why is that?" Uncle Snap asked.

"It's a hot spot that needs to be monitored, not swept through. Not until we get our hands on some bastards who will talk," I explained. "But I'm working on that, Unc. So check it. I was going through some things, and Absolan had a routine. I was in my head, thinking that we retrace his steps, and by we, I mean you and I."

"Hmm . . ." Uncle Snap rubbed his chin in thought. "What's these spots?"

Now, we were getting to some shit. I leaned back in my chair and pulled out the intel sheets. "Let me see. He hit up his church shit and was running that. Two black mofos walking up in his church ain't going to work, so I'm sending some of our inconspicuous people up in there."

"A'ight, nephew." Uncle Snap chuckled. "Go on."

"So, you and I can hit up a couple of his favorite spots. He wasn't known to hit up the chess spots like Cavriel, but the fact that he liked to hit up the spa lets me know he had some other vices outside of being a mobster."

Rolling around NYC as two black men, one older, I knew that whatever we did, we had to make sure we knew what areas we had flexibility in and what areas we didn't. Commission or not, you rolled up in the wrong spot and it could be lights out or you'd be locked up. So a brotha had to think this shit out. Whoever was able to get to Absolan had to have some form of privilege where he or she was able to move in his zone in a cloak of invisibility. Which meant I had an idea that whoever had him wasn't a person of color.

"You sure, nephew?"

"Yeah, all I need to do is get close enough to the spots that have Wi-Fi, and I can hack into the shop's security."

"And then I can get in old school. Be slick about how we ask questions and then walk out."

I looked at Uncle Snap with a grin. "Exactly."

The OG leaned so that his arms sat on his knees, and then he reached into his jacket and pulled out a flask of what I knew was moonshine. He unscrewed the silver top, then took a swig. The scent burned my nose hairs as he said, "Then let's get into some fun, nephew."

Shit must have tasted like water for the old head, because he downed that gulp with no flinching or anything. I remembered how I used to drink like that. But now I knew I couldn't even risk a taste of anything, for fear of it triggering my addiction. The thought took my mind to Inez. I knew Shanelle would keep her leveled out. I hadn't called her. Didn't want to stress her out. We'd learned in our addiction meetings that stress was a trigger. I didn't want to risk it. Loved her too much.

"Yessir, and maybe Von will turn over stones as he does his thang as well." I glanced toward my brother and noticed him coming our way. "Everything good with Shanelle?"

"For now, yeah. The house is protected. Jojo is still closed off, but outside of that, she's holding it down," Von explained. "We need to get through this shit as quickly as possible. Let me run down some things me and Unc were talking about."

"A'ight, I'm listening."

I sat there as he told me about how some shit in Pop King's journal wasn't lining up. Compound that with what was going on now with the Commission, and to me, shit seemed suspect for sure. I guessed this go-round in NYC, we were going to be helping out the OGs and those from the past to salvage the foundation. Otherwise, more troubles would be coming our way.

Chapter 10

Javon

A lot of things weren't making sense to me, and I hated to be placed into a situation where the mastermind behind all the madness thought we were stupid motherfuckers. That insulted my intelligence. It insulted my interest. It also insulted the time I had put out there. So, after flipping through the journal in my hand, I tucked it away, then exhaled and tapped my foot against the knuckles of a man who was testing my everlasting nerve.

"Paulo. That's your name, correct?" My gaze scanned the urban skyline that was Queens. The sun was bright, though chilly weather encapsulated us. It caused our breath to vaporize into steam and leave nice little clouds in the air as I spoke and Paulo frantically panted.

"Yes. I . . . I don't know nothin', man . . . nothin', understand? I was just checking out his groceries, as usual, and walking them to his home. That's on everything."

A simple crate sat under me, while my dark jean-clad leg was stretched out, crushing Paulo's hand. I had on a tailored black overcoat that had a black hoodie lining. The hood covered my head, and the tails of the coat were parted, because I was leaning forward. My hands were covered in black leather driving gloves, and the black boots I had chosen to wear were causing hell, thanks to the waffle bottoms.

"No doubt. I believe you, Paulo. I do." My brother had pulled through on his surveillance. "But you were the last person to see him, correct?"

Paulo was stretched out wide on top of his grocery store roof, as if being prepped to be tarred and feathered. Lucky stood to the left of Paulo's body and was chewing on a Twizzler while slowly walking back and forth with his hands in his pockets.

"Several men linked to working with the kidnappers were also seen exiting your deli," Lucky said as he strolled up to a stretched-out Paulo. He squatted near him, then hit him in the face with his Twizzler. "Have you lost your loyalty to us, Paulo? Or were they scoping out Absolan's places?" That Twizzler tapped against Paulo's jaw in tandem as Lucky taunted the shaking and anxious man. "What did you see that you aren't saying, my friend?"

I gave a deep chuckle and pressed my foot down harder, until Paulo screamed. Lucky was fucking with Paulo , seeing if the man was broken enough to spill out anything.

"Please don't kill me. Please. I have a family," Paulo pleaded.

The sky was a light gray. The smell of incoming snow had birds fluttering above us in confusion. Cars zipped around, and people walked around without knowing what was going down on the rooftops above them. The occasional scent of food and coffee mixed with the smell of trash and of the onset of winter.

Only texting with my brother and watching Lucky toy with the man before me kept me entertained. From what I was reading, Uncle Snap had Cory shuffling around, as if they were Jehovah's Witnesses passing around the Watchtower. It was a good ploy and a good cloaking mechanism. Judging from the texts that had been sent, Paulo had given the men only sandwiches and whatever else they had ordered, which meant that only the deli had been scoped out and nothing more.

"We all have families, my man, but what that gotta do with a piss in the wind?" I pointed down to where a large wet spot had formed under Paulo. I spun my cell in between my hands and kept cool. This dude was an interesting type, which meant to me that he wasn't a goon of any importance.

"T-this is all I know. I . . . I transport Absolan, and I bring whatever meals or necessities he needs." Paulo spoke the words between the chatterings of his teeth. "I . . . I don't know nothin' 'bout no other goons, on my word. On my family."

Lucky circled Paulo. "I know that you've been questioned already, but tell us, did you see anything odd or questionable in your time working with Absolan leading up to his disappearance and after?"

"N-no. I had ma brotha take ova the counter. I packed up his favorite minestrone soup, a pastrami sammie, some pastries, and a coffee." Paulo turned his head to try to look at us both through his swollen eyes. "I then went next door to grab his groceries. Then I walked out. Saw nothing that day. Was stone quiet. Yeah . . . yeah . . . I rememba thinkin' that was strange, 'cus we ain't never had a quiet block round his home."

"And you saw nothing?" Lucky asked quickly.

"N-no. Nothin.' Hand ta God," Paulo squeaked.

"Shame, because I've seen this before." Lucky pushed at Paulo's waist, making him turn to show me a crest on the flank of his back. "Been seein' that pop up a lot now."

I leaned and then tilted my head to the side. My gaze went to Lucky, and the look on my face said, "This motherfucker right here."

Paulo began rambling. "That? That ain't nothing. I-it's just an order, something to protect our neighborhood. Yeah. Nothing that's a threat, I promise." Paulo pressed his hands together and shook his head.

"Paulo, Paulo. See, I'm inclined to believe you, because we all have families, ya know, but, ah, because of how I grew up, I've heard about the Knights of St. Assisi, who are associated with, eh . . . the Vatican. Something that was once linked to Absolan." Lucky scratched the side of his jaw, looking like *The Thinker*. "If my history is correct."

In the research I did when I first came into everything, I had learned that the Knights of St. Assisi were a sect of goons who were like the Forty Thieves. Professional muscle used by those connected to the Vatican, and overseen by Absolan himself, before they were dismantled. According to rumors, they lost themselves in an excess of greed, counterfeiting, trafficking, and a shitload of murder and mayhem.

The fact that the Knights' emblem was on Paulo was interesting. The second fact that we had learned earlier in the day was that a specific type of shell casing associated only with the Knights had been found in Cavriel's home. It was that crest, with its rearing horse and a multitude of crosses, that made me finish texting everything that we had just learned, then stand to shift my foot and press it against Paulo's throat.

"Now . . ." I tucked my cell in my coat. Looked around while pushing my sleeves up and talking nonchalantly. "If we were to exhume the bodies of the men we saw entering your deli, would we find that same harmless crest on them?"

"God," Paulo grunted. Spittle flew everywhere. He gritted his teeth as tears slipped down his face.

"Would we?" I asked, pressing.

"N-n-yes. God, yes!"

I looked at Lucky; then he thumbed his nose. In a flash, his gun was out and was pointing at Paulo's skull. "I hate fucking liars."

Without blinking, Lucky pulled the trigger. It was a clean shot between the eyes. Shock frozen in eternal rest was on Paulo's face.

"Round up Paulo's brother Frankie," Lucky ordered. "If he's suspiciously disappeared, grab the kids, grab the mother, cousins, aunts, uncles, friends, and so on, and end their lives."

One of the Forty Thieves with us gave a quick nod, then disappeared.

Stepping over Paulo's body, I slipped my hands in my coat pockets. "It's like that?" I asked while looking out at the view.

"Can't be nothing else but that." Lucky was looking in the opposite direction as we stood shoulder to shoulder. "A king's descent was put out on us. The Knights are a part of that. Therefore, cousin, what they put on us, we put on them in return."

I turned my head and looked at the side of Lucky's face. Dude had a skull cap on that obscured his face. His jaw was clenched tight, as was his posture. Shit was like looking in a mirror with how I was a year ago. Lucky was a nigga hell bent on extracting vengeance and protecting his pops. I didn't blame him, not a bit.

If people could be reincarnated, then on my life, the way Lucky spoke made me think of Kingston. A light chuckle came from me as I thought of that, because if reincarnation was real, then King would be a spiteful motherfucker in this current life if he came back through Lucky. It would be fitting as well.

"What do you know about the summer of nineteen eighty-five?"

Lucky gave me a look of curiosity. "Not a damn thing, other than that being around the time King died, right? I was born five months later as well."

"The old man talk about that time to you yet?"

"Naw, but he needs to, considering what I know now, cousin," Lucky said with a slight tinge of abrasiveness to his voice.

"Yeah, I said as much to him when I found out yesterday." I added emphasis to the word *yesterday* to let the nigga know that he had to chill with me and that family secrets seemed to hit me last minute as well.

"What's your angle?" Lucky asked me, turning to slide his hands in his pockets.

All this shady shit had me thinking, could I go there with Lucky? Revealing a little crumb while holding back my true agenda wasn't nothing to me. I just needed to shape that shit to work out in favor of family first. Mama's and now King's words were teaching me that.

"Don't have one." We both moved to allow Paulo's body to be removed. We then headed down from the roof. "But like you, I'm being hit with a lot of history." I paused on the steps and looked at him. "History that feels like it's repeating itself."

"What do you mean?"

I cracked my neck as we walked. "Just that last time a nigga went missing, he ended up dead in a fire, body burnt to toast, and all due to a call to meet with the Commission."

"Hold up." Lucky grabbed my arm.

I looked down at it and up at him slowly, which had him drop his hold quickly.

"My bad, but, ah, explain that last part, okay?" he said.

"Nothing to explain, yet," I coolly stated. "Just some shady shit that I'm noticing that is familiar to me. Like these Knights."

"Were they around back then?" I heard Lucky ask me.

A quick glance Lucky's way had us stopping directly in front of our ride. "I don't know, cousin. Were they? Might need to have that talk with your pops about that time, including the ins and outs of your birth, I'm just saying. These old heads did a lot of shit that we're just finding out. And it's shit that shaped the very foundation of both our united groups, and our lives, man. Don't you have questions?"

I watched Lucky stand in a stoic silence. His jaw twitched while he studied me, deep in thought. Again, it was like some mirror shit. A cool chill whipped around us. We both quietly climbed into our unassuming ride, an everyday SUV. Appearances were everything when playing invisible. Once we had sat down and the SUV had pulled off, the change in Lucky's body language answered all my own inner questions.

Dude had just had weight dropped on him, and like I'd had to when I first came in, Lucky now had to assess his entire world.

"Yeah, I have questions."

Resting my arm on my knee, I watched the streets while Lucky drove. "Now answer me this. When you find out what you need to know, how will your loyalty go?"

"Man, I don't even know, Von."

Lucky was watching the lights, while gripping the steering wheel.

"Are we good? That's all I need to know, because there's shit I gotta find out as well," I explained.

"We're good, especially when ya unc keeps a closed mouth around my mother."

I chuckled at that shit. "As you learned, they have history, history deeper than the two of us. Can't do shit about it but make sure neither draws on the other."

"True that." Lucky stretched a fist out and slammed it on the roof. "So, you think the Knights might have taken out King in the name of the Commission?"

"Didn't say all of that, but I am noticing some patterns. The Commission was good to King, as far as I know, but some funky shit did occur around the time they reached out for an unplanned meeting. Kinda like was done to me and my fam during our shit."

"A'ight." Lucky rubbed his hands together, then gripped the wheel again. "Well, let's get the universe to unravel some more knowledge for us. Case in point, since the Knights seem to be our lead in finding Absolan, who the fuck pulled them outta retirement?"

"Time to find that out. Maybe Frankie got the answers." I sent a text to Cory, then sat back in thought while relaying coded information to Cory and Uncle Snap. Heavy was the head that wore the crown.

Sweat dripped from my chin to the floor. The room I was in smelled of must, mildew, burning flesh, and something like the scent of an electric current. I stood saturated in my own sweat. Spatters of blood decorated my tank and gray sweatpants. My knuckles were covered in bloody bandages wrapped in thumbtacks, metal screws, and sharp nails.

"*Kuya*, hit that current in his ear." By *ear*, I meant the gaping wound on the side of Frankie's head where his ear used to be.

Cory sat on a crate by Frankie's swinging body, with a pair of jumper cables in his gloved hands.

"No," Frankie screamed, pulling at the chain that he was hanging from, arms pointing to the ceiling. That rattling chain was wrapped around his wrists and his neck. His body was covered in bruises and cuts from where my fists had met his flesh. His ribs had cracked from the force of my punches.

"Oh, now you hear me, nigga," I spat out, tired of working this fucker up. "Now we can get somewhere, correct?"

"Or does my friend have to slice another appendage from your body?" Lucky stood face-to-face with a hanging Frankie. His face was covered in blood, and in his hand was a butcher blade. "Matter of fact . . ."

Lucky reached his hand out and snapped, motioning to one of his men who held a tablet. "You bastards want to wipe out my line without consequences? Huh?"

"Oh no . . . no . . . come on, man," Frankie cried as he looked at the tablet. On it was Paulo's family and Frankie's.

It was apparent that the nigga was heartbroken by the way his face was a ruddy color, but when it darkened and his face contorted, I knew the real deal was climbing to the surface.

"*Fotti tua madre,*" Frankie spat out in fury at the scene of his wife being shot. "And ya family, ya fucking mook. Ain't nothin' that you can do to me. You fucking mutt will be cleansed from this earth, and with it, everyone that accepted you on our throne."

Sinister laughter came from Frankie. "I sliced that Jewish bastard's throat. Watched him look at me in surprise over it. Know why? Because I had gotten in where no one could. The Commission will fall, and once we're done, we'll move on to the rest of you niggers."

Lucky tilted his head to the side, looking disinterested. "Oh, is that what this is? You tell me to fuck my mother, then throw in the racial cleansing bullshit as icing?"

Cold as ice, Lucky leaned in toward Frankie. He spoke low against Frankie's ear. "*No mi interessa un cazzo, puttana.* My blood comes from survivors and adapters. My family will always come back and each time erase you bastards. So thank you for exposing yourselves. That's all I wanted, *figa.* Light him up."

A smirk spread across my face. I dropped into a squat near my brother as he muttered, "That ninja is crazy as shit."

I gave a nod and pressed my hands together, watching. "Just like us, huh?"

"Every bit as crazy as us, *kuya*. But check it. What did he say?"

Cory had humor behind his eyes, I guessed to stave off the intensity of this situation. He calmly looked Frankie in his eyes, then tapped the charges together before pressing them against the man's flesh.

Screams rent the room. Behind me Uncle Snap sat watching with a dazed look in his eyes. It was as if he wasn't here, but when he said, "He said that he didn't give a fuck, nephew, and called the bastard a whore and a pussy," I realized that he *was* here. And I realized something else.

"You can speak Italian?"

Uncle Snap glanced at Lucky for a moment, then pushed off against the wall. "Consigned myself to learnin' after meeting Luciano. Wasn't 'bout to have my woman talked about and me not know. Though she knew the lingo as well."

When the screaming stopped, I looked at Uncle Snap with new regard and respect.

"Clamp the nigga's balls, nephew," Uncle Snap suggested with a casual flick of his wrist, pointing. He had his flask of moonshine again and took it to the head. "Ah . . ." He wiped his mouth, then signed, "He'll talk quicker if his nuts pop."

Cory chuckled. "Ooh wee. Unc got lessons. All right, Frankie man, say good-bye to your manhood, homie."

Lucky moved out of the way, annoyed. He haphazardly slashed his butcher knife against the man's back. "You got this mook fucked up."

When Lucky bent down to pick up a big white jug, then threw the liquid in it on him, Frankie let out screams, his body pulling at the chains, until he gave. "I lied," he screamed in agony. "I didn't do it. B-but I know some people who may know something. Old Parish. Where Five Points began. There's a church there. . . ."

"Uh-huh, you just gotta keep fucking with me. But that's all good, my friend. I got something real nice for your racist ass." Lucky gave a quick nod. "Finish his people."

When Lucky said that, Cory clamped the cords and hit the power. We watched quietly as Frankie screamed and gyrated. Foam gathered around his mouth; then his eyes became red as liquid spilled from him. We watched the force of the charge make him bite down so hard that his teeth broke. It was then that I remembered the old man's request. I motioned for the power to stop; then I pulled out his tongue and sliced it off, for Cavriel.

"It's always a good day to watch a cracker fry," Uncle Snap said in cold malice.

As for the rest of Frankie's people, they all were wiped out as Frankie watched and then was fried alive.

Chapter 11

Claudette

"Cece. Come here! Toya almost here."

This little town was gonna be my death or the cause of the rest of my insanity, I swear ta God. Hearing that my godchild Toya was on her way here had set a pit in my stomach. Not of fear, but of the desire to off the man who had dared put his hands on that child. I didn't need to see her right now, but I needed to get to her home and put a nice talking to her mother, my old friend Betsy, on why she wasn't keeping Toya off the streets while I was here. I didn't need Toya seeing what I had in store for Lonnie.

Which made me think of my husband. God, it was good to hear his smooth, velvety voice. He always knew how to calm the wave of rage that was ready to come toward me. It was like he knew what was in my mind. Not what I was thinking, but what was actually in my mind before I could even birth it into a thought. That was something he had always been able to do, and it was sexy as hell. It was his voice and ways of soothing me, with a bottle of moonshine and Prince on the radio, that had me pregnant with his child a year ago. It was the sweetest memory and later the saddest.

"Deedee," I screamed at the top of my lungs. "Tell me why this little girl is coming here to your home, where this pedophile lays his head, huh?"

"That child neva comes this way, not until, I guess, she got wind that you here."

Deedee was in the kitchen. I could smell something frying. I glanced in and saw sliced green tomatoes and a brown paper bag with flour handprints on it. I guessed she was craving chicken.

My ignorant-ass sister stepped from the kitchen, wiping her hands on the apron that was wrapped around her swelling belly, and she looked at me, confused. "Which got me worried, Cece. She looks like a broken doll. Lonnie hurt that girl badly. She might not be the same little gal that called ya Auntie."

What she said was true, and that worried me. It also pissed me off. When the light banging of a fist on the porch screen came, I exhaled.

"I need you to follow what I said to a T, Deedee," I said with melancholy in my heart.

"Why? What you finna do, huh? That gal needs you, not me. She hates me."

"That's your own fault, and you know it. I need you to go make sure your simple-ass husband is still at the bar."

Deedee gave me a confused look. "I kicked him out the house, baby sis. I don't wanna see his disgusting face."

"His face wasn't so disgusting when you married that bitch, then allowed him to touch you with his sick ass," I spat out at her.

I could be very petty, especially when pissed.

"I told you—" she began, but I held my hand up and shook my head.

"You told me that you were hiding and keeping a baby from one man, only to stupidly marry a rapist and known child molester and, looking at you, a wife beater." Anger had me feeling light-headed. "For a change, can you accept your foulness, huh? I'm here to

clean it up, but accept ya shit, sis. Anyway. Let me get this baby."

As I walked away, I saw Snap watching from the top of the stairways. *"Snap, can you walk with my sister and keep her protected? I'll be safe and fine here."*

"You sure?" he asked, slowly coming downstairs.

From my peripheral, I could see Deedee taking off her apron and turning off the stove.

"Yes, I'm very sure."

"Then I'll protect her, as you asked." Like that, he bounded down the stairs and headed to the back. I heard him say, *"Ms. Deedee, come on with me."*

After I watched them exit, I gave a deep sigh and whispered, *"Jesus, help me."*

I quickly moved to the kitchen, poured two glasses of ice water, grabbed some cookies and the fresh tomatoes my sister had sliced, and put everything on a tray. Then I walked out on the porch. Toya sat on the front step, with her face pressed against her knees. She looked so tiny, so fragile, so unprotected, and it hurt my heart.

Quietly, I sat down next to her and laid the tray down behind us. I rested my hands on my knees. I had long since removed my gloves and changed out of my travel clothes. Currently, I wore jeans and a cropped MJ's "Bad" T-shirt. I had no shoes on, which was a childhood habit while I was home, and my hair was up in a bun.

"Baby girl, tell me what you want me to do," I said gently.

When a woman, let alone a child, was raped, oftentimes she couldn't compartmentalize what had happened to her, let alone why it had happened. And oftentimes, she—we—had no one to act as our voice for when we couldn't talk.

I knew the feeling well. Lonnie had taught me that lesson, and I had been too afraid to tell even my own *father, because of how innocent I had been. I didn't want my daddy taken away from us or Mama for killing that monster.*

So, in order to protect him instead of myself, I had kept my ten-year-old mouth shut, and I still kept it shut, until now. My sister knew the truth. And despite that truth, she had still married that bastard. My heart was heavy, and the disloyalty was like a bleeding open wound.

Light sniffling was all that could be heard, and I sat in the stifling silence. I had learned long ago that silence could be healing when it came to therapy. It could also be suffocating.

"I wanna go with you, Auntie. I wanna leave this place," she eventually whispered.

Fifteen years old and no one had protected her.

"What does your mother have to say to that? Have you asked her?" I gingerly questioned.

Small shoulders shrugged, and I wanted to pull her to me.

"All right. I'll talk with her. I think it's beyond time to get you out of here, and as I have always told you, baby girl, if eva you need me, I'll come."

"I wish you coulda have just come an' got me instead of visited." Toya's small face finally turned toward me.

Her tiny oval-shaped face was a battleground. She had broken, swollen lips. Her left eye was black and blue, and the whole right side of her face had a fist imprint. It took all my spiritual knowledge, all the training I had, to keep a poker face, all my strength to keep me where I was and to sit by this child's side.

This goddamn town was trash. They let this child walk around like this and didn't make that nigga Lonnie disappear in the night? Oh, hell to the naw. I realized just how deeply changed this town had become. The real heavy hitters, the real old elders had passed on, leaving this once feared town crippled, and it was a shame. Toya's attack was testament to that.

"Auntie is here for you now." Carefully, like holding fragile china, I held Toya's chin in my hand and gently tilted it up so that she could look me in the eyes. "I know it feels like you're alone, but I'm here for you, and I will keep you safe as best as I can, okay? Do you trust me?"

"Yes, ma'am. That's why I came here. 'Cus I knew you were here." Toya had a tiny voice, like a blue jay's. It hurt that the light in her had been broken.

"Tell me of Betsy. Did she try to shoot him?" I asked, thinking of my old friend.

"Yes, ma'am, but I stopped her."

I knew why too. Because her mother was all she had, and that broke my heart. "Why don't you let me take you home?" I looked at the sky and watched the darkness overtake the fading orange light. "I'll bring dinner with me, and you and Betsy can eat and start packing."

For the first time since she had sat down by my side, I saw hope shine in Toya's eyes. "Yes, ma'am. You're really gonna take us to Atlanta?"

"Yes, I am. I promise you." I made sure to let her know that I always stood by my word by looking into her moist eyes. Oftentimes it was up to us women to show our young daughters or girls that they were not alone when wronged. It was these delicate moments that could forever break a young girl. I knew that well. So, I tried to give Toya my strength through my words and by being here with her in the moment. I had nothing to hide from her or lie about and I knew she understood that when she looked into my eyes.

Toya's arms wrapped around me. "Thank you, Auntie."

I wrapped my arms around her and held her to me. "You're welcome, baby girl."

Afterward, I walked Toya to her home, where I had a long talk with her mother as Toya slept in her room, with her bags packed around her. Snap called Betsy's house from the juke joint and told me that Deedee was back at the house and that he was watching Lonnie as we spoke. I told him to continue watching him while I handled business.

"He hurt my baby girl, sister. He hurt her." Betsy stood in the middle of the room, crying and filled with brittle rage. "That nasty bastard followed my baby from school, then snatched her up when she tried to run."

Betsy was still a beauty. Five-six, slim, and the color of clay, with a short hair style like Anita Baker. I had learned that my old friend was a schoolteacher and that she had stayed in Creek Town to keep watch over her mother, who'd passed two months prior. When I offered to set her up in Atlanta, she happily took it. I figure, she could be a good asset to the neighborhood, especially to the children whom me and King mentored.

But for now, our minds were on Toya. Betsy was pacing, with a mason glass of brown liquor in her hand, while I had moonshine in mine. B.B. King played in the background just to drown out our conversation so Toya could rest without reliving what we spoke about.

"Tell me the rest," I said quietly.

"He choked her, beat her until she couldn't move, and then he . . . he . . . he hurt my baby, sis. My only baby girl . . . hurt her and changed her. I want him dead, Claudette. I want him strung up in the town to cook in the sun as the birds eat his eyes and foul dick. Told her she was a special, sweet thang . . . ," Betsy said as tears ran down her face.

It was the same thing he had told me. I was sure it was the same thing he told all his victims. And it was those words that had me leaving Betsy's house in the middle of the night with purpose and heading toward the juke joint. My feet moved with purpose, kicking up gravel. In my right hand was a closed glass full of clear liquid; against my back, my pistol; and in my left hand, my engraved switchblade.

I felt the fieriness of vengeance in my spirit. In this world, where women were becoming less protected by the day, sometimes only sisterhood could get shit corrected. My Kingston understood that in me, which was why he had made me his right hand in the Syndicate. I didn't fucking play. I intended to show that to Creek Town by holding Lonnie's esophagus in my hands while a dog ate his dick.

Chapter 12

Shanelle

Justice and Honor were in their baby rockers, pacifiers in their mouths, fast asleep. Worry had my head hurting. Anytime Javon, or any of my family, stepped out to handle Syndicate-related business, I worried. I often pondered what I would do if Javon never made it back home. How would I go on? How would I raise Honor alone? How would I keep the family going? All that shit constantly bombarded my mind. It was a natural process, I knew, but sometimes it just got to me more than other times.

I walked back into the kitchen to check on the shrimp and grits I had cooking. Dinner was going for the family and Ms. Lily, our next-door neighbor. She had been a little sick the past few months, but like clockwork, every morning she showed up to have breakfast and to sit with the babies. This morning had been no different. She'd gone home only to nap. She'd be back soon, I was sure.

The kitchen door opened, and with a gust of wind, Inez came in. "Hey, sis. How's Jojo?" she asked.

"He got up, got dressed, and headed to school like normal. After he spent time with Justice, of course," I answered her.

She hugged me, then kissed my cheek. She smelled of lemon verbena and honey. I smiled at her. It was just a year ago that we thought she and Cory had died. Finding out she and Cory had been addicted to drugs and in a mutually abusive relationship—none of us had even known they were in a relationship—had caused Javon to snap. Once Javon found out his brother had been laying hands on Inez and had been on drugs, he and Cory had fought. More like Javon had given Cory some tough love, then had tossed him and Inez out on their asses.

Soon after, Cory and Inez were attacked by the Irish, leaving us to believe they'd been killed. However, we found out they'd survived with the help of Ms. Lily, who also happened to be one of Mama's friends. The injuries they'd sustained were severe. Both had been scarred up and down their bodies. Skin had been ripped from their faces because of the accident caused by the Irish attacking them. The skin grafts Inez had had done to her face had healed nicely. While Cory had decided against getting reconstructive surgery for his injuries, I was happy Inez had gotten hers. She would always be beautiful, no matter what, but I knew the injuries to her face had bothered her.

Inez pulled her trench coat off. I smiled at the white scrubs she had on. She was back in med school. I was proud of her, to say the least.

"So, you want me to stab that bitch or not?" she asked, attitude clearly in her voice as she went into the dining room.

I knew she was checking on the babies. The plan had been to kick Dani out, move her next door with Jojo and Justice. But Javon had decided against that once he saw the problems they were having. He wanted to keep Jojo close for fear Dani would push him over the edge.

"No, don't do that, Inez. Especially since I don't know Jojo's mental state right now. I mean, I figure he's pretty broken up about that shit, but I need him to actually talk to us and tell us."

"Tell us what?" Navy asked as he breezed through the kitchen door.

I took him in. His silky auburn hair was down. He had on gray sweats, a hoodie, and a pair of fresh white Nike Air Max shoes.

"Where the fuck have you been?" I snapped at him.

He stopped abruptly, then gawked at me. "Was at the office. Javon gave me a list of shit to do, and I had to cover Jojo's shift."

"All night and half the damn day?"

"Yeah. All night and half the damn day."

I gave him a side eye. Since he had broken up with his girl last year, he had kind of turned into a workaholic. Even still, he knew he should have at least checked in before now.

"I'm sure you know Javon had to leave on emergency business, so I need to know where you are at all times. Understood?" I asked.

Navy tilted his head to the side, then looked at me. My paranoia mixed with my overprotectiveness was showing.

"I'm aware, Shanelle. I'm aware. Again, a nigga was at the office. Feel me?"

I gave him a stern look, then nodded. He knew how I got anytime Javon left. They all did. So, I was grateful that he didn't give me any lip.

"I heard about what happened with Dani and Jojo," he said, snatching up a hot shrimp to put in his mouth.

I swung the tongs at him. He chuckled but rushed out of my swinging range.

I asked, "He called you?"

Navy nodded. That didn't surprise me. He and Jojo had always been close and had grown closer over the past year.

"Anybody heard from Monty?" I asked.

"Yeah," Inez said, walking back into the kitchen with Justice in her arms. "He and Trin were at the rez with Nighthawk."

Trin was a leading member of a gang called Rize whom Javon had brought under the umbrella of the Syndicate. Over the last year, she and Monty had gotten closer and developed a relationship.

"When did you speak to them last?" I asked.

"Last night," she said.

"And no one has heard from them since then?"

Inez and Navy looked at one another. Navy's shoulders tensed a bit.

Inez answered, "No. Why?"

"Something going on?" Navy asked.

I shook my head, then turned back to give the grits one last stir. "Javon had to go to New York last minute because some shit is going down with the Commission. I need to make sure all of you are accounted for at all times . . . just in case, is all."

Just as I said that, my phone vibrated. I wiped my hands on my apron, then rushed to the table to pick it up. Javon's face popped up on the screen.

"Hey, baby," I answered. "Everything good?"

He sighed before saying, "Can't really say, baby."

"Talk to me."

And he did. I listened to him relate what he had read in King's journal. I was a bit stunned and taken aback. He couldn't stay on long, but he told me what he needed from me, and as always, I was set to oblige.

"Shit," I mumbled once he and I had hung up the phone.

"What is it?" Inez asked just before her phone gave a shrill ring.

"They made it to New York, but not without some fire," I said as I turned the stove off. I hurriedly untied my apron. "We need to get Monty home. Once that is done, we get Ms. Lily over here to sit with the babies. Until Javon hits me back and lets me know more of the details of what's happening, none of us make a move."

Navy and Inez nodded.

"Why do we need Ms. Lily to watch the babies?" Navy asked.

"Just in case," I said.

"Just in case what?" Inez asked.

"Just in case we have to move in Javon's absence. If the Commission called in Javon, then some heavy shit is going down, and we need to be prepared to put calls in to the Syndicate at a moment's notice, which means we need to be able to move without restrictions . . . and Ms. Lily has an arsenal at her disposal. I know she'd protect the babies with her life."

"That old biddy is dangerous," Navy said, then peeked out the kitchen window. "Thieves are out here thicker than normal. I see some Rize guards as well. Von must have already clued them in."

"She is dangerous, but she's declared herself Justice and Honor's fairy godmother. And you know Javon is never going to leave us unprotected. No matter what. I need to go make a phone call," I said. "Find Monty. He's got to be on the move, since the Thieves are here and he's head of security," I said, heading up the stairs.

I got to Mama's old room and picked up the phone to call someone whom I'd become closer to than I thought I would.

"Hey, you," she answered. "And please don't tell me one of you has gotten arrested. It takes away too much energy for me to deal with y'all in that capacity," she joked.

I smiled. "No, Jai. No one has been arrested, but meet me at the house as soon as you can."

Jai was the family's attorney, who no one knew about until Jojo, Navy, and Monty got arrested last year. She was able to pull strings to get all charges reduced and later dropped against all three of my younger brothers.

The noise in her background faded, and she dropped her voice to a conspiratorial tone. "What's up? Talk to me."

"Not over the phone. You know that. Get here as soon as you can."

About an hour later, Jai walked in. She was dressed in jeans, a tank top, a leather jacket, and running shoes. Still as beautiful as the day I met her. She smiled when she saw me and Inez. I had to admit, it was good to find peace with Jai after that incident in our front room when I attacked her. Yes, a huge reason I'd attacked her was that I thought she had snitched on Jojo, leading to his arrest, and another reason was that I thought she was after Javon. In hindsight, it was stupid to think that, but my emotions had been high and I hadn't been thinking clearly.

Ms. Lily sat in the corner next to the window and between the babies. Anytime she was here, she never let those babies leave her sight. If they had to have a godmother, I was glad it was a crazy German woman who was once an assassin.

I had pulled a large round table into the front room. A small feast had been set out.

"We're waiting on Monty," I said. "I wanted everyone here."

Jai nodded, then pulled her leather jacket off and hung it on the coatrack next to the door.

Navy sat in the chair next to the stairs, with head-phones on and a laptop on his lap. Jojo was not too far from Ms. Lily and the babies. There was no emotion in his eyes. His face was stoic as he checked the orders of his poppers. He and Navy had set up a system where they had college-age white kids delivering orders door-to-door. Meanwhile, they worked for Javon as a cover. It worked out perfectly.

A few minutes later, Monty walked in. Just as tall as he was broad, my little brother wasn't so little. He smiled at us as his hair curtained his face. Dressed in all black, he looked like the security he had spelled in white block letters across the shirt on his chest.

"Sorry I'm late, sis. Nighthawk and his lessons ran a little over," he said.

I hugged him, and once everyone was settled with food on their plates, I said, "I'm going to keep this short and sweet. So, Javon is in New York. Shit is hot, and that heat may well trickle its way down to us. I want us to be prepared and ready to go. I need to tell you guys something that you didn't know. Mama has a sister, and she is in New York."

Jojo stopped eating to look at me. Navy removed his headphones, mouth full of food. Monty tilted his head and frowned.

Inez said, "What?"

"And that's not all," I said. I told them about Javon's suspicions about King's death and who might have been behind it. While they were all sitting in stunned silence, I turned to find Ms. Lily watching me. I wasn't surprised.

"What do you know about the summer of nineteen eighty-five, Ms. Lily?" I asked her.

She glared at me for a long time, like she was looking through me instead of at me.

"That's when they killed King," she said.

"Who are *they*, Ms. Lily?" I asked.

"So, the fire didn't kill him?" Monty asked.

Ms. Lily nodded once. "Fire had help killing him," she said.

"Do you know for certain who did it?" Jai asked.

"Claudette didn't find out until he was dead for a few months. You know that the Commission called that meeting with him on the day he died," Ms. Lily said. "But when she asked Acardi about it, he outright denied it. Said neither he nor anyone in the Commission had called a meeting, since they'd already had a summit a few months before."

I looked around at my family and said, "So someone lied."

"I knew King," Ms. Lily said. "And King wasn't a fool man, ya hear? If he said them fools called a meeting, then someone from that camp called a damn meeting."

"It's odd Mama never found out who killed King, though," Navy said. "I mean, don't you think? After finding out who she really was, wouldn't it make sense that she would have had enough pull to find out who killed her husband?"

There were nods of agreement around the room.

"She did look. She looked until she damn near drove herself crazy. Claudette damn near drove herself to the nuthouse, looking for who killed that man. That's how she met that FBI agent, Monroe. Damn case went cold on her, though. Me and Snap had to beg her to lay off. She spent the first five years after his death taking over the Syndicate and looking for that man's killer. Claudette turned into a monster, something I ain't know she had in her. That damn rage and grief made her do shit. . . ." Ms. Lily stopped, then shook her head.

She went on. "I'll just say she was a motherfucker. She ain't take no prisoners. She wiped out families, kids and all. That woman lost her mind when King died. She even went head up with Acardi. She was fit to kill him too, but some kinda way he convinced her he ain't have nothing to do with killing King."

I felt my blood pressure rise. To hear Mama had gone through so much grief that it turned her into something else was alarming. It made me think of what I would do if something happened to Javon. I'd no doubt grieve the same as Mama, if not worse than her. I'd turn hell inside out looking for the culprit.

"And she never turned up nothing?" Jojo asked, surprising me.

I'd thought he was still in his feelings over Dani, well, too in his feelings to care about what we were talking about. Guessed I was wrong.

Ms. Lily looked at me, then back at the babies. "Just like Javon, King was a black man with a lot of power. Ruffled lots of feathers in the underworld."

"He wasn't the first black man in the drug game with power, Ms. Lily," Inez said.

"Yeah, but he was a black man with the protection of the Commission, which meant he had power to walk where no black man had before," Jai added.

Ms. Lily nodded. "She right. King could walk in New York City, Philadelphia, New Jersey, New England, just like the Italians and the Jews and the like. This was back in the sixties, seventies, and early eighties. He was a made man. You know how mad that made the who's who in La Cosa Nostra?" she asked. "No matter how times had changed, ain't shit changed. Get my meaning?"

"That would make them mad enough to kill him?" I asked.

"Sho'. And they did kill him. I know it was a hit because of who King was. He wouldn'a just went to no meeting alone like that. That's why they ended up coming for him."

"According to my folks, there was talk about it for a long time, sis," Jai said. "You know my bloodline and my pedigree. Stories still get told about how they killed him."

"You get that Monroe on the line. That bastard knows something. He was a rookie back then, easy to manipulate, but I bet you get on his ass and he'd tell ya something," Ms. Lily said.

I nodded, knowing she was right. Monroe was very familiar with this family. Since he had arrested Jojo, and we had found out he had been on Mama's payroll, he was an asset. So, calling him up didn't seem like a bad idea at all. Any information I could send back to Javon to help him, I would.

Chapter 13

Lucky

I looked at my uncle lying in that hospital bed with all those tubes running in and out of him. I thought I knew so much shit, but I finally realized I had no idea. My sister watched me from the window. After finishing Frankie with Javon and his team, we'd all come back to the hospital. Sleep escaped me.

"You should go rest, Lucky. You look a fucking mess," she said.

"Later," I said to her.

"You still mad at Mommy?" she asked.

"Yes, Giana and I will be for a long fucking time. All this time she lied to us."

"To you," Giana said softly.

I cut my eyes at her. "What the fuck does that mean?"

"She told me who that woman was to her a long time ago."

"So why the fuck you ain't tell me?"

Giana's face softened. "You know how Mama is, Lucky. You know she hated that Claudette favored you so much, and you were crazy about the woman yourself. If I didn't know better, I'd think you were in love with her."

I looked at my little sister like she had sprouted three fucking heads. "What?" I blurted out.

"She doted on you, Lucky. Shit. I'm surprised she didn't leave you at the head of the Syndicate. Anytime she came to New York, it was Lucky this and Lucky that. Mama hated that shit."

"So because she hated that the woman loved and respected me, she decided to not tell me Mama Claudette was her sister, my aunt?"

"You know how Mama is, brother. You know she's selfish as fuck at times."

"I don't give a shit. That was pivotal, crucial information."

Giana didn't say anything. She glanced out the window, then back at our uncle.

"Stay out of Javon's face too. You barking up the wrong tree. Don't let Ma get your shit knocked back," I warned my sister.

She pursed her lips, then folded her arms. "What's that mean?"

"That means his wife will kill your ass. Trust me," I said, remembering how Shanelle had drawn on my men when Javon and I fought in that parking deck. I'd been going after Shanelle, and he'd found out about it. Decked me right in my fucking face. And after I sliced his arm, he shot me in mine. "I don't want beef between the families because Ma on some other shit. Javon ain't like other niggas no way. He can't be swayed with pussy and a pretty face."

"Well, then, you ain't got shit to worry about."

I sighed, then looked at her. For some reason, I felt like what I had said had gone in one ear and straight out the other. She was going to have to find out the hard way. I turned my attention back to my uncle. Rumor had always been that he wasn't really my uncle, and that his brother, who had been killed in a shoot-out with the Feds, wasn't really my father.

The jokes about how I looked more like my uncle than the man who was said to be my father had always resonated with me. The fact that Uncle Luci had always been around and had always taken care of me and Giana was a red flag too.

I didn't look up when my mother walked into the room. I smelled food, and my stomach growled.

"I brought your favorite," she said softly. "Cajun shrimp and chicken pasta with roasted tomatoes."

"You know you shouldn't be going out of here alone," I said coolly.

"I wasn't alone. I had men with me."

"Still, you need to stay put. Stop moving around." I felt her looking at me, but I refused to meet her gaze.

"I'm not one of your little flunkies, Lucky. You don't get to boss me around like you do them."

Now I looked at her—more like glared. "What part of 'someone is trying to kill Uncle Luci' don't you understand? Or do you not care?"

She drew in a breath and acted as if she was offended. "Don't you dare accuse me of such a thing. Of course I care."

"Then act like it. Stay put. Don't draw attention to yourself or lead any wondering eyes back to this area."

"Don't piss him off anymore, Mama," Giana said. "He's on one or two."

My mother huffed as she set trays of food up on the small table in the room. "We're all upset," she said as she took out plastic utensils. "No need for him to behave like an ass," she quipped. "Lucky, you need to sleep. To rest. That way you—"

"Is he my father?" I asked, cutting her off.

Her eyes widened, and her posture stiffened. She clutched at the pearls around her neck, as if I was standing in the middle of mass and cursing the Pope.

"W-what?" she asked.

"Is Uncle Luci my father?" I repeated.

"Wh-why would you ask me such a thing? You know who your father is."

"You're such a fucking liar, Ma. Even after finding out Mama Claudette was your sister, you're still lying to me. You're looking me in my face and lying to me."

She said nothing. She just stood there, clutching her pearls, with tears rolling down her cheeks.

"You know someone is trying to wipe us out, the whole familial line, because I'm black? Because there are blacks in the Luciano-Acardi bloodline?"

"Don't be ridiculous," she whispered aggressively.

"He's not being ridiculous. He could very well be on to something."

I jumped, then looked at my uncle or father. I didn't even know what to call him. I stood, then moved closer to the bed. I checked the monitors to make sure he wasn't overexerting himself. He looked weak and fragile. Nothing like the man I'd come to revere and know. Bloodshot eyes looked up at me.

"You shouldn't be trying to talk," I said to him.

"You need rest," was his reply. "You can't run on low fuel." His voice was low, and he sounded groggy, sounded as if he was on his last leg.

"You'd better not die on me, old man," I demanded.

He chuckled. Well, he tried to. The chuckle came out like spurts of jagged breaths. "Going to take more than a bullet to the chest to take me down, son," he croaked out. His eyes roamed around the room to settle on Giana.

She smiled at him. "You want water or something?" she asked him, a soft smile on her face as she watched him.

"No, baby girl," he responded. Then, to my mother, he said, "You can stop lying to them now."

My mother rolled her eyes and huffed. "You tell them, since it was your idea to hide it to begin with. I'm tired of being made out to be the bad guy here."

"It's not about being the bad guy, and you know it. I did what I did to protect them. You did what you did because . . . well, you're just you." He said that last part like he was somewhere between disgust and resignation.

"So, you're my father?" I asked, just to be sure.

The man I'd known as Uncle Luci my whole life turned his eyes to me, then nodded once.

I looked at Giana, who cast her eyes downward. That told me that Ma had already alerted her to this. I felt like my mother and my sister were my enemies in that moment. Yeah, it was probably stupid of me to feel that way, but no way I would forgive my mother for keeping this shit from me. The fact that my sister knew told me my mother was intentionally fucking with me. Why, I didn't know.

"I hid that to protect you. My brother, no one would bat a lash if he had half-breed children. He was a wild-card child. Always leaving his seed wherever he laid his hat. Was easy. But me, leader of this crime ring, we have to keep an image of purity. Fuck black women on the side, yes, but don't . . . don't bring home any mooks for kids. All hell breaks loose. I could make your mama a kept woman easily. Many in the mob have done and still do it, but 'Always marry your kind' is a rule."

I knew that already. He really didn't have to explain, but I guessed my problem was, they couldn't have told me? I knew the rules and would have followed them if that meant protecting my mother and sister. Everyone knew I was some kin to Luciano Acardi, anyway. He didn't make that a secret, but I guessed having me as a nephew was safer than having me as a son.

I needed to take my mind off the feeling of not being good enough. I didn't want to go there in my mind. Didn't need to rehash all the shit my sister and I had had to endure as kids at family functions because we were half black. Didn't need to think about all the times Uncle Luci had had to smack a family member to make them mind their manners when it came to the things they would say to us.

"What happened in the summer of nineteen eighty-five" I asked him.

Uncle Luci looked shell-shocked for a second. "What do you mean, son?" he asked.

"Who killed Kingston McPhearson?"

Ma gasped. I looked at her. She avoided my eyes. Started straightening things that didn't need fixing. She knew something.

"We . . . No one ever found out," Uncle Luci answered.

"Someone killed one of the biggest kingpins in the South, and no one knew nothing? That's kind of hard to believe."

"Leave it alone, Lucky," Ma said from across the room.

"Leave what alone?" I asked.

"Let sleeping dogs lie," she shot back at me.

"Claudette damn near killed me about that man," Uncle Luci said. "His death turned her into a madwoman. Crazy woman tried to slice my fucking throat," he continued but then stopped when a coughing fit took over.

My mother and sister rushed to the other side of his bed. I remained silent as they made a fuss over him.

"She thought I'd called a meeting with him," he said once Ma and Giana had calmed him down. "I did no such fucking thing. I told her this. She didn't believe me. Never had to fight a woman the way I had to fight her for my life that day. Crazy bitch—and I say that with love—locked us in a room and came at me like she was possessed. That was the day I knew she loved King in a way she could and would never love me."

"So you're saying with one hundred percent certainty you did not call a meeting with King on the day he died?" I asked.

"Yes, son. We'd already held a summit weeks before. Wouldn't have been a need for me to call another so soon."

"Then who made the call, Uncle Luci? Because Javon just found out about that so-called meeting, and he's got the scent of blood in his nose. So, I need to know if you did this, Uncle Luci. That way I know what side of the friendship line—"

"I did not kill King, Lucky. You know me. Ain't I always been a man of my word? Even when my bullshit stinks, I'll own it. I did not call a meeting with Kingston. Same as I told Claudette. On my word and my honor. I respected the man, his skin color be damned. He was an astute businessman and brought millions of dollars in for the Commission. Besides, I'd have never wanted to hurt her that way."

"By *her*, you mean Claudette?"

"Yes. I would have never wanted to be the one to bring her such pain."

His response made me look at my mother. "You know something," I said to her.

"Lucky," she said with a frown.

"Ma, if you don't tell me what you know, I'm going to let Javon and Raphael in here and tell them you know more than what you're telling, and then we can watch all hell break loose. Because you know how they will react, and then you know how I'm going to respond. This room will be lit up like the Fourth of July. And then you can live with knowing you got your only son gunned down because he was trying to save you, even though you didn't deserve saving."

By now, she was full-blown crying, chest heaving up and down like it was hard for her to breathe.

"I—I—I . . . saw Cavriel and Absolan that day," she said.

"What?" Uncle Luci said.

"I saw them. They were in Georgia that day," she said. "When Claudette got the call to come because King was in trouble, we all rode back with her and Snap—me, Toya, and her mama. Well, Claudette dropped us off and then took off to find King. Cavriel actually came to Claudette's house maybe thirty or so minutes later, looking for her. He said that he needed to see her and that it was important, a matter of life and death. He looked spooked. I told him where she had gone, and he left like hell was on his ass. Then, that same evening, I saw Absolan. I was in West End. He was in full priest's garb, rushing into a black sedan."

"And you never thought to tell Claudette this? She could have killed me, woman." Uncle Luci had all but tried to sit up and reach for my mother.

She jumped back and bumped into Giana, who grabbed her to hold her. I helped Uncle Luci lie back on the bed. His machines started beeping erratically. Nurses ran into the room.

"She wouldn't have listened to me. She was out of her damn mind, crying over King. She lost her mind that day, and everybody knew it. She cried over his burned body in the middle of the street. Wouldn't let nobody touch her or his body. I—I—I . . . didn't . . . wasn't even thinking. I'd done some messed-up things to my baby sister, but even I didn't want to see her like that. That was a heartbreaking sight."

"So why not tell her when you saw she was looking for his killer? That could have helped," I all but yelled. "Why are you this way?"

Ma lifted her head and clamped her lips together. Her pride would let her take only so much prodding and castigating.

"I was scared," she said. "Absolan and Cavriel saw me that day. Two days later, in the apartment Claudette had put me in, I woke up to a severed horse's head on my pillow. At first, I thought it was a joke. Thought some kid had seen *The Godfather* too many times, and then I opened my door to find fish with their eyes gouged out. I knew what that meant. Scared me to death. I was pregnant with you, Lucky. No way was I going to do anything to get killed, get my baby killed. Shit, it could have gotten Claudette killed. I kept my mouth shut, and when Claudette put me on a plane to New York, I never looked back."

Chapter 14

Uncle Snap

I frowned as I looked at Javon, then Cory. We had been standing outside of Luci's room and had heard everything.

"She knew something. That bitch knew something this whole time and said nothing," I said to Javon.

I think I was fit to be tied at that point. Lucky had asked his mother a question that Claudette had been trying to figure out the answer to for years. Why was Deedee the way she was?

"You know that means that all the shit that is happening now could be connected to what happened in the summer of nineteen eighty-five, right?" Cory asked.

Javon nodded. "Cavriel and Absolan were in Georgia the day King was killed, and now Cavriel is dead, Absolan is missing, and someone botched a hit on Luci. It's connected, but I feel we're still missing something."

"Why in hell would Absolan be in full priest's garb in West End, Atlanta, the same day King was killed?" I asked.

Cory added, "And what in hell had Cavriel so spooked that day?"

"Yet Luciano swears he didn't call a meeting that day. Some shit just ain't adding up," I said.

Javon looked at his phone when it beeped. "Shanelle just said Ms. Lily told her Agent Monroe was on the case back in the day."

"King's death brought in the FBI?" Cory asked.

I nodded. "Yeah. He was found in one of his stash houses. Drugs, money, weapons, all of that was found in there."

Javon said, "Shanelle just told me she sent him a nine-one-one page, so she's going to—"

Before he could finish, Deedee walked out of the room. She looked at me, then balled her lips before saying, "Please don't say shit to me, Raphael. I've beat myself up enough."

I stared at her for a long time. "I will never understand you and the way you treated my woman."

"I'll never understand how you claim to have respected King and sniffed around his woman like a lovesick puppy," she snapped back at me.

"At least I loved and respected her."

"And I didn't?"

"You had a funny way of showing it. You saw how much pain she was in behind his death, and you didn't open your mouth."

"So it could get her killed?" she asked.

"Don't pretend you gave a damn. You kept silent for you."

"Yes. Yes, I did. I kept silent for my son, myself, and for my sister, and I don't give a flying monkey's ass if you believe me or not. She had already gone mad. I was not about to tell her what I saw, so she could go on a suicide mission. Any fool could see she wanted to die along with Kingston just to get back to him. Don't you get it? She wasn't head of the Syndicate yet. She didn't have the backing or the firepower she needed to tackle the Commission. And I was not going to be the reason she leapt to her death."

"So you came up to New York and became a kept woman to the man who could have very well had a hand in killing King," I said.

"Luciano did not kill King, and Claudette believed him."

I grunted. I wasn't sure of anything anymore at this point, and I didn't say anything else to the woman. I let her go on about her business.

I looked at Javon. "This is going to get messier before the endgame."

He nodded. "I'm aware and well prepared."

"You and Lucky may end up on opposite sides of this here thing. What if his father is lying and had something to do with King's death?"

"Lucky and I already discussed that," he said.

"And you cool with either outcome?"

Javon smirked a bit. In that moment, he reminded me of King. King never talked about what he was going to do. He just did it, and if someone made the mistake of crossing him, he or she lived to regret it. Too bad my mentor fell the way he did. He was an evil genius when the need called for it.

"Just be prepared for anything, Unc. You never know the way the dice will roll with this one."

Chapter 15

King

I turned my nose up at the woman in front of me. This would make the second time she had tried to offer me and my men her daughter in exchange for drugs. My men knew not even to breathe in the direction of a young girl or any child in a sexual manner, or I'd gut them myself. Cheryl was one of the only white women who lived in the hood. She had a sixteen-year-old daughter, whom she used as a pawn when she didn't have money to get drugs. She mostly went to my rivals, as she knew the only thing that talked this way was money.

"I told you the last time you tried to sell me your daughter that there would be problems, didn't I, Cheryl?" I asked.

We were in my office. The sun was still high in the sky. Anxiety had me antsy.

She shrugged. She had the jerky movements of a dopehead, and she kept licking and twisting her lips. Her daughter stood next to her, dressed in hooker attire similar to her mother's. They both had on clear six-inch hooker heels, short skirts that showed neither one wore any undergarments, and bras that showed that the summer sun had done nothing to tan their pale skin.

Judging by the way the young girl was twitching and was barely able to stand, I could tell she was high out of her mind.

"Go fetch Lily for me," I told Cleophus.

"Yes, sir."

"Tell her I need my trash taken out."

Cleophus nodded. "Of course, sir."

I walked to the basement door, then yelled down, "Ella."

She came rushing to the bottom of the stairs; sweat drenched her face. "Yes, sir, Mr. McPhearson?"

"Come here. I need you to do something for me."

She wiped her hands on her skirt, which was now covered in dust. She came up the steps two at a time. "Yes, sir?" she said when she reached the top of the stairs.

"I need you to take Amber to see Ms. Dutchess. Tell Ms. Dutchess that Amber will be needing room and board until I say otherwise."

Ella nodded, then took Amber by the hand.

"Ella," I called out.

She turned to look at me. I handed her, her switchblades. "You'll be needing these for the journey."

Ella smiled, then took her weapons. She quickly hid them on her person, then took Amber's arm. The girl could barely walk.

"Nighthawk," I yelled.

A few seconds later, the boy came from the basement. He was just as dusty and dirty as Ella had been.

"Yes, sir?" he answered.

"Shadow them. They'd better make it to Ms. Dutchess's place unharmed, and then you and Ella get back here."

Nighthawk nodded, then headed out behind them.

"Mama," Amber's soft voice called as she went. "I don't . . . I don't wanna go. I'll do whatever you need, Mama."

"Take her on, Ella," I ordered then watched them leave.

I shook my head, then looked at Cheryl. "You're the worst kind of mother that I've ever come across. And I try not to be a violent man, I do, but you just keep

*pushing my buttons. What I should have done was sent
Amber to Ms. Dutchess the first time you brought your
trifling ass to my men, trying to sell your daughter's ass.
But you told me you were going to send her away to her
father."*

*"And I did, King. I did send her away, but she ran
away and came back to me. My girl loves me," Cheryl
said.*

"Eh. Too bad you don't love her."

*"I do love her. Why you think I show her the ropes?
Better me than some pimp, yeah?"*

"She's a child, Cheryl. She's your child, your daughter."

*"She gotta learn some time, King. The streets don't love
us womenfolk, and you know it. Ain't no man coming to
rescue my white ass. I'm trailer trash. I grew up—"*

*"I know your story, Cheryl, and we all got one. Hell,
my wife has one, but you see what she does? She
helps children. She doesn't continue to perpetuate that
fucked-up cycle."*

Cheryl sniffed. "I know, and . . . and I'm sorry."

*I went into my top drawer and pulled out the fix she
wanted. "The fuck you apologizing to me for? You see
that young girl who just walked out of here? You should
apologize to her."*

*Cheryl's eyes glossed over as she eyed the pure uncut
heroin on my desk. Her nose started leaking, and she
wiped the back of it with her hand. That was right
before she started junkie scratching.*

*She nodded her head my way. "Wha-what I gotta do
to get that?" she asked.*

*Just as she asked that, another white woman walked
in. Lily was short. Her blond hair was pulled back into
a bun, and she had glasses on that made her look like
a schoolmarm. She was dressed like she had come to
collect the trash—blue coveralls and some black steel-*

toe boots—which was in stark contrast to her *Playboy Bunny* looks.

"I came to collect the trash," Lily said.

I nodded. In Lily's hand was a roll of plastic, and she had on a tool belt that housed tools. Tools that did things to the body that were ungodly.

"Come sit over here, Cheryl," I said.

Cheryl's eyes were still on the heroin as she moved to sit in the chair next to my desk. Lily unrolled the plastic and covered the floor. I tossed Cheryl the heroin. She looked up at me, aghast. She was so astounded by the notion of getting high that the fact that Lily was lining the floor with plastic didn't register.

"I . . . I ain't got but a little cash on me, King, and it ain't nowhere near enough for this. What chu want me to do for this?" she asked. "I been out whoring this whole time, so I know you don't want—"

"Ugh." I turned my nose up, disgusted she would even think I'd want to lay with her for any reason. "Don't flatter your fucking self," I spat. "Take the hit, but only under one condition."

"Yeah?" she said, licking her dry lips. "What's that, King?"

"Leave your daughter alone. As a matter of fact," I said, going into my drawer, pulling out paper and a pen, "give Ms. Dutchess custody of her. Let the old lady help get her clean and give her a shot at a decent transition into adulthood."

I glanced at Lily, who had taken her tool belt off as she walked on the plastic.

"You can't take my baby, King," Cheryl said.

"I ain't taking her. I'm asking you to do the right thing. Let Ms. Dutchess clean her up, get her on the right track."

"Then I can come back and get her?"

"No, Cheryl. You can't come back and get her."

Cheryl bit down on her bottom lip and started rocking back and forth. "That's . . . that's my baby, King."

"That's your moneymaker, you mean."

"I mean, yeah, she makes me money, but that's my baby, ya know," she said, then smiled, showing stained teeth. "Ain't nobody gon' love her like I do. I know, I know you think I ain't shit as a mother. That's all the women in my family done ever been is crack whores. So you can take her and do whatever you think ya can, but she gone end up a whore, anyway, because it's in our blood, ya know?"

I studied the woman and could see she really believed what she was saying. Even if what she was saying was her truth, her daughter deserved to know some sense of normality. She should have been doing what other girls her age was doing. Going to school, planning outfits and hairstyles, talking about boys, make-up, and shoes.

"Sign her over, or I take my stuff back," I said.

She looked at the heroin in her hand and started shaking her hand back and forth. Lily stood with her back turned to us. I could see she was putting something together. Cheryl snatched the pen from my desk, and I watched as she signed Amber over to Ms. Dutchess. It would take nothing for me to get the paper notarized and to make sure Amber was in a safe place at least until she turned eighteen.

Once Cheryl was done, she sat back, went inside her tethered brown bag, and pulled out what she needed to shoot up. Normally, I didn't allow that kind of shit in my presence, but shit happened. I watched Cheryl tie a rubber band around her arm, then shoot up. What she had in her veins was pure uncut heroin. The least I could do for her daughter was to make sure her mother felt nothing when death came for her.

I moved to the hall as I watched Lily walk behind Cheryl and then proceed to blow her brains out. Cheryl fell face forward onto the plastic, spoon and lighter falling from her hands, while the needle was still stuck in her arm. I'd warned Cheryl the last time that if she ever tried to sell me her underage daughter again, I would kill her. I'd meant that.

Lily rolled Cheryl's body in the plastic and taped it up so no blood would get anywhere or on anything in my office. She lifted her body and took it out back to her truck. Lily was a lot stronger than she looked.

"Look in the cigar box on the top shelf for your pay," I said once she was done.

Lily stood and looked at me. "Free of charge," she said.

Ever since Claudette and I had saved Lily's life, she had been indebted to us, and not because we'd deemed it so. The woman had been sent to kill me years ago. Because of fate, my wife and I had ended up saving her life. Since then, she had been our personal hired gun. Anytime we needed the trash collected, we called in Lily.

"Take the money, Lily," I said.

"No. Any woman, any mother who would sell her child for drugs, I'll charge nothing to send her to hell," she said.

I leaned against the doorpost, then lit a cigar. "I need you to stick around the area for a bit."

"Need more trash taken out?" she asked.

I took a puff of my cigar. "I'm not too sure yet, but I can feel something in the air today."

"Claudette okay?"

I nodded. "Yeah. She's in Creek Town, handling some business."

Lily studied me for a moment. To someone watching us, it would look as if she was checking me out in an intimate manner. But I knew better. She was trying to assess me and listen to what I wasn't saying.

"You feel like some heat coming your way?" she asked.

"I just don't—"

Before I could finish, Ella came busting into my office, a wild look of panic in her eyes. Nighthawk wasn't too far behind her.

"Somebody attacked ya men over near the tracks by the post office," Ella said.

"Denton and Tracy got hit, boss," Nighthawk said.

Tracy was another one of the men on my payroll. He was a nice kid, had come from a rough childhood. It hurt to hear he had been taken down with Denton.

"Some white men in a black car rolled up on them and took 'em out!" Ella exclaimed.

"We couldn't hear the shots, but we saw them go down," Nighthawk added.

"Silencers on their guns," Lily said. "Means they don't want to be seen or heard. Sounds like a hit, King."

"And we found this," Ella said as she held up a chess piece.

It was a black knight. Lily's spine stiffened.

"Found it where?" I asked.

"One of the men tossed it out of the car as they drove away," Nighthawk said.

I knew something was off. I'd been feeling it in the air all day. I opened the closet door and grabbed my assault rifle. I called all my men inside the office and gave them a rundown of what Ella and Nighthawk had relayed to me.

"Lock the town down," I ordered Cleophus. "You four, go with Lily, come up around Southlake Parkway, crossover Morrow Industrial, and get down to Highway fifty-four. You five, come with me, and I'm going to come up Lake Harbin. If the men who did it are still in the area, we can corner them. Nighthawk, Ella, y'all lock yourselves in the basement. Don't come out until *you hear me come back and specifically call your names. You understand?"*

Both kids nodded. I tossed Nighthawk a shotgun and Ella a Beretta.

"Anybody come down those stairs that ain't me, shoot to kill," I ordered. "Now go," I said after they nodded.

I waited until I heard the locks turn on the basement door before I and my men headed out. By the time we made it to the scene of the crime, whoever had killed my men was long gone. Denton and Tracy had been with me for years. They had been ambushed and left to die like animals. I got out of the car and walked over to see the carnage. Bullets riddled their bodies. Denton had died clutching his son's picture.

Just as I got ready to open the car door to remove the picture from his hands, a shot rang out. It hit the door of the car and narrowly missed my head.

"Get down!" one of my men shouted as he tackled me to the ground.

I looked around wildly, not knowing where the shot had come from.

"Came from on top of that church across the street, I believe," Cleophus said as he covered me.

I nodded, as words escaped me at that moment. It was a sick feeling to know someone was gunning for me and I had no idea where they were coming from or when they were coming. Blood trickled down the side of my face. I touched the right side of my head to feel where the bullet had grazed me.

All I could think about was that I had been a split second from never seeing my wife again. I needed to get to a phone to make sure she was safe. I needed to know that none of this heat had come for her. She needed to know to take extra care in watching her back. I regretted not sharing my thoughts with her earlier.

"We need to get into the Laundromat. That's a safe haven. We get in there, we can get to more weapons," Tiny Tim, another one of my guards, said.

"I don't think that would be a good idea. We go in there, and we're caged in. Out here we can move," I said.

"Yeah, but we're sitting ducks, boss. We don't know where these motherfuckers are or how many there are," he said.

"I realize that, but would you rather be closed off and cornered in that building or be out here, where you can run and move freely? Clearly, they were set up in this area. We don't know what they see, what traps they've set out."

As those words left my mouth, a car pulled up to the stop sign. I aimed, ready to shoot, until I saw it was Lily. Her hair was down, glasses still sat perched on her face, and she had changed out of her garbage collector attire. She looked at me, then gazed straight ahead. She sped across the tracks toward the church.

She parked and got out of the car with a bag hooked on the crease of her arm. The tall heels on her feet made her look taller than she was. She looked as if she was going to mass. She walked into the open building and disappeared into the shadows.

"What now?" Tim asked.

"Wait for it," I said.

No more than twenty seconds later, we heard a man's screaming voice, just before his body went flying from the roof the church. I looked up to see Lily standing on the roof, looking down. The wind whipped her hair around as she looked at me. I hopped up and jogged across the street. The man wasn't dead, but the stab wounds to his neck and chest probably made him wish he was. His leg was bent inhumanely, and his arm was twisted behind his back.

"Who sent you?" I asked him.

His already pale skin drained of any color it had left. He tried to spit on me, but his saliva ended up landing right back on his face. I stood there and then kicked him in his already mangled leg. He yelled out in pain. I heard heels clacking against the sidewalk and knew Lily was behind me.

"King, you need to see something," she said. She kneeled and yanked the man over, then lifted his shirt. I didn't readily know what I was looking at.

"What is that?" I asked her.

"Knights of St. Assisi mark. You know how the Vatican has the Swiss Guard?"

I nodded. "Yeah."

"Think of this as the rogue faction. They're killers, King. Assassins. When Ella showed you that knight chess piece, I had a feeling they were here."

"How do you know this?"

Lily looked uncomfortable before she turned and lifted her shirt. She had the same mark on her back. She turned back to look at me.

"I never knew who sent me to kill you before," she said. "We get the orders, and we move out, but whoever wants you dead has tried before, through me. And now they're trying again. This is a hit squad. They want you dead by any means necessary."

Chapter 16

Javon

When I can't sleep, I pace. Usually, I also go and take a hot-ass shower, so as not to wake Shanelle or Honor. But since I was in NYC, I was in a bed by myself, with thoughts that wouldn't keep quiet. King's journal started out like any normal journal, with a discussion of his childhood and some of his adolescence, but the pages devoted to his adulthood were much more interesting. I learned a lot about the man who was a myth in our house.

Some of what I learned was, he loved the very air around Mama Claudette. Learned he saw her in some place called a juke joint in Creek Town, and then the rest was history. I learned King liked to shave by steaming his face with a cup of hot water, using a straight edge, then rubbing his face down with coconut oil. King had a love of reading crime novels to the kids in the area. I learned that Mama hated when King would leave his old records around and not put them away carefully. I also read a little about some intimate sexual shit between him and Mama, but then I skipped those pages. These were the private things I learned about a man called King.

All of what I learned, including who his allies were, which codes he used, how much money he had in savings, and more, kept me deep into King's voice and vision. So, it was hard to read about his downfall. I had to stop the moment I read about the Knights. It was too hard to

continue, and I realized why Uncle Snap had never read
any further. King was a true type of dude. One whom
others could hold to his word. If he was going to do something, he'd always do it. But in all of that, he was a loving
husband, a best friend to his wife and to those few whom
he chose to keep in his private circle, and a damned good
businessman.

He and I had gone through some similar shit, especially losing a child. It was crazy to read his thoughts on
that and see that we shared similar views. All we wanted
was for the women we loved to be cared for through the
loss, and that was what we did. King was about honor, so
why did motherfuckers have to snuff his light out?

I rose from the sheets of my king-size bed. The light of
the moon was peeking in through the tall paneled windows of my room. After opening them, I glanced at the
night beauty that was Manhattan. The view from the
building was incredible, but it was shady. Shady, as if
something sinister was going down in the underbelly,
and it was.

My arms crossed over my chest. I stood wide legged
in gray sweatpants and no shirt. Something from what
I had read in one of King's chapters—a chapter that had
been written in a rush, which was evident since it did not
have the usual smooth style of King's writing—sparked a
memory in my head. Lily had been there with King. Had
she been there for his last breath?

That question made me glance at the leather-bound
book that was King's. I still had a lot of questions, a lot of
thoughts going on—

"Hold up," I muttered to myself.

Quickly, I took two strides to the book, picked it
up, and cradled it in one hand while the other flipped
through the pages. King had said that Ms. Lily had once
been sent to kill him. That she was a former Knight. *Fuck*

my life. I had glossed right over that reveal in the journal as I'd been too tired at the time I read it, and so I had not tripped off it. But here it was written and underlined twice by King's hand: *Knights of St. Assisi.*

As I stared at those words, I thought of Mama. If only she had read the book this far. . . .

Then I called Shanelle immediately. She'd told me that Ms. Lily was there, so I had to get my woman up to date and ask Ms. Lily what the deal was.

"Baby, I'm sorry if I woke you," I said when she picked up.

"No, you didn't, babe." Shanelle's voice was soft and gentle. It made me miss her suddenly, like I missed our daughter. "We're still up discussing everything." I heard her say.

"Perfect . . . Wait, it's two a.m. there, and y'all still discussing?" My brow lifted; then I chuckled, remembering to stay on point. "Is Ms. Lily still there?"

"She just put the babies to bed, so yes, let me call her down. And you know that we have to stay up though, Von. I had to wait for everyone to show up."

I glanced at the clock, then chuckled again. CPT—colored people's time—mixed with hustler hours did make us hard to reach as a unit, so I got what my baby was saying.

"Listen, Elle, I have some things to update you on. While you're calling for Ms. Lily, go get your copies of Mama's journal and what I sent of King's."

"Okay, baby."

As she did that, she stayed on the phone with me, and I broke down everything for her that I could on our secure private line. Even though I was telling her everything, it was framed in a coded context that only she and I understood.

"Are you messing with me, baby?" Shanelle asked in a shocked tone when I was done.

"In no way am I messing with you. I need you to talk to Ms. Lily and see what the okeydoke is. Right now, I don't feel that she is a threat, since it's written repeatedly about how protective and loyal she is to this family, so you know my mind, baby. See what you can learn."

"I'll do my thing. I promise."

"Thank you, baby."

A sweet pause in our conversation happened. I could hear papers rustling. When I heard a light creak, I could tell that she was in our bedroom. Mama's old room.

"They had an incredible love, huh?" she finally said.

"No doubt. Memorable too."

"If something like that happened to you, I want you to know that I'd make Mama smile, because I would burn the world to find out who came for you. I love you that deeply."

I gave a light chuckle at how down my baby was for me. "I love you, baby, because that's some real shit right there. It's the same I would do for you. Annihilation isn't even strong enough for me to use in what I'd do."

"You better." Shanelle's light laughter relaxed the muscles in my neck. "Tell me the page in King's journal that you want me to look at."

I did, and then I waited as she read King's words to herself.

"Are you fucking kidding me?" she said when she was done reading. "Okay, let me get Ms. Lily. I'll talk to her and get back to you. For now, please rest. I know you. Honor knows you. When you're up, she's always up."

"Even with me gone?" I asked incredulously.

"Yes, baby, even with you gone, so sleep. I'll call you back. I love you. Come home to me."

"I love you too, and I will, on both accounts." With that, I hung up.

Something in me kept having me glance at Mama's journal. So, since my spirit was talking to me, I read it. I knew that Mama's journal contained pages that were blank or had illegible scribbles. Before I had read anything from it, I had leafed through her journal and had noticed those pages with the large scratched words "They killed my soul. They killed my King. . . ."

Those scratches were saturated with pain, and it hurt to see them on the rumpled and tearstained white pages. Now, after reading all that I had of her journal, I finally understood why the final pages were wrinkled and torn. It was all because of King's death and Mama's grief, which had turned her into a raging angel of death.

It would be a while before Shanelle called me back. I had texted her that I was going to sleep and to just hit me with a "Call me" later. I climbed in bed and fell into a deep sleep. Once I did wake up, which was sometime around seven in the morning, I showered, shaved, and brushed my teeth. Then I left my room, King's journal in hand, and went into the kitchen, where I found the OG Snap drinking a cup of coffee. He stood solemnly, as if in deep thought, watching the city from a large open panel window, with one hand in the pocket of his slacks.

Sometimes when Uncle Snap was like this, he looked like he was in his late thirties. It was wild to me, seeing the young man he once was, not that he looked overly old or anything. But right now, he was how I had imagined he looked in Mama's journals, standing just like that, keeping Mama protected while she stood by King. The image in my mind was something like a trinity to me. Two brothas deeply in love with their queen.

Blowing out steam, I shrugged my shoulders, dropping the classic hood love story in my mind. The need to protect one of the lasting tomes was heavy in my heart once again. Losing Uncle Snap would add to the crack in my heart. I didn't need that.

"There's fresh juice, espresso, fruit, cheese, and some pastry thang with an egg cooked in it and some cheese on top." Uncle Snap took a drink from his coffee mug and kept his gaze ahead. "The chef is bringing some scrambled eggs, meats, and other stuff shortly."

I took a glance at the mini-spread on a long kitchen island. Plates, glasses, and utensils had also been placed on the island.

"Hmm. Looks like they are pampering us, but can we get some toast, grits, and country ham in this trick?" I jokingly asked, walking up to the island to get a cup of espresso and that pastry. "How you feeling, Unc?"

"Just living, nephew." Uncle Snap gave an amused deep chuckle. "And, yeah, I said the same thang 'bout break-fast. That's why I sent that chef on back to the kitchen. We all grown-ass men up in here and got the hunger of a wolf pack. Can't be up in here feeding us air."

Uncle Snap was wild. I laughed hard, then took a seat at the table. "So, I got something that I need you to read, if you're up to it, Unc."

I watched the humor in my uncle's eyes disappear as he walked over to me. "Which one? King or Mama?"

"Eventually both, but right now, just King. I need your thoughts about something as you read it."

In my hand was that egg pastry. I almost put it down on my plate when I thought the egg was runny, but when I poked it and saw it was set, I was all good. Once I took a bite, I put it down. It was really good, but I needed more than this. I reached for King's journal, which I'd placed next to me on the table, and set it down across from me for Uncle Snap to grab. "The page is marked for you," I said, studying him.

It was going to be hard for him to read that, but I needed his guidance.

"Good thang I got some moonshine in my coffee, then," he said, sitting down across from me at the table. He opened the journal. He reached in a pocket of his slacks and pulled out a pair of wire glasses. Once they sat on his nose, he sat back and began to read.

"Cory still asleep?" I asked, getting up and filling my cup back up with coffee.

"You know ya brotha."

I laughed and headed to his room. "Sleeps until the hogs can't be called anymore, as you say."

"Fa sho', nephew."

My fist banged on Cory's door; then I opened it. Cory was under a heap of covers. His foot hung off the side of the bed, and his subtle snoring could be heard.

"*Kuya*, wake your ass up. We got some planning to do." I kicked his bed, then stepped back, just in case his ass pulled steel on me.

"Bruh," was all he said as he groaned. His hand reached out from under the sheets to grab his tablet, which lay near him. "Found some more shit out that's leaving me with questions."

"So did I. Hit us up in the main area. Got some food coming, and I sent a text to Lucky."

"A'ight." Cory stretched, then climbed his naked ass out of the bed.

I shook my head, then walked out, chuckling to myself. The old Cory would have found a way to have some female in the bed with him. The new Cory was just a tired-ass negro, due to all the running around we'd gone through last night. I owed my bro some fun. I had to squeeze something in there.

After a few, we all sat around the kitchen table. Cory was now reading King's journal, while Uncle Snap had his silver flask out now, and I was eating a mound of scrambled eggs and cooked meats.

"What's your thought on these Knights? You ever run across them during your years with Mama?" I asked, waving my fork in the air.

"Outside of Lily, and those I first met through the Commission, can't say that I have. . . ." Uncle Snap leaned in his chair, thinking back. "Wait now. Yes. When Mama turned dark, shit, we ran across a couple but didn't thank nothing of it, 'cus they weren't gunning for us and didn't give off cues that they had any thang ta do with King's murder."

"How you come about seeing them?" Cory asked before I could.

"Let's see. Saw a few after the summer of eighty-five. They were hangin' around the Irish territory. After that, there were some in NYC, but that made sense because they were based here." He paused, took a sip from the flask, then continued. "There were a few in ninety-five in Vegas. That was 'bout the time Mama began shifting her dealings and started changing up her identity with the Syndicate."

"So that establishes a pattern, yeah? They've been watching in the cut," I said quietly.

"Mmm-hmm. Mama always felt watched, always. She just doubled up her protection and kept the Syndicate as her backing. Me, I just made sure those eyes kept their distance. Killed a few but never checked for crests. Now I know I should have. Damn this life."

"It's not even your fault or hers."

I studied my Uncle's face. The drinking had him looking haggard. His usually smooth face had creases and lines now. His face had a gentle scowl, and his eyes were sad again. I was about to ask him about more of his thoughts, but the interruption of a knock on the door kept me silent.

Cory smoothly slid me the journal, and I left the kitchen to lock it away in my suitcase back in my room.

"Bring ya ass in here," Uncle Snap called out as I walked back into the kitchen.

It was Lucky with his sister. I scratched the side of my jaw in hidden annoyance, not wanting to deal with her flirtations. Out of respect to Lucky, I was doing my best not to wreck the girl, and by wreck, I meant fucking with her emotions and breaking her ass down right when she thought she could get the gold. But that was the old me. The new me had already told her up front what it was, and in no way or form was I even tempted. She wasn't my type.

"Breakfast on point?" Lucky moved to the island and grabbed a plate of food. The homie looked just as exhausted as we all felt, and just as haggard as Uncle Snap looked.

"Everything is all good. Cooked well too," I answered.

When Giana grabbed some fruit from my plate and sat by me, watching me, my eye began to twitch. It was then that I forgot that I was sitting with my shirt off and not in a tank. *Fuck my life.*

"What questions did you have for me?" Lucky asked, giving his sister a look. He smoothly grabbed another plate of fruit and slapped it down in front of Giana, who laughed at her brother.

"Did Absolan have any family? Wife? Children? Side ho?" I paused and glanced at Giana. "Brother, sisters, or cousins?"

"Absolan has a little vice, one that he enjoys a couple of times a month," Giana answered. Everyone at the table turned their attention to Giana, who had interrupted Lucky and prevented him from answering me.

I glanced at Cory, and he spoke up for me. "And what's that vice?"

"He loves his libations, women, and sex," Giana explained.

"Not surprising at all, and the drinking was a clear type of thing," I said to her.

"No, it's not, but it's the sex that's the thing. Absolan has a little thing for Korean sex slaves. Especially, ones who can tailor themselves to his Catholic guilt and need for power." Giana gave a smile and popped a piece of pineapple in her mouth. "There's a private club that caters to the priests of NYC who have particular vices."

I sat back in thought. That was an interesting bit of information. "And could he have been taken from this place?"

Giana gave a slight shrug. "Possibly, or hiding, or anything."

Lucky set his fork down. The brotha looked tense, so tense that he ran his hand over his face, then stared at his sister. "Why do you know this?"

"Mama isn't as messed up as you think she is. I mean . . . she is . . . she does things that only she gets off on, for whatever reasons. But even so, she has our best interests at heart."

"Is that so?" Lucky asked. There was unspoken communication going down between brother and sister.

Shit was as familiar to me as it was to breathe. Having a brother close in age, then later picking up several other siblings, would teach one how to pick up nonverbal cues.

"Don't start, chooch. Please." Giana glared at Lucky, then slapped her hand on the surface of the table. "Just everyone, get dressed. This spot, from what Mama says, is very retro, and if you're not in the know, then you can't get in."

"Don't call me a jackass," Lucky grumbled.

"Well, ya actin' like one," Giana countered.

"Now, how are you going to get five black men and yourself in where, I'm pretty sure, melanin ain't the right currency?" Uncle Snap asked.

Pushing up from the table, I looked at everyone. "It don't even matter. If she can get us in, or close enough to watch the spot, then that's what we need to do. Either this nigga was kidnapped or something else is up with his fingerprints all over it."

"Everyone, put on your best. I'll go make some calls to get our ins." Giana smiled as if she had done something amazing. She winked at her brother, then walked out with a pep to her step.

"Dead ass . . . I swear to God, she's problematic as fuck." Lucky gave a sigh. "I'll meet up with y'all when it's time to leave. I need to check in on my pops."

"Is he all good? Vitals doing better?" I asked, still standing with my hands in the pockets of my sweatpants.

"For now, yeah. The medicines they are pumping in him keep him drained and out of it, but he's still fighting," Lucky explained.

"Us old gangstas don't fall down as quickly as others wish." Uncle Snap slowly stood, then headed to his room. "I'll put my best on."

I solemnly shook my head, wishing Mama hadn't fallen. "Check you on the flip side, Lucky. Tell the Old Italian that we got him and we are breaking this down as best as we can."

There was a call to Shanelle I had to make, and I wanted to get back to her quickly.

"You know I will, and he knows it." Lucky headed to the door. He paused to give Cory a handshake; then he walked out.

Lucky was walking on a familiar thin line. I knew it well because I had just healed from my own shit. The weight of our family's past still weighed on his shoulders. Hopefully, what we would find would help push this plan of ours ahead.

Chapter 17

Cory

When Lucky's sister said she had an "in," she meant that shit. We stood outside of an old Gotham-style building. Standing before twin medieval-looking black doors, a hulking, chunky guy in all white and with a long ginger-colored beard watched us. The alleyway we stood in was moist from the freezing rain.

Our unmarked ride was parked in front of us as a shield, just in case some shit went off. We all stood in our best dressed. Behind me was a biracial member of the Forty Thieves named Alex. Dude was dark haired and could pass for white, so that was why he was here in the front, while we looked like his entourage.

Shit was working my nerves, but it was for a reason. The side of my face itched, so I scratched it. After I first was burned, I did get grafting done, but the shit was stressful, so I stopped. My face was scarred but not in a manner that disgusted anyone. It just gave me a unique look, which I didn't mind, even though I knew it made me stand out.

"I think I'm going to get my face worked on," I muttered to Von. I had added a prosthetic to disguise my looks.

"Why?"

While we waited on Lucky, Giana, and her "in," I shrugged. "Makes it easy to ID me, if ever we get into some shit we can't get out of."

"It was hard on you, *kuya*. You sure?"

Von had on all black. He stood in a meek manner, like he was an everyday businessman, with a suitcase in front of him and glasses on. This was his cover. He was here to talk security financial protection.

My cover was also my former everyday work, the law. "Yeah, but I can handle it. Besides, you'll put me up with nothing but the best, right?"

"You know I will." Von gave me a quick nod.

I returned my focus to the hulking bouncer.

"We're guests of Don St. John," Alex told him calmly. He flipped out a laminated business card that was red and was emblazoned with a crest. It didn't match the Knight's crest by far.

The burly, ginger-bearded, bald bouncer gave us black folk the one up and down. "Don St. John is inside. Welcome to the Chain and Silk."

He did a quick text on his cell, then conveniently ignored Alex and searched us darkies, as was written across his face. Muthfucka had the nerve to test me by fucking with my nuts. He did the same with Von as well.

"I'm pretty sure that I cannot hide a weapon against my ball sacs, friend. You should move on," I said as properly and as calmly as I could.

Fat boy gave a sharp grunt; then, once he saw we weren't strapping, he stepped his girthy ass to the side to allow us inside.

Smoke rolled into the street when the twin doors opened. I looked at my cell and saw Uncle Snap's text.

Clocked in and working, nephew.

That was code that he was already inside. Giana had managed to get the OG in as a washer in the back kitchen. I quickly sent my own text.

Entering my meeting.

"Everything is accounted for," I muttered to my brother, and he gave a nod of acknowledgment as we stepped inside.

Darkness filled the hallway, until splashes of red guided us up into the hidden club. Once inside the secured place, all I heard was old white music. Like Frank Sinatra, some jazz that didn't have real soul. Red silk draped the walls. Old-ass paintings that put me in the mind-set of some PBS period show shit stared back at us as we walked through. I had expected to see women servers all over the place, but that wasn't the case.

"Welcome Mr. Bernard and guests. Please follow me this way to Mr. St. John," said an attendant.

There were separate booths where old white guys sat drinking and smoking cigars. A few of those tables had chains on them, with women of various races locked in them. These women looked up at us with no life in their eyes and fake, plastic smiles. They were virtually naked, except for the silk draping their crotches and over their breasts. On their arms were bangles, and they wore little things that made them look like naked nuns, such as cross chokers.

The servers in the place were men, and they were dressed like waiters from the sixties. My shoulders felt tense as I looked at this shit. We continued walking through the elaborate place. When we rounded a corner, more women appeared. Many were on pedestals, like statues. Others danced on tables in a slow, hypnotic manner. Water streamed by our feet against smooth, modern-painted walls. The water was lit, and as we walked down the hall, white light greeted us like a door.

When the attendant reached out, he laid his gloved hand against a panel of carved glass, then directed us outside. On some real shit, my mouth dropped open.

Before us was nothing but greenery. We had stepped into a Roman/English garden, with columns included. This was where the rest of the silk-covered women and men were, the slaves. They all had chains and sat on their "masters'" laps or at their feet.

Familiar faces dallied around the luxurious greenery. They were familiar to me only because we always did our homework before visiting specific cities where we had business. There were a few doctors, lawyers, and other professional men, but the majority of the men who were here were men of the cloth.

Across from a huge water fountain sat Lucky, with Giana. Both were draped in luxury, especially Giana. Next to Giana, twirling his fingers through her hair, was her "in," Don St. John, as he was called here. When in the streets, he was Armani Rossi, just one of Luciano and Giovanna's old friends from the old world

Everywhere we moved, I made note of the exits. We walked over and sat in front of Armani. He stretched out a hand and grinned. "Have a drink, my friends. Thank you for heeding my call."

He was playing the game well. That was my clue to send a message to Uncle Snap.

Seek.

After that, I stood and asked, "Where are your bathrooms?"

"Julie." Armani snapped his fingers and a curvy pale chick with red hair that matched Armani's came over to me. She wore nothing under her silk panel. I could see her bare slit, and the pink nipples under the silk swath of fabric did a piss-poor job of holding her tits up.

I gave a smile. "Thank you, Mr. St. John."

"You're welcome, my friend. Enjoy the fruits as well. Take this." Armani held out a gold chain to me that was connected to the collar around Julie's neck.

No lie, but the dynamic was fucking with my mental, but I played along and let her lead me to the bathrooms. Once we rounded the corners, I pulled on my "slave's" chain.

"Stay here and say nothing, do you understand me?" I said.

"Yes, master," was all she said as she slumped down to kneel like some sort of pet.

Shaking my head, I strolled into the bathroom, then walked right on out behind Julie's back. I smoothly took note of the many faces that watched me. I nodded and took my time to become invisible to the onlookers. Once that happened, I found myself by the kitchen. I peeked in and didn't see Uncle Snap, which was good. I then checked my cell and found a message with a location mark.

Crest on statue near draping tapestry. Statue is real. Going inside.

Uncle had pulled through. After that, I went back to gather Julie. She slinked up my body like a cat. I gave her a dissatisfied frown, and then I went back to the crew. By that time Von was done talking acquisitions and whatnot. I handed Julie off and smacked her tiny ass; then I took my seat.

"What a salacious establishment," I said in my dorky proper tone.

Everyone gave a good chuckle; then I leaned toward Von and whispered everything to him. When he slid a note in the guise of a folder to Armani, Lucky glanced down, then walked off. The plan was for him to back up Uncle Snap, while we waited to follow. This freaky-ass jawn had a lot of secrets, and we planned to decode them.

Chapter 18

Shanelle

"Ms. Lily, you feel up to talking some more, or do you need to rest?" I asked once the old lady had hobbled back down the stairs.

She looked tired, but she smiled up at me once she made it down the stairs. "Listen now, I needs my rest so me and the girls can have playtime in the morrow. So ask me what'cha need, and then I wanna carry my tired ass home," she fussed, but there was a twinkle in her eyes.

Jai laughed. "You are a trip, Ms. Lily."

"You need me to get you anything?" Jojo asked her.

"A nice hot mug of whiskey may do me some good," she said.

Monty shook his head. "Nighthawk's father drinks his whiskey hot too."

Ms. Lily smiled as she ambled over to her favorite chair. "He does like his fire water hot. He taught me the trick, the old bastard." Ms. Lily studied Monty long and hard; then she tilted her head to the side. "You look like ya mama, ya know."

Monty cocked his head to the side. He glanced at me before turning back to Ms. Lily. "My mama?"

Inez sat forward, and Navy stopped tinkering with some new e-cig gadget he and Jojo had been working on. Jai looked at me before turning to study Monty.

"Yeah. She was a hellcat, that one. I remember the day she and ya pappy had their first fight. Was right out in the middle of town, in front of King's office. Y'all know where downtown Jonesboro is, down there by the old courthouse?"

We nodded as Jojo came from the kitchen and set a mug of steaming whiskey in front of Ms. Lily. She thanked him, and he nodded.

Monty moved closer to Ms. Lily. "You knew my mother?" he asked.

"Sho' did."

Monty waited for her to say more, but she didn't. I could see it in his eyes that he wanted to ask more questions. He'd never met his parents, and it had always bothered him.

"What was her name?" he asked her.

"Ella was her name. She 'bout cut ya pappy a new asshole back when they was fourteen. He yet got the scar to prove it," Ms. Lily said. She rocked in her chair with her mug, laughing like she was remembering the day she spoke of. "They clowned real bad out there. He was mad I 'spose 'cus Ella was bragging about her Indian blood. But she was black, ya see. Pretty dark-skinned black gal. She had long hair and light eyes. She was Claudette's little foot soldier. Spoke real proper English when she wasn't mad. Ya piss her off, and the country came outta her quick."

As much as I wanted to ask Ms. Lily about what Javon and I had spoken about, the look of utter elation on my brother's face silenced me. It was the first time he'd heard about his folks.

"Ya pappy was right proud of his Indian blood. He always hated when the little black girls claimed Indian just 'cus they looked mixed or had long hair. Ya pappy was a lot like you. He still is. Manuel boxed, you see?

He put many grown men flat on their asses. Made King a right nice amount of money. Big-ass Indian, even at fourteen. Voice deeper than King's at times."

"What happened to my mama, Ms. Lily?"

She looked at Monty, and her smile faded a bit. "Racist cops got to her. She died fighting, though. Protecting you. Ya father beat a cop to death with his bare hands. Was in prison for some time afterward. Ya grands had you for a while, but ya grandpappy was an old drunk. He beat you and ya grandmama's ass. One day ya granny got fed up. Came over here with you. She was busted up and bleeding. Told Claudette she wanted to leave. Claudette sent y'all away for a while, but then ya granny died, so you had to come back here. Ya grandpappy got some issues, so he ain't want you. Claudette sent you to Ms. Dutchess. You remember her, I know."

Monty nodded, but his hands shook and his eyes held unshed tears. Ms. Dutchess was who Monty had lived with until the old lady died; then Mama had taken him in. I remembered the day his big ass came walking in the house. I chuckled at the memory of him looking at the rest of us kids with a scowl on his face. Head full of wild hair and clutching his boxing gloves for dear life. If I wasn't mistaken, he had been only about eight or nine.

Ms. Lily continued, "Anyway, one night ya mama was on her way back to the rez when these cops pulled her over. Cops always used to harass the Natives. Ya mama ain't ever liked the cops. They yanked her out her car, tried to violate her body, but not Ella. Good ole Ella and her switchblade tagged ass. Sliced one of those officers real good. Took him outta here. And was set to do the same to the other one, until he shot her in head."

"Damn," Navy said, vocalizing what the rest of us were thinking.

Jai winced as she gasped.

Ms. Lily went on. "No matter. Ya daddy was crazy about that gal. Walked right in that cop's house and beat that man to death in front of his wife and kids. He knocked the shit out the wife too when she tried to hit him with a bat. He damn near folded that lady in half. Caved her mouth clean in. He killed a cop. They wanted to kill ya pappy, wanted him to fry, but not on Claudette's watch. She couldn't keep him out of prison, but she knew the judge who sentenced him. Instead of life or the death penalty, the judge gave him fifteen years. Pissed a lot of folk off, but Claudette was queen by then. Nobody was gonna test her."

"My daddy still in prison?" Monty asked.

Ms. Lily shook her head. "Naw."

"Where is he?"

"Closer than ya think. Ya know, he fought 'side King on the day he died. Him and ya mama. Them two kids fought to save King, until he made them leave him. We got outnumbered. King made me take them to the rez. Made me leave him too. Boy, that damn Ella jumped from the roof of the office on the back of a man and stuck him good. Bled him like a gutted hog, ya hear? Manuel was tagging ass too. That damn Indian was big, but he moved light as hell on his feet. If they didn't see him coming, he laid 'em down. But King sent us away. Told me if I didn't get them to the rez, he was going to kill me. I hate that I left him. That man and Claudette was the only two real friends I ever had. I lost both of 'em." Ms. Lily's voice croaked as if she was about to cry.

I went over and sat next to Monty, who looked as if he was somewhere between grief and happiness. Sad because he had finally found out what had happened to his mother, and happy because his father was somewhere out there and, according to Ms. Lily, he was close. I held his hand, while Inez sat on the other side of him and did the same. Navy and Jojo flanked us and laid hands on his shoulders. Jai ran her hand over his head, then kissed him there. It was a sobering moment.

In all that, Ms. Lily had just about answered the questions I had wanted to ask. It was good to know that on King's last day, he hadn't had to fight alone. After I made sure Monty was okay, I got down to what I wanted to ask Ms. Lily.

"What do you know about the Knights of St. Assisi, Ms. Lily?" I asked the old woman.

She frowned, then sat up straighter. She studied me for a moment. "You already know the answer to that, don't chu?"

I nodded.

She said, "They killed King."

"Who would have sent them?" I asked.

"A priest . . . someone from Vatican City."

My head jerked back. "Why would Vatican City care—"

"The mob runs deep, baby. King's family always ran with the big dogs, the who's who of the underworld. I ain't never know who sent me to kill him the first time, if that's what you hunting after. Back then, you get an order, you carry it out. No questions asked."

I could tell that bit of information had shocked the rest of the family by the way they all got wide eyed. I was kind of disappointed Ms. Lily couldn't shed more light on who could have given the order to kill King. But she was old now and probably didn't remember a lot of things. However, I was grateful for the bit of information she had given us.

A few minutes later, Monty, Jojo, and Navy walked Ms. Lily home. I was mentally exhausted and knew everyone else was too.

***

The next morning, Nighthawk showed up at the ass crack of dawn to get Monty for his training. However, Monty couldn't leave until he made sure the Forty Thieves and the guards from Rize had checked in. He took his job serious. Since Cory had come back, Monty was no longer head of security. He was now cohead, and he always made sure his end was on point. Once a weapons check and a head count were done, we all sat down to breakfast.

While they ate, I made sure things at J.M. & Co. Financial Security were running smoothly. I didn't work for Javon, but I could run his company just as good as he could in his absence. Since I had to be on strict bed rest while pregnant, I hadn't had time to set up my real estate business. However, I did do financial consulting on the side, and it brought in good money. I also still ran all the legit businesses Mama had left behind. No one could question where our money came from, since everyone in the family had legitimate jobs.

Ms. Lily was a little late this morning, but she showed up, as always. The first thing she did was head to the girls. However, I had Honor latched on to my breast, while Jojo sat feeding Justice from a bottle. Ms. Lily was all smiles as she went from me to Jojo, speaking to the girls in German.

"Hurry up with feeding them," she fussed. "I promised them some good stories today. Y'all holding me up. Jojo, you have to hold that baby's head better than that," she said while helping Jojo to adjust Justice's head better. I didn't think Jojo was doing a bad job, but when it came to her girls, Ms. Lily had to have everything perfect. Then she looked at Nighthawk and said, "How you doing?"

Nighthawk, dressed in jeans and a T-shirt that showed pride in his Seminole heritage, nodded at Ms. Lily. "I'm fine, Lily. How are you?" he asked.

"Can't complain, really. I'm just old as hell and wondering how much longer I got here."

She kept studying Nighthawk like she was trying to figure something out. She smiled, then took a seat in her favorite chair. She started humming as she looked out the window. Ms. Lily was finicky like that. One minute she seemed happy. The next she withdrew into herself, like she had traveled back to another time.

"Shanelle, ya wanna know more about that day in the summer of nineteen eighty-five?" she asked after a while.

I took Honor off my breast, covered myself, then proceeded to burp her. "You remember something else?"

"No."

I sighed. Was kind of annoyed. "So why did you ask, Ms. Lily?"

"Because I'm sure Manuel does," she said.

From where I was sitting in the front room, I could see into the dining room. Monty's head snapped up. He dropped his fork and damn near toppled the table over as he abruptly stood. He rushed into the front room.

"You know where he is?" Monty asked Ms. Lily.

She looked at him and tilted her head. "Course I do," she said.

When she said nothing else, I could tell Monty got annoyed. He scratched his head, ran a hand through his hair, then switched his weight from one foot to the other.

"I meant to ask last night but got caught up in my emotions. But where is he, Ms. Lily?" he asked her.

Nighthawk took a deep breath, which drew my attention to him.

"Manuel, you ever gon' tell this boy you his pappy?" Ms. Lily asked.

At first I thought the lady had lost her mind. Maybe she had gone senile, and we'd missed the signs.

"I know you never wanted Mama to tell him who you was 'cus you was ashamed of going to prison and all. Mama and you argued about that, remember?" She turned to look at Nighthawk. "I don't know why ain't nobody put two and four together to get eight yet," she said. "The boy may look like his mama, but he every bit of you in height and build."

"Oh shit," Jojo said.

Navy quipped, "Jesus H. Christ." His mouth was agape as he looked from Nighthawk to Monty. "Yo! I always thought . . . Yo!"

I had no words. I felt stupid. How could something so obvious have escaped all of us? I mean, granted we had met Nighthawk only after Mama had died, but still, the fact that it took Ms. Lily pointing out the obvious blew my mind. Ms. Lily turned back to face the window.

Monty's whole body stiffened as he gazed across the room at Nighthawk. A barrage of emotions flittered across his face. His chest heaved up and down heavily.

"Why didn't you say something?" Monty asked.

Nighthawk looked at his son. "I would have . . . eventually."

"Eventually," Monty repeated, like he hadn't heard him the first time.

Nighthawk relaxed his stance. "I'd rather we do this in private. I don't want us to speak about this the first time in front of others. Not when your emotions are this raw."

"For over a year, I've been coming to the rez, doing lessons and learning about my Seminole heritage, and every day you looked at me, knowing I was your son?"

Nighthawk nodded.

"You heard me vocalize wishing I'd known my mother, and you ain't say shit," Monty said, his voice hardening by the second.

"It wasn't the right time," Nighthawk said. "You're what? Nineteen now? I spent fifteen years of your life in prison. I got out a year before Mama died, and when she took me to your school one day to show me how much you'd grown and I got to see you happy and thriving, I didn't wanna ruin that. I didn't have shit to offer you. You were happy here with Mama and the kids you'd come to love as your siblings. What did I have, Monty? A drunk father and a small house on the rez?"

"You would have been enough," Monty said. "Just you. Just knowing you were my dad would have been enough."

Nighthawk shook his head. "No. I had to have something to offer you other than just my mere presence. I owed your mother more than that, owed you more than that. Mama put me back on the payroll, but she told me not to even glance your way if I wasn't ready to be your father full-time, and I knew I wasn't ready. Then she was killed, and I knew I had to be a part of your life some kind of way. Javon putting me in a seat at the table of the Syndicate worked out perfectly."

Monty was about to say something, but just then Ms. Lily spoke up.

"I remember they wanted King to call Claudette," she said.

"Huh?" I asked. "Who?"

"The Knights who had come to kill him."

Inez asked, "Why?"

"That's kind of odd, to ask him to do that while trying to kill him, unless they wanted to lure her back," I said.

"I thought it odd then too," Nighthawk said. "But when I cornered one of the men around back of King's office, he was talking into a walkie, saying Claudette wasn't there."

Ms. Lily eyes widened as she turned around. "It was to be an ambush. They . . . they wanted to kill them both. Claudette was s'pose to be there. It was to be a double tap. Double tap for our kind meant like a two-for-one special."

"But she got that call about her goddaughter being raped," I said, remembering Mama's words from her journal. "So she wasn't in town."

"I always said King had a sixth sense when it came to protecting his woman," Ms. Lily said. "That man knew something . . . some kind of way he knew she needed to get 'way from here. We always joked about how his family's voodoo roots worked for him a lot."

Inez shot up from the couch. "What if Javon being called to New York is a setup, sis? What if they were lured there?"

My heart damn near leapt out my chest onto the floor. "That makes no sense. Why kill Cavriel and try to kill Luci just to lure Javon in? And where the hell is Absolan?"

"It's a king's descent," Ms. Lily said.

My whole body shook. I tried to stand and fell back on the couch. I knew what a king's descent was. I'd read about it in Mama's and King's journals. "They don't just take out the king. They wipe out the whole bloodline," I whispered.

"But Javon isn't any kin to any of them," Jojo said.

"Oh, but he is," Ms. Lily said. "Lucky is Claudette's nephew. Javon is Claudette's son."

"By adoption, not blood," Navy said.

"Don't matter. She claimed the boy as her own," Ms. Lily continued.

"That means that Cory and Uncle Snap will get hit too," Inez said, sheer terror etched on her features. "I . . . I can't lose Cory," she said. "And we can't lose Javon or Uncle Snap."

"We have to warn them," Navy said.

"But the whole bloodline?" Jojo asked, fear creasing his brows. "Don't that mean they could come for us too?"

Inez said, "Technically speaking, they lured the king and his right-hand men away from his family. . . ."

"We're sitting ducks?" Monty asked, but it came out more like a statement.

I looked at Honor and couldn't imagine a life where she didn't know her father's touch or his love. I also couldn't imagine having someone take me from my child. That cycle had to stop. I shot up from the couch and grabbed my cell. I dialed Javon, only to get no answer. I tried another three times and got the same results. I tried Uncle Snap, only to have his phone go straight to voice mail.

"Cory ain't answering," Inez said, panic lacing her voice.

I did something I had said I'd never do. I called Lucky, praying that he answered. Maybe he would know where Javon was. Maybe he could calm the voice in my head that was telling me my man was in distress. However, Lucky didn't answer his phone. My gut told me Javon was in trouble. Thinking about the fact that I wasn't there to have his back caused my whole world to collapse.

Chapter 19

Claudette

My dearest King, let me tell you through my words, my memories in this journal of mine, that I always could feel you. In my dreams, my mind, in the wind, the land. I always felt you, even when you were not near. And that night, as I went after Lonnie, it was no different. I felt you all in me, through me, the sweet, endearing chuckle of your voice in my mind. . . .

2L#

Kitty's Juke Joint was only a block straight from Betsy's house. Everything around me was quiet as a soundproof room. The dark skies twinkled as the moon revealed itself in its full, beautiful majesty. It was strange to me because I was in a clear, lucid zone.

Though it was close to midnight—it was 10:30 p.m. when I left Betsy's home—it didn't feel like it. My feet were thumping on the street, my breasts bouncing, as my walk was mean with purpose, I tell ya. I looked left, then right, plump lips set in a mean look, like that of a hunting wolf. I could see a few elders watching from their houses. It made me glance at them in response.

"I got rights. Rights all y'all were too scared to handle yaself. My Big Daddy Haynes is no longer on this earth to enact law, but I got rights as his blood and surviving child."

There was a rage in me, and the town needed to know it.

"I call the old law up in here, and y'all all knew it when I came home. Don't y'all call no one, undastand me!" I shouted. "This is sundown rights, hear me?"

When the doors to some of the elders' homes opened and I saw them pull out chairs on their porches and flash lights in support, I kept my strut right up to the large former train depot that was now Kitty's Juke Joint. A flashing sign of a cat flickered with the rhythm of my beating anger. I could hear Patti LaBelle crooning with Michael McDonald, until the tune switched to Janet Jackson trying to sing about somebody being nasty.

Cautiously, I put my gun against the small of my back, palmed my switchblade, then walked into the smoky club. Cigarette butts and walnut shells were scattered on the oak floors of the joint. There were the occasional spills as well, which made the floors sticky. Now, I knew Vernon Kitt, the owner, was particular about keeping his place clean, but since he was up in age, I could see that things had changed a bit.

At the right and left of me, I saw a couple of elders—Mrs. Wilks, who flipped on some Muddy Waters, and Mr. Wilks, who sat in a booth, cradling his favorite Colt 45 bottle with a shot of moonshine.

The old man was leaning. He clapped his hand on the table with the beat, then started crooning, "Well, I been settin' here drinkin'. I'm just as lonesome as a man can be."

Mrs. Wilks walked on by me with a glass of something in her hand. She had a carefree smile on her face and a blunt between her lips as she swayed to the music and waved a hand in the air. "Well, if it ain't sweet Detty," Mrs. Wilks said with a drunken, sweet smile.

Detty was the name all the old people had given me, completely ignoring the nickname that I did like, which was Cece.

Mrs. Wilks gave me a look over, then chuckled in the way of an old wise woman. "'Bout time ya came fa blood." Her glass-holding hand ran in front of me as she spoke. "I see it in ya eyes. Ya got ya daddy fiya in ya . . . and sumptin' else. Humph . . . 'bout time."

"I call sundown rights," I said as calmly as I could. By this time, I was so high on rage that my fists were clenched and my eyes were twitching.

"That nasty bastard is up over cha in the corner, thankin' no one will see him. Just vile. Hiding in the open. Nasty bastard." When Mrs. Wilks swayed to the music up out of my way, she looked over her shoulder at me. "Gawn take ya time wit' him. No one got nuffin' to say gal 'cept 'Handle yours.'"

"Yes, ma'am," was all I said as I left Mr. and Mrs. Wilks singing the blues.

To the left was a hall that led to the main part of the bar. An antiquated-looking wraparound bar, with various drinks on a wooden shelf with a mirror behind it, dominated the room. At one end of the bar sat Snap. He sat with his hat low, hunched over a cup of what I knew was a mix of whiskey and moonshine. Smoke danced around his face and caressed his lips. From how he leaned, with a glass in his hand, I could tell that he was watching the room, his gaze focused to the left of me.

Music played on, with more Muddy Waters crooning about some champagne and reefer. I turned and gave a nod to Snap, then took my slow stroll toward a private covered booth.

Mr. Kitt, who was sitting by the bar, coaching his son and watching my ass as I walked on, gave a curt chuckle. That old man wiped at his brow and said,

"*Shit . . . She done grown up very well. Gawn and crank up that music, son.*"

Ignoring them, I turned and slammed my fist with my blade on the booth table before me. "Hello, Lonnie."

"Aww . . . shit," Lonnie said and turned the color of tired khaki. With muted brown eyes that sagged from too much drinking, and hands marred by cuts and gashes, he looked up in his drunken and high state.

That foul-ass nigga slid back against the corner of the booth he sat in, as if trying to melt into the wall, as he stared at me with bloodshot eyes. Sweat touched the temples of his salt-and-pepper hair. His stained finger-nails scraped the surface of the table as he watched me.

"Cece . . . the fuck you doing here, huh?" he tried to bark at me with his stale-smelling breath.

"Oh, you still feeling a bit strong, huh?" I crooned.

"Fuck right, I do. Like I said, what you bring ya ass down here for, huh? Ya cheating-ass sista finally went on and did it, huh?"

I chuckled low, then slowly climbed in the booth, holding on to the table, and leaned in his face. Muddy Waters's "Mannish Boy" played as I leaned into the booth. Long ago, Lonnie was supposedly a fine mother-fucker. High yellow, hair that coiled on his head, and a slick smile that drew all the women. Some of that was still faintly in his face, but for me, all I saw was a devil.

"Did you not think this day would come?" I said sul-trily. "Didn't my daddy's last breath say that you'd die by a Haynes's hand?"

Lonnie was so gone that he didn't know what to do with himself. His gaze dropped to my breasts, which peeked out as I inched closer; then they went to the knife I held flat on the table.

"Damn, ya still a pretty thang. Shoulda been you as my wife," he said, then blinked, shaking his head. "But you ain't nothing but a nasty bitch who fucked that Kingston nigga."

"Fuck right," I said, then slammed the blade of my knife into the palm of Lonnie's hand.

A loud shout came from him, and I tossed the mason glass of liquid in his face, then spit at him. The affront was enough to pull out the real monster that was Lonnie.

"Bitch. My face!" He swung out, then pushed me out of the booth.

I fell on my back, breaking a chair in the process, while the glass from the mason jar shattered behind us. A record would scratch in an ordinary joint, but here everyone knew he had this coming, so they minded their business. Flashing a satisfying grin, I looked up as Lonnie tried to pull the knife from his hand. His face was beet red. Burns were already showing on his face, and the smell of lye on his face almost made me gag.

"Moonshine and lime bastard," I said, cackling from the floor. Pain shot up me, but I didn't care. I was here for a purpose, which was why I pushed up quickly, jumped back in the booth, and sent my fist into Lonnie's face.

"Didn't . . . my . . . daddy . . . say . . . that a Haynes was going to be your death?" I spat out between each punch.

Lonnie twisted and turned to hit me with his free hand. The force of his punch was so strong that it made me stop my hits to pull the knife from his hand. Once free of the knife, Lonnie grabbed my neck and squeezed, forcing me out of the booth. Lonnie's face contorted with clarity as he snarled. Cigarette ash flew in the air, along with liquor and his spit.

"Get cho dirty-ass hands off me, whore! Yo' sista a whore, and so are you," Lonnie spat at me. "You think I wouldn't get me some fresh fish afta ya lying-ass sista tried to play me? Huh?"

My eyes rolled in my head. I could see Snap rushing forward, glass shattering everywhere as he had dropped his cup.

"You had no goddamn right to put your goddamned tainted hands on my sister, or the girls in this town or elsewhere, motherfucker." Twisting, I felt the blade in my hand. Music blared in my ears, and I screamed as I stuck the knife in Lonnie's side, then swung up to scrape my nails down his face.

Screaming, Lonnie let go. A right hook from me made his face turn right with a harsh snap. Then I swiped my blade against the side of his neck. That was when Snap dropped low and jumped him, making them both fall back to the floor. Panting for air, I slowly sat up, feeling my gun at my side. My head was ringing. Blood splattered my clothes, and I was wet from the spilled liquor on me. Something in me wailed. I rose to my feet and stumbled, and when I did, I looked down as light flashed over Snap and a scrapping Lonnie.

I walked forward, then stopped. My vision was blurry from the stinging alcohol. When I raised my gun to send a bullet into Lonnie that hit his shoulder, I stopped. My vision was a mess. It made me see Kingston for a second. There was a look of intense fury on his face, and slight fear. Fear that he wasn't going to make it from wherever he was. Blood dripped down his face. I could see that his body was battered and bullets had connected to my man's regal body.

Stunned and in shock, I didn't hear when I dropped my knife. All I could do was stare at my husband as he scrambled on the floor for his life. He lifted his gun and fired a shot, screaming. His handsome face was contorted in pain.. Hot tears fell down my face. I gripped my chest and felt my heart slamming against my rib cage.

When the flash went away and I saw Lonnie trying to go for my knife on the floor, I acted without realizing it and placed my foot in his face, cracking teeth and his nose. I heard myself scream, "You hurt another child. Another girl."

Shaking my head, I tried to get my thoughts together. I wasn't sure what I had just seen, but I felt as if time was slowing.

"Kingston . . . ," I whispered, looking around in a panic.

"Sista," I heard Snap say.

His voice was so raw that I had no choice but to look his way. Snap sat on Lonnie's back, with his bulky arm squeezing Lonnie's neck, like a snake ready to kill.

"Mama," he shouted at me again.

When I blinked, I nodded. Something was going on with Kingston. Our breaths were one, and though I was in southern Georgia, I could feel his touch on me as if he were with me. Pain ripped through me. It made me stumble against a chair and grip it.

"Go!" Snap ordered, with his hand against Lonnie's face in a way that showed that he was about to make that fool sleep a bit. "I'll finish this fah ya."

"Thank you . . ." Taking deep breaths, I turned and ran out of that juke joint with purpose. I could still hear the blues in my ears as I ran toward my family home. Satan was on my tail, as the elders would say, because I sprinted down the street as if I could fly. My lungs burned from the exertion.

"Kingston," I muttered.

When I burst through the front door, Deedee shot up from the couch, looking at me as if I were a ghost.

"Did you do it?" I heard her ask.

Frantic, I looked for the phone, then grabbed it and hurriedly dialed.

"Sis . . . did you—"

"Yes, *Deedee. He's handled,"* I screamed, shaking.

No one was picking up at the house. I slammed the receiver down, then picked it up to dial again.

"What's going on, baby girl?" I heard Deedee ask me. It had been years since she called me that. I knew she had finally caught on that I was operating in fear, which was why she had called me that.

"Did Kingston call?" I asked, shaking. No one was answering at his business. I watched my sister slowly shake her head. I made another call but got nothing. I knew this was not normal, and I knew this meant only one thing.

Holding the receiver in my hand, hearing it making that "dropped call" sound, I screamed, "Kingston!" My life crumbled before me, and I felt as if all the air in the room was compressing. . . .

Kingston, baby . . . that was the day I was no more. I fainted dead on that floor. I fainted . . . and . . . and . . . I died with you. I . . . I can't write no more, baby. I can't.

They killed my Kingston. They killed my light. . . .

Chapter 20

Uncle Snap

I left the kitchen in search of anything that would point us in the direction of Absolan. There was no way the nigga had just dropped off the face of the earth. There had to be some trace of him somewhere.

Once Lucky had joined me in the dark hall behind the kitchen, everything was going according to plan. We checked out some of the rooms without being noticed. We were doing good. Getting in and out, undetected. Everything was all fucking good, until Lucky got a message on his phone.

"Shit," he said.

"What is it, nephew?" I asked.

"Absolan," he said, then showed me his phone.

Absolan had been tied to a chair and beaten. His body was badly bruised. The old man looked as if he was barely holding on to life.

"Damn," I said. "They done fucked him over good."

The only thing was, we didn't know if he was being held against his will or if that old freaky-ass priest was enjoying what was happening to him.

I asked Lucky to hold his phone then showed the woman Absolan's picture. "Have you seen this man tonight?" I asked one of the timid women walking past us in the hallway.

She shook her head after looking at a picture of Absolan.

"He's been here before, though, right?" Lucky asked behind me.

The girl, a blonde with bought tits and a rail-thin shape, nodded.

Lucky asked, "When's the last time you seen him?"

"Yesterday," she said.

Lucky and I looked at one another before he asked her, "Did he walk in here on his own?"

She frowned. "What do you mean?"

"Was he in distress, or was he in here partying in this BDSM establishment?"

The girl looked to be high out of her mind, so it took her a minute to register what Lucky was asking her. She scratched her head and furrowed her brows. The broad was dressed like she had walked out of one of those old Conan the Barbarian movies.

"Um . . . ," she said as she glanced behind us. She pointed. "They brought him in."

Lucky's phone dinged again. "They know we're here," he said.

We had walked into the club expecting to find some shit about the Knights and had ended up running right into those motherfuckers. As we turned to make our way down the hall, motherfuckers in clerics robes met us halfway. A hailstorm of bullets rained down on us. We'd gotten caught in some shit we weren't expecting. There was no time to pussyfoot around. I raised my gun and drew first blood, shooting one of the men right between his eyes. Lucky was a good shot. Following my lead, he took out another one.

He flipped his phone and showed me a picture of him and his sister walking into the club.

"We gotta get back to Javon and Cory," I said.

I was worried that neither one of them knew the shit had hit the fan.

Screams lit up the hall as an alarm went off. Lucky and I took off full speed ahead down to the end of the hall. We were outnumbered, no matter how we looked at it. And when those priests pulled MAC-11s and AK-47s out from under their robes, I snatched Lucky and pulled him into one of the occupied rooms in front of us. We fell inside just as bullets chased us down.

A slew of half-naked women were scattered around the dimly lit room. Lucky shoved one of the women into a closet and out of the way. It would have been funny, given the way he slapped the girl in the back of the head and pushed her in there, if niggas wasn't on our asses.

There was a bed against the wall that was big enough for four overgrown men to sleep in. A crucifix in the center of the room looked as if it had been welded to the concrete floor. Pails and buckets of God knew what sat haphazardly around the room. There was a man tied to a chair, with his nuts ensnared in some kind of contraption. He was gagged and had his hands tied behind his back, and the pale nigga had on a red wig, lipstick, and gaudy eye shadow.

"What kind of freaky shit y'all got going on in here?" I asked to no one in particular.

I heard Lucky give something of a chuckle as he kicked over the chair the man was in. The man's muffled screams could be heard as gunshots rang out in the hall. I looked around for another way out. No way we wanted or needed to be trapped inside a room with a hit squad outside the door. There was a door that looked as if it led to another room, but there were too many locks on it. We'd waste ammo trying to shoot the locks off, and that would take too much time.

Lucky looked stressed, more stressed than I'd ever seen the young man.

"We're pretty much trapped in here," he said as he looked around.

"We got two options, nephew," I said. "We dive through that fucking window and hope we hit that damn pool below, or we try to shoot our way back up out or this room."

He shook his head. "We didn't bring that much ammo between us. We need to get downstairs, where I have men set up." As those words left his mouth, bullets lit up the doorway.

I said, "Looks like we taking a dive, then."

I raised my gun to shoot at the glass, praying that shit wasn't bulletproof. As the glass shattered, Lucky and I heard a loud explosion. We took a running leap through the broken window and flew through the air just as the door to the room burst open.

Instead of hitting the water, it felt as if the water punched the fuck out of me. Lucky and I hit the water hard, causing instant chaos. We knew bullets would soon chase us, but because of the crowded bar area, it made it easier for us to get out of the water and get lost in the crowd. Water weighed down my clothes as Lucky and I shoved people out of the way, trying to get to the room where we'd left Giana, Cory, and Javon. With bullets lighting up the floor after us, we didn't have time to call or text.

"This way," Lucky called as we ran toward the more private area of the club.

Just as we got ready to pass the kitchen, the doors flew open. As I yanked Lucky out of the line of fire, a bullet tore into my shoulder, sending me flying backward. I let out a roar that showed the pain I felt. Something like fucking sharp electricity danced through my body. Felt as if my shoulder had been ripped from my body. I ground my teeth and took sharp, ragged breaths.

I looked up to see Lucky get to his feet, then cover me. His gun game was on point. Anything he aimed at, he hit. The young buck yanked me from the floor, shielding me as he shot at anything in a black robe. Clearly, at that point, the boy didn't give a damn who could get it. And the nigga was a helluva lot stronger than he looked.

"We gotta find another way," he said.

"Naw, we gotta get out," I said.

"We have to get Javon and—"

"Naw, son, trust me. Von would want us to get out," I croaked out, pain making slobber drip from my bottom lip.

He nodded. "Can you shoot with your left?"

"Yeah," I answered.

"Then let's shoot our way the fuck up outta here."

Whoever the hit squad was, they had played us like chess pieces. They knew we were here. They waited until we separated and then moved in. Javon and Cory had been meticulous in the way they had set this sting up, so it had to be someone from Lucky's camp who had dropped the ball, since they had pictures of him and his sister entering the club. We were missing something. Had to be. This shit reminded me of how King had been left on his own in the end. No way was I going to let Javon, Cory, or Lucky get taken down like they did King. I'd throw myself in the line of fire first. That made me think about someone I'd left back home.

None of the kids knew I visited that whorehouse. They had no idea that I disappeared every Sunday and sometimes Saturday to spend the days with the whore who looked like my woman. She was of no relation. That I was sure of, but over the past year, she had been good to me. After a while, she'd stopped charging me, but I still paid her, anyway. Had to keep shit in perspective. And yet I couldn't help but think I'd want to get back just to see her again.

A bullet whizzing by my head cut those thoughts real short, though. Lucky pulled us into a corner, behind one of the statues. I took the pain, leaned around to the left. I sent a bullet right into the heart of a shooter who had emerged from behind the curtains. Erupting gunfire from the other side of the club told me there was another fight going on.

"I'm almost out of ammo," Lucky said.

"Yeah, me too, nephew."

"There's too many of them, and they've blocked us off from getting to the other side."

"I know. I gotta make it out of this bitch alive. I gotta take care of my woman's children, nephew. She wouldn't want me to leave 'em, and she wouldn't want me to leave you, either. Ya mama ain't shit, but I wouldn't wanna bring her dead son back to her. So listen," I said, then looked out at the chaos. "There is a dead Knight about two feet to ya left. He's got a MAC-11 and probably some more weapons on him. I'll cover you as you get to him. Get his weapons."

I watched Lucky look to where I was directing him. The boy took direction well. He ran in where I told him, while I made sure to keep the heat off his back. It happened quicker than I expected. While he went for the gun, I emptied mine, shooting at the opposition. Lucky picked up the MAC-11, and as if his name was Tony Montana, he let that pretty bitch spray the air, taking down Knights and anybody else who got in the way.

My shoulder bled like a stuck pig. I felt myself getting weaker, and my shoulder felt as if all feeling was dissipating in it. Men in robes surrounded us. It seemed for every one man we took down, three more showed up in his place. Lucky looked at me as he dived behind the pillar where I was, and in that moment, I could tell we were thinking the same thing. It was quite possible we had met our end. That shit scared me. I wasn't gon' front about it.

Lucky tossed me another MAC-11 from one of the downed Knights. A year ago, I'd been 'bout ready to go be with my woman. But after coming across King's journal again, remembering how she loved him, it was safe to assume that if there was an afterlife, Mama was back with him. Shit saddened a brother on some real shit. I was a lonely-ass old man. And that was probably why I had been seeing Rowena more. She filled a void in me, a void that the kids couldn't fix.

Something similar had crossed Lucky's mind. I could tell by the way his brows furrowed as we came together and then stood back-to-back.

"I figure if we gone die, nephew, we may as well take as many as these motherfuckers with us as we can. You ready?" I asked him.

"Naw. Not really. I hadn't planned on dying tonight, but, shit, if it's war these motherfuckers want, then let's show 'em how we get down," he spat.

"Let's do it," I said.

Lucky went left, and I went right. If I was gonna die tonight, I'd go out fighting.

Chapter 21

Javon

If predictability could be a watch, then that shit was always on time in this world. I sat back under a secluded Roman-style cabana, and as I sat there, I stared at a motherfucker who kept watching us. See . . . I knew coming up into a place that felt like a hotbed of fire ants, namely, a spot that *possibly* was associated with the Knights of St. Assisi, was a gamble. But, hell, I could play a mean game of Yahtzee, so I rolled that die. I knew that no matter what, I'd come out with the information that I wanted and needed.

So, as I sat there, playing the scared financial security analyst, I made sure to be ready. Silk-clad bodies with various curves and of different ethnicities undulated before us, dancing for "Don St. John's" entertainment and flinging silk panels toward us. I watched, in thought, as a stick-thin sista who had sad eyes fed Armani wine from a goblet with her lips. Another dancer, a white girl with brown hair, landed in a handstand and tried to make her tiny ass shake. Meanwhile, a third tired, thin Latina with overly bleached hair that didn't match her complexion fanned Armani.

This shit up in here was wild. "Master and slave" was thrown around like everyday bullshit, while "servicing" was done, with pride on display, in the cabanas next to us for anyone to see. Glancing at my brother, I was ready to go. I knew that Cory was going to be effective in scoping out the joint. That would then lead Uncle Snap to get a little deeper in the belly of the beast. After that, I knew Lucky was going to back him up, which would possibly cause some shit to go off, and that, too, paid off.

Undoing my jacket as I slowly stood up, I kept my attention on a man who felt familiar to me. Off in the distance, amid a group of businessmen, stood an unassuming man in a dark gray suit and a white open-collar shirt. His dark hair was pulled back in a man bun. He had a slight pale brown hue to him, which suggested either that he had just come back from a trip where there was plenty of sun or that he might be Sicilian. For me, it was possibly both.

Light from the open pavilion danced at that nigga's feet until it flashed in my face. With steely eyes and a sharp jaw, this nigga looked like the poster boy for a Valentino advertisement.

Ain't nothing happenstance, Von. In life, every bit of information thrown at you can be in the form of a sign, misuse of a word, or action. You have to just be smart enough to read those cues. It was Mama talking to me, reminding me what I needed to do versus what I wanted to do.

So I listened. My memory was fucking with me, because I knew that I had seen this bastard somewhere. When recognition hit, I moved near Cory.

"Get Giana to safety," I said in a low voice to Alex, then looked at my brother.

Like the trained assassin he was, Alex remained low key as he took Giana by the arm. "Yes, sir. I'm being told there's a scrabble going on in the club, sir."

"Wait, wait . . . What's going on?" Giana said, looking confused and stunned. She reached under her dress, fiddled with something near her crotch area, then pulled out a gun.

"That's Lucky and Unc. I feel it in the air. Keep her safe, and, Giana . . . fuck some shit up, Mama. Just don't get hurt or die," I ordered.

With a quick sleight of hand, making it look like I was going for my drink, I leaned down to grab my suitcase.

"What's up?" Cory asked, looking toward where I was staring. "Hold up. That's Absolan's personal guard. His adopted heir, ain't it?"

"Yeah. I believe his name in Fabian O'Neil, and judging by the way he's quickly getting up, and how his security, Luciano's men, are texting and grabbing him, he realizes that we shouldn't be seeing him."

Last year, when I met the Commission, my meeting Absolan's personal right hand had been a quick thing, because the guy had been on his way to the Vatican. The fact that this nigga hadn't been accounted for when Absolan was taken and only now was on the radar made the pieces of this tricky puzzle come together, because at his side were two dudes from Luciano's security team. This shit was an inside game, and the proof stared at me from afar.

"Cory," I said calmly, still watching Fabian. When that nigga gave a slick smile and nodded my way, I felt a chill of awareness run down my spine. "Follow him."

"Already on it," Cory said, then walked toward the crew. "Bitches are running. Be on alert."

I nodded at my brother, then looked down. "Mr. St. John."

Lounging in la-la land, while eating a palm full of purple grapes, Armani rolled to his side and looked at me.

"I believe it's time for you to escort me out."

"Wha-a . . . Why?"

"Get your bumbling, entitled, borderline sick ass the fuck up *now*," I barked, then cleared my throat, looking around. I could hear screams kicking off and behind that bullets being discharged.

"Oh, shit! Who's shooting?" Armani quickly shot up from where he was lounging. The casual Roman-style robe he wore shifted in a manner that made his balls and his ass end up on display.

My eyes turned into quick slits out of annoyance. "If you're trying to stick around to find out, then by all means, keep being stupid. But if you are really as smart as our Commission friends seem to think, then you'll—"

Before I could finish, Armani flipped over his table, reached down into a pile of pillows, then tossed something at me. "Perks of VIP legacy membership," he said with an amused look on his face, pulling out some other things.

When I caught what Armani had thrown, I saw that it was a pump shotgun. Without even a blink of an eye, I widened my stance, pressed that shit against my shoulder, and quickly pointed it toward Cory's back. My brother was rushing into the crowd, which seemed to swarm him like bees from a hive. When he pivoted, trying to cut through the people, I aimed over his shoulder and let out several rounds toward Fabian's crew.

My aim was on point, as was shown by one of Luci's turncoats gripping his shoulder. I watched Cory disappear in the crowd. Hands came out of nowhere in the mix, and I saw that it was Cory who sliced a blade against the throat of another one of Fabian's people, almost snatched at the nigga, but was forced back by security hands. I pumped off another round. Armani was at my side, aiming at people who were rushing in and shooting back at us.

Fabian was being flanked. He shouted out orders that had a few of his men breaking off and going in different areas, while some came our way. In the middle of the chaos, he took the opportunity to disappear behind a statue.

"Shit. This is like the good old days," he said, laughing. He then flung back the bottom of his robe to drop to one knee in some type of desperado-looking move. He grinned wide, aimed his guns, and shouted, "Don't harm the pretty flowers, assholes."

My mouth pursed. Dude was crazy as a coon, which reminded me of something. "We need to clear the area now. Left a little present, which is about to go off," I said.

"All right," Armani said, hopping up. As he did so, he took two fingers and put them in his mouth and whistled. "Young man, come flank your family."

I saw Cory look my way. I gave a nod, and I watched him turn while pulling on one of Fabian's men. The hell was my fam, my people? I wondered. My eyes searched the open area, found nothing. Uncle Snap and Lucky, where the hell were they?

"Where does that statue lead, Armani?" I pointed away from me, strapping my shotgun to my back and taking a pistol that was being handed to me.

Armani gave a look and frowned while he pulled out a final gun. "Leads to the BDSM zone. You don't need to go that way. You'll get lost up in those halls and caged in."

"But you do know the way out through there, correct?" I asked. I just needed to know as I followed him to a wall of flowers and vines.

"Yes, son. But I don't want to die today, so I'm taking you out through the emergency exit route," Armani explained. He motioned for us to follow him. "The halls are purposely narrow for situations like this that might occur."

"No doubt," was my only reply. I watched him move the planter vases to the side and push against a hidden panel. The panel sank into the wall and revealed a dark entryway. A set of stairs appeared, and I could see windows that gave a view of a back alleyway. Behind me, bodies peppered the lush green garden. Something had gone down. It made me worry about Uncle Snap.

Shit. I even had concern about Lucky. I knew and had faith that they each could hold their own. There would be no way that they would be alive today if they couldn't manage on their own. I just didn't want either of them dying on my watch for coming into this cesspool. But above anything else, I couldn't take it if something went down with Uncle Snap and I lost him.

"U-up ahead has the mark of St. Assisi." That was Cory. He was panting, with a mixture of sweat and blood running down his face. He had exerted himself by running and dragging by the throat a nigga who was trying to struggle against his hold. When he'd snapped that fool's neck forward to slam him against a wall in the corridor, I calmly stepped in front of the guy.

Just then that loud explosion sounded— one of my babies snuck in, in my suitcase. The force was intense. We could hear feet thumping around and men shouting about where we all could have disappeared to. I used that moment to reach back in my suitcase. Once I got what I was aiming for, I calmly slapped the chest of that dude I was standing in front of, the one Cory had slammed against the wall.

Anger was reflected in the periwinkle hue of the man's eyes before me, and I stood there in his face, silent. My jaw clenched. Armani was up the stairs, locking down the passage. All we could hear were loud blasts and shouting, and then it sounded as if screams were coming from the walls. During all of that, we were in flickering red light and darkness.

Finally, ready to talk, I kept my voice even and without emotion as I stood face-to-face with a traitor. "Hello. I believe your name is Stefano?"

Cory squeezed, and a ruddy undertone washed over Stefano's rough features. I could still see that he was fighting, but he was losing due to having issues breathing.

"At any time I can tell my brother to crush your esophagus. Because it's hell above our heads right now, I really am trying to be logical about this shit. So, let me repeat myself. Your name is Stefano, correct? A soldier and protector to Don Luciano."

"Y-yes," Stefano answered.

"Tell me . . ." I slowly slid my hands into my slacks and kept my stance before continuing. "How do you find yourself working for Fabian and turning your back on Luciano? It's Fabian who's after Luciano, am I correct?"

Once again, Stefano bucked. A sharp cough came from him. He strained, and tears fell down his face.

"Talk and we can finish this," I said calmly as Cory squeezed, then twisted his blade into Stefano's side. "We all can go about our business and forget this happened. You know who I am, correct?"

Stefano nodded.

"Then you know I stand by my word, correct?"

When Stefano nodded again, I smiled. "So explain."

Cory loosened his grip, and Stefano coughed. "For my family, I do everything."

"What does your family have to do with this?" I asked. "Is it about loyalty to Absolan versus Luciano?"

"Yes," Stefano croaked. "Absolan . . . Absolan is the true heir. And through him, the Commission will be purified and made great again."

A deep chuckle came from me. *Here we go with this bullshit*, I thought. "So Absolan wasn't kidnapped, huh?"

When Stefano lunged forward, I moved to the side and slammed my fist in his throat. I watched the man almost crumble to his feet, which allowed me to slam my knee in his face. Calmly, I snatched his head back and snarled.

"I asked a question." Tapping the disk, which was a bomb in disguise, against his chest, I watched lights on it blink rapidly. "Absolan wasn't kidnapped, huh?"

"Solummodo ex vera pura possint imperare a sanguine omnium nostrum," Stefano gruffly spat out. He tried to pull at the bomb. He looked at us, then smiled. "Militum laudibus St. Assisi."

I reached out and cracked his head against the wall. "I am about tired of this shit." Each blow was harder than the last, until blood decorated the wall. Pissed all the way off, I punt kicked that nigga's body. "The fuck you say, little nigga, huh?" I shouted in annoyance. "What Latin shit was that?"

"Let's go before we blow the fuck up, *kuya*." It was Cory's voice. He grabbed my arm and pulled me so I would stop stomping on that nigga's body.

"My bad," was all I could muster. I was pissed all the way off.

"I feel you. This is some round about fuck shit right here," Cory said while rushing forward. I followed him.

When we ran into Armani, we pulled that fool with us.

"He said, 'Only the blood of the true pure can rule us all. Praises to the St. Assisi.' Luciano will erase them all. Now go left," Armani shouted.

As we did, we burst through a set of double doors that led down to another level of the building. We ended up in a large room with nothing but gilded mirrors, several chandeliers, and slick wooden flooring. It was a ballroom.

"Straight ahead," he ordered, rushing through the large, empty ballroom.

The abrasive sound of guns going off grew louder. "Where is that coming from?" I asked.

Looking over his shoulder, Armani frowned. "There's many ways to get around this club. I believe that's from the BDSM area. You can get to it from here."

It was at that moment that I heard a loud crash and the boom of my bomb. When we all looked, we could see several bodies flying down past the large paneled windows in the ballroom. The route we had taken to the ballroom was turned into rubble from the impact of the bomb. We had to get up out of here, and without the fun gunplay, but I knew that bomb was going to draw others, so I counted our blessings and readied myself.

"Whoa. Was that Lucky?" Armani asked incredulously.

"Hell, if we know," Cory said, rushing forward to look. Then he laughed, shook his head, and gave a nod. "Yeah. So. Let's bounce, because Uncle Snap just flew by too." Cory made a falling motion with his hand while whistling, indicating that Unc had fall out the window too.

"Oh, shit," I said, shocked. There was no way that I couldn't laugh at that.

"Over here," I heard someone shout. The voice came from over by one of the several decorative mirror panels on the wall. Each one vibrated; then two slid open.

"A'ight. Let's go," I shouted.

Both Cory and I pulled out our Glocks. We shot off rounds and shattered the mirrors as we jogged to the stairway that led to the exit below. Shards of glass peppered the smooth flooring. We could see men in robes hunkering down behind the open doors that were mirrors. Others stepped forward in the same black attire that matched that of the men who had chased us when we first landed. This shit was pouring out like roaches from a wall, and a truth was finally settling in my mind. All of this was too close to home, and the reason for this was that Luciano no longer had secure backing.

"We need to get Uncle Snap and Lucky, then get to the hospital." I rushed out to Cory, and he then ran by my side.

I popped off my shotgun and then swung it into my bag so that I could grab the Glock that I had on me, thanks to Armani.

"Got you covered. . . . Shit," Cory hissed. His neck was bleeding, liquid seeping from where he held his hand to his neck. "Bitch grazed me."

"Move in front of me," I told him.

"Naw."

I gave my brother a look, then slowed down and allowed him to get in front of me as we ran. "Nigga, move."

Cory shook his head at this move of mine, then helped me shoot at those who were chasing us. We paused on a set of stairs and pointed our guns upward at the robes that followed and the black-clothed soldiers. We shot at them, and they fell like rain around us.

"Fuck!" I shouted, moving to the side. I patted my brother's shoulder, and we rushed down the stairway as fast as we could. Red liquid was dripping down my brother's shirt. He kept shooting behind me, but there were too many soldiers.

As I turned, I felt a hand push me, causing me to fall forward. I felt my hand slam into the face of one of the soldiers, and I grabbed him as I fell. Now, when I say I fell, I mean, my ass plummeted to the first floor of the building. I had been on the second floor. Because this nigga was attached to me, I was able to use his body as a cushion and soften the impact.

"Von!" I heard my brother yell, until I went splat against the floor.

Nothing but darkness was my friend for a moment. I felt pain rip through my body. I had been shot. My side was aching, and the back of my head felt like hell. But under me I felt the nigga whom I had held on to slowly moving.

When his groan hit my ear, I heard a voice in my head. *If you don't get cha ass up, I'll shoot you in ya pinkie toe, boy, then whup ya dumb ass.*

"Mama," I moaned, then tried to open my eyes. My eyelids fluttered, and all I saw was white light.

You heard me. Don't let these niggas end ya life, I heard her say.

When I looked up, I could see a woman whose beauty almost made my heart stop. She smiled, and when the corners of her eyes crinkled, I realized that I was staring at a younger Mama Claudette. Her hand touched my chest, and her lips kissed my forehead.

Take your lessons, son. Tell everyone how much you've learned, and you let them know how much I love them. I'm watching. Mama gave me a gentle wink, an enduring one. *Tell that man of mine that I love him even now and that what he needs is coming for him in this life. I will always wait for him too.*

"Mama?" I moaned again.

Tell my Raphael that, my Snap. Now getcha self up. I ain't letting these bullets hurt my babies anymore. There's a gun to ya right. Get it. When she slapped me, I sat up, reached beside me, and fell off the goon beneath me.

I felt that nigga punch me, then struggle for the gun I held. We scrapped and fought each other. My head slammed into his masked face. His hand slammed into my ribs, making me spit. The pain was crazy, but I was on one. I felt Mama all through me, so when I hit the goon on top of me with my arm, then kicked him back, I sent several bullets into him. At that same moment, Cory finally made it down the steps to the first floor.

Sweat dropped down my face. I felt my brother reach down and grab me, then help me stand so that we could rush out. As we escaped through the doors, I swear on everything that I saw Mama, in white, standing on those steps, looking like a young Iman, while by her side was a brotha, also in white, who made me think of Jesse Williams with a head full of hair. He gave me a nod as he stood by Mama's side on the stairway. Wherever he touched, debris fell, causing the goons who were chasing us to stumble back. In Mama's hand was my suitcase, and I could glimpse the rest of my bombs, which were blinking rapidly.

Chapter 22

Cory

My brother, who wasn't so out of it that he couldn't run, was mumbling something about Mama as I helped him from the building. I could hear something ticking as I hit the doors, hoisted Von against my shoulder, and ran like Ricky from *Boyz n the Hood*. It kind of also helped that I swore that I felt a pair of hands push against my back. When I turned my head, I swore I smelled Mama's perfume.

A powerful blast followed. The heat of it and the force made me stumble. Shaking off the vibe that Mama was with us, I looked ahead. Armani was with Giana, who stood with our Forty Thieves member Alex. A large black SUV ran behind him. Once they saw us, Alex rushed forward to help me with Von.

"He's hurt," I said, rushing to the car.

"So are you, man," Alex said with concern.

"Don't matter. Just take care of my stupid-ass brother," I said with a frown.

Had he not moved me out of the way, I would have been the one to fall. It should have been me, and not him. Panic and worry had me pissed the fuck off, so I was snarling at Alex, ignoring the fact that I was bleeding from my neck and was light-headed.

"I got you both, regardless," Alex simply stated, helping us into the SUV.

Giana was teary-eyed while pulling at us both to get us in the car. When she hovered over us to blanket us from any gunfire, I saw her pointing a gun back at the blazing building. More men were coming, men in all black, who, I knew, were Knights. Giana's face contorted, and she let off rounds, which made me think of how people described Mama in battle.

"Start the fuckin' car," she yelled, a thick accent taking over her voice.

Tired, I reached under her and pulled out my Glock to help her. At the same time, I felt Von, who was leaning against me, shift. When I heard a third gun, I realized it was him. The three of us had our arms stretched out and were blasting niggas with the car door open. Alex revved the ride, hit reverse, then forward, ready to get us the fuck up outta there. Armani keeping Giana balanced on the seat as she kept shooting.

As we got ready to ride off, the car almost ran head-on into Uncle Snap and Lucky.

"Holy shit!" Armani shouted, slamming his hand against the roof of the SUV. After turning, he pushed open the back door on other side of the SUV. "Close that door, Giana."

Giana did as she was instructed, and her weight shifted off our bodies. She sat on my lap. I got ready to say some ignorant shit, but she seemed focused on my neck, against which she placed part of her ripped shirt.

"Damn," I muttered as I watched Uncle Snap climb in, holding his shoulder. "You got hit too."

"Got slammed like Cheney going hunting," Uncle Snap grunted.

"Lucky, you hurt?" I said between my teeth. My neck was on damn fire. All the running I had been doing, I hadn't pay it any attention, but now that I was sitting, I could feel it.

"Hurry, man," Armani told Lucky, who had only half his body in the SUV.

"Shut the fuck up, Armani. I'm trying," Lucky hissed. "Yeah, I'm hurt. Fucking bitches ain't playing."

Alex chose that moment to speed off, with Lucky half hanging out of the car. It took Armani pulling Lucky in and then struggling to grab the door handle for the door to close.

"Get us the hell outta here!" Giana shouted from my lap.

She motioned for me to hold my neck, then climbed back over the seat to work on Uncle Snap and Lucky.

"We'll need to go to . . ." I listened to Giana shout out instructions to a second location in order to lose the Knights.

Von groaned by my side during that time, until he sat up coughing. "G-gotta get to the hospital. Lu . . ." He paused, gave a cough that rattled even my own lungs. "Luciano is in danger."

"True that," Uncle Snap grunted. "We done found out that these assholes are running deep. That this has to be an inside thing. Show 'em, nephew."

Lucky shifted in his seat while his sister wiped his face. He took out his cell phone, pulled up a picture, and showed us a battered and bound Absolan.

Ninja was hunched over, looking like the worst human being on earth. Bruises marred his face. Blood was caked on him, and I saw some gashes. A part of me felt bad for the old man, but another part was confused as fuck. The longer I stared at that picture, the more I realized that this shit had to be a setup.

When Von laughed, I knew that we were on the same wavelength. "Just had a bastard pledge some allegiance to the Knights. Said Absolan is the way . . . some pure blood shit again," Von stated.

"He's not telling lies." I looked at Lucky. "Was one of your own. Stefano."

"What? Stefano?" Lucky looked incredulous, then pissed. His jaw clenched, and his nostrils flared.

"Some of your people are on the Knight's side, and ya boy Fabian is linked to it. Saw him with your men," Von explained. His voice was deep and tired. "So it's like this, man. You can only keep who you know without a doubt is blood tied to Luciano and will die protecting him, because they want him dead and erased."

"Daddy . . . ," Giana gasped, in shock. "Get us to the hospital." Her eyes were wide, serious. She looked past my shoulder, then patted Alex's shoulder. "They're behind us. Go through this light and make a left ahead."

"Yes, ma'am," Alex said, maneuvering us through the congested traffic. Towering buildings were on the left and right sides of us. On the right side was outbound traffic. It was gridlocked as the vehicles waited for the signal lights to change color.

It was Alex and Giana who got us out of the fucked-up situation we all found ourselves battling. When Alex took Giana's advice, she led us to a huge parking garage. We sat quietly, watching and waiting. Once we saw the Knights in their rides, Alex hopped out of the SUV, helped Lucky into the front seat, then switched seats with Armani.

Giana sat on Uncle Snap's right. She and Alex rolled down their window. It was then that that crazy-ass friend of mine behind the wheel sped after the Knights. I watched Lucky finesse the SUV to get behind the Knights.

"Wish we had more of Von's bombs," I said, watching Von chuckle.

"Mama took 'em," he said with a smirk. His head lolled; then he shook.

This ninja had a damn concussion. I knew it. "Let's get them done and get to the hospital," I said, watching my brother and feeling worried. "I'll call our Thieves to keep him flanked. Got another hospital we can move him to?"

"On it, and yes, tell some of the thieves to hit up Harlem," Lucky said. He gave me an address as he whipped the ride wide, making us glide. He straightened us out, hit the gas again, then coasted up against the bumper of the Knights' ride.

"Armani, call our boys in blue and black to keep those not at our pay grade off our asses," Lucky added. He hit the Knights so hard, it made them swerve, whereas our ride ended up directly at their side.

"Yes, boss. Luciano would be very proud of you," Armani said, then got to dialing.

It was then that Giana and Alex sat up, got a clear look at their targets, and pointed their guns toward the Knights. Everything then moved like something from an action movie.

Giana pushed her hair from her face, waved, then said, "Bye, bitches," as she let off her rounds from the two silver pistols resting against the palms of her hands.

I smirked. She was a baddie.

Because Von didn't want to die, I guessed he decided to get his loopy shit together and help out. My brother grabbed his shotgun, rolled his shoulders, then expertly let them bastards know not to fuck with any of us, especially the head of the Syndicate.

I was impressed by my brother, proud, and worried too, because that nigga had hit his skull hard. Either way, I helped out by watching our backs. Bullets rained, and the Knights looked shocked and fucked as they crashed and burned.

"Goddamn. You're just as crazy as your brotha," Snap said, chuckling, as we peeled off and headed to collect Luciano.

Chapter 23

King

Life comes at you fast. That was the only thing I could think of. Time was of the essence. After killing the man Lily had thrown off the roof, me and my men headed back to my office to suit up, only whoever was out to kill me was two steps ahead of us. As Cleophus and Tiny Tim trotted up the front steps of my office, behind me, two shots rang out, killing both men, just as I opened the door to my office.

I fell through the front door, kicked it closed behind me. As soon as I did, I saw ten of my men. All had been shot in the head or the heart. My heart rate sped up when I looked and saw the basement door had been kicked open.

"Manuel," I yelled. "Ella."

I didn't know who was trying to kill me. Didn't have time to think about it, either. I hit my fist against the wall panel next to my bookcase. The wall slid open to reveal a weapons room. A cold chill swept across the back of my neck. I was going to die today. I felt it in my bones. That was what that strange feeling I'd been having all day was about.

I'd never see Claudette again; I was sure of it. I needed to talk to her. Hear her voice one last time. I snatched out a duffel bag, a Beretta AR70, and two Magnum Research Desert Eagle semiautomatic pistols. I put the *strap of the AR70 around my shoulder, then tossed the duffel bag behind my desk and picked up the two pistols.*

I rushed to the basement stairs. I looked down and saw four dead men in priest robes. Two had shotgun blasts to the face, and the other two had bullet wounds to the chest and abdomen.

"Manuel," I called out again. "It's me, son."

I heard movement in the basement. Just in case it wasn't Ella or Manuel, I aimed my Desert Eagles. The shotgun was the first thing I saw, then Manuel. Behind him, Ella eased around the corner, Beretta aimed perfectly.

"You two kids okay?" I asked.

Manuel nodded. "Yes, we ran out of ammo, though. What's going on, sir?"

"Trouble. I need you two to get out of here and get to the rez—"

The sound of vehicles approaching cut me off. I peeped from my blinds. Men all dressed like priests, armed to the fucking teeth, were exiting the vehicles.

"Get up to the attic right now!" I yelled at Manuel and Ella. "Now. Go!" I rushed them into the hall, snatched the string for the attic door, and pulled it down. I looked up. "Pull the fucking door closed behind you and stay put. Don't fucking come out for no reason," I ordered.

Once Manuel and Ella had gone up, Manuel yanked the door closed. I snatched the string down and tossed it into another room. I was outnumbered. My men had been taken out. My survival instincts kicked in. I tucked my Desert Eagles against my back and took the AR70 into my hand. I flipped my desk over. Papers and folders went flying, and as the phone clanged against the floor loudly, I saw Claudette in my mind. I wondered if she had tried to call while I was out.

Baby would know something was wrong, and she would come running. However, I wanted her nowhere near what was about to happen.

I counted down to when I knew the front doors would come flying off the hinges.

"Five . . . four . . . three . . . two . . ."

Before I got to one, a shotgun blast tore a piece of the door off. As soon as three robed figures walked in, I lit their bodies up with a flurry of bullets. Those motherfuckers shook like electricity and lightning had taken possession of their bodies.

I chuckled. "Oh, you gotta be quicker than that," I said.

I unzipped the duffel bag and grabbed three grenades.

"Let's dance," I quipped.

I stood, then grabbed one Desert Eagle from my back. I shot the window out. Pulled the pin on one of the grenades, then tossed that motherfucker into the middle of the circle of cars. I took great pleasure in watching my killers scatter. As they scrambled for safety, I aimed my AR70 and let 'er rip. That pretty bitch sang beautifully as she lit assassin priests up.

"Hail Mary, full of fucking grace," I spat. "May you sons of bitches and whoever sent you rot in hell."

As I said that, I passed the dangling front door and tossed another grenade outside. The explosion from the grenade gave me butterflies. I laughed to myself. A bit of madness had overtaken me. When a man knew he was going to die, all his senses left him. My father had told me that once. I didn't understand what he'd meant then, but now the meaning was in full Technicolor.

Now that I had their attention, I stepped onto the front porch and let my AR70 do the talking. I caught two gunmen as they raced up the steps. I used their craniums for target practice, making holes in their faces as if they were Swiss cheese. I used that automatic weapon like she was the hand of God, taking out as many of the men as I could. I spent the magazine in the AR70, then tossed it.

I grabbed my Desert Eagles and jumped over the ledge of the porch when I saw robed men. The branches from the trees and shrubbery cut my face and head, and I hit the ground hard. I took out two more men as I rolled over, then took cover behind a car. I kneeled and aimed over the hood. I pulled my triggers so hard, my knuckles were white, with the skin threatening to rip from them.

There were nine rounds of .357 ammunition in each Desert Eagle. The recoil was a motherfucker. The auditory sound exploded in my eardrums like claps of booming thunder. But I'd been trained for this shit. Was used to the shit. I was with the shit.

Ten men with various weapons came for me like it was the running of the bulls in Pamplona, Spain. I pulled the trigger, aiming at the nearest one, and watched the bullet slam into his face. I took out the knee of another before giving him a kill shot to the heart. They were coming so fast that some of my shots missed, but before my ammo ran out, I took down at least six.

I was so busy trying to add another clip to my gun that when the bullet hit my shoulder from behind, the pain blinded me. I roared out, then slammed against the car I had been hiding behind. One of my guns went flying over the car.

"Shit," I spat, spittle flying from my mouth. "Goddamn," I said, trying to catch my breath.

I looked up to see a gunman running for me. With my shoulder injured, I couldn't quite get the new clip in as fast as I wanted to. No way I was going let that Michael Myers—looking motherfucker take me out on my knees, though. I struggled with the clip as another bullet went into my leg. I fell back, gritting my teeth. Water in my eyes blinded me. I blew out a hard breath.

The gunman was closer now, and just when I thought that big pale motherfucker was about to end me, something came flying from the roof. It wasn't until I saw black Mary Jane loafers, white schoolgirl socks, and a school uniform pleated skirt that I realized it was Ella. She jumped on that big summa bitch's back like a rabid pit bull. Sticking, sticking, sticking him in the neck.

Blood spewed like a faucet as the man twisted and turned, trying to get Ella off him. He grabbed her hair and flipped her onto the ground. She jumped back up. Hair wild and teeth bared, like she was a goddamned she wolf. The man's eyes were wild as his gun fell to the ground, and he clutched at his neck.

Ella attacked again. She was quick. She went low and attacked his legs with her switchblade, hitting pressure points and main arteries. She came back up. A stab to the chest. Then one to the abdomen. She ran around him and jumped on his back again. She stabbed him in the neck until he went down on his knees. Then she sliced his neck with a surgeon's precision. The girl stood over his body; the shooter's blood had decorated her clothes and face.

She looked at me, wild eyed. Claudette's training could be seen by the way the girl's eyes roamed. She was taking inventory of how many men were still out. She grabbed the felled shooter's gun and rushed to kneel beside me. After she handed me the gun, she helped me to sit up and then kneeled as she looked over the hood of the car we were hiding behind.

"There're seven more men in the yard," she said. "Manuel took out three behind the house. But I see more cars coming."

"I—I told you damn kids t-to stay in the fu-fucking attic," I fussed.

Ella looked at me. "If the patriarch dies, it leaves the women and children unprotected."

I stared at the young girl. "Only if the matriarch is weak. Our . . . our matr-matriarch is anything but we-weak," I said.

"Our matriarch isn't here," Ella said. "The queen isn't here to protect the king."

Just as she said those words, a loud explosion lit up the night. Ella screamed. I grabbed her and pulled her close to me to protect her from whatever was coming. I turned when I saw a shadow approaching us from behind the house. I lifted the gun to shoot, but then I saw it was Manuel.

He baseball slid next to me and Ella. His knuckles were bloody, and his shirt had been ripped. It hung haphazardly on his upper body. His face also had a few bruises, which showed he'd been in a fight. I handed Ella off to him.

He said, "Lily's here."

I chuckled. Of course she was. I told Manuel to help me up. Once he did, I stood as best I could. There, in the middle of the street, was a little white woman, still dressed as if she was going to church. On her shoulder was a rocket launcher that looked as tall as she was. The cars that were approaching flipped as she shot another missile toward what looked to be a motorcade.

Lily dropped the rocket launcher. She pulled the gun strapped to her back in front of her and started dropping gunmen like dominoes. The woman had to be out of her damn mind to be out in the middle of the street, in the open, shooting. But there she was, laying niggas out like it was a sport to her.

"You and Ella have to get to the rez," I told Manuel.

"Never leave a man behind," Manuel said.

"When at war, who are the two most important beings to keep safe?" I asked him.

"The women and children."

I looked at Ella. *"Then as soon as me and Lily clear a path, get Ella out of here. Don't fight me on this."*

Pain caused me to blink rapidly and grit my teeth. I handed Manuel my Desert Eagle. I pointed to the clip on the ground, knowing he knew what to do with it.

"The recoil is a motherfucker, but you can handle it," I said. *"Stay here until I give you the signal to run. Hear me?"*

He nodded. I stared at the two kids, who had tried to beat the shit out of one another earlier, and gave a pained smile. I glued their faces to my mind, alongside Claudette's. They, along with all the other children in the neighborhood, had become my children. Claudette and I couldn't have any, so we took in the kids who came from broken homes or those who didn't have fathers. They came to us for any and everything. I licked my dry lips, feeling . . . knowing my time had come.

As unshed tears clouded my vision, I moved out. Through the pain, I used both hands to aim the Glauberyt submachine gun and took out three of the men still in the yard with ease. I heard a scream behind me and looked over to see Manuel fighting with a man, while another dragged Ella by her hair.

The distraction was costly. A bullet to the back staggered me. The impact was so hard, I did a full 360-degree spin, the gun in my hand firing haphazardly. Even still, I took out another two shooters.

"King!" Lily yelled.

"Get the kids, Lily!" I yelled back, staggering.

She came running, gun blazing, and took down anything in a robe. Another bullet to my back damn near took me down. The gun fell from my hand. I refused to fall. The man I was, the fight I had in me, the need to talk to my wife again kept me on my feet.

"The kids, Lily." I staggered again just as she reached me.

She ignored me, threw my arm over her shoulder, and half dragged me—the bullet in one of my legs making it hard for me to run, but not impossible— back toward the house.

"Manuel, Ella," she called out.

I looked over to see Ella straddling a man and using her switchblade with ease to cut the man's face and neck. Manuel had another man on the ground and was pummeling him. Once Lily called their names, they jumped up and followed her as she helped me up the front steps. Once we were inside the house, Manuel closed the door as best he could. He and Ella quickly pushed a bookshelf in front of it.

"More are coming," Ella said. She looked frightened. No matter how proficient she was at fighting, the fear in her eyes made her look every bit of the child she was.

I was drained. I felt paralyzed. My wounds made me feel as if my body was caving in on itself. Blood trickled down my face from where I'd jumped through the trees to get behind the car. I was barely able to sit up in a chair.

"Get them out of here, Lily. Get them to the rez," I said.

"Claudette would kill me if I left you here—"

I looked her square in her eyes. "I'm going to kill you if you don't get Manuel and Ella to the rez safely, and I've always been a man of my word. Don't test me, Lily."

The headlights of fast-approaching cars caused me concern.

"Go now, Lily," I said.

Before she left, Lily went to the weapons room, retrieved two Glock 18s, and handed them to me. I motioned with my head for the duffel bag that was behind my flipped desk.

"*Grenades,*" *I said.*

Lily's face had reddened. Her eyes were red. "Let me stay. I can help."

"*You have to stay alive for Claudette. She's going to need you.*"

"*She needs you too, King. This neighborhood. The Syndicate. Nothing will be the same without you.*"

"*Keep in . . . in mind, I am . . . the man I—I am because the right woman loved me,*" *I said, my body shivering as chills set in. "The queen can always move any-anywhere she wants on the board. Take care of my woman, Lily.*"

Once I'd gotten what I asked for, I watched Lily and the kids run to the back door. Ella and Manuel turned to look at me, with tears in their eyes.

"*I'll be fine,*" *I lied. "Go.*"

I could tell they knew I was lying, because through tears, Ella said, "Thank you, Mr. McPhearson, for being the father I never had."

I winced and nodded at the girl. Manuel gazed at me for a long time.

"*Until next time, sir. May the great spirit keep you well rested,*" *he said before he grabbed Ella's hand and disappeared into the night.*

I sat in that chair and waited for the grim reaper to take me. When the men finally made their way into the house, a face among them somehow didn't shock me.

I looked up into the man's face and chuckled weakly, then asked, "Why doesn't this surprise me?"

He was dressed in a bespoke Italian suit, with expensive loafers to match. He was what many women considered tall, dark, and handsome. I aimed my Glock 18 at his head.

"*I knew you'd be a hard kill, but by God, man, just go down already,*" *he quipped, then blew the smoke of his Cuban cigar in my face.*

"If I go, you're going with me," I said.

He gave a smirk, one similar to mine. "I figured you'd say that. So, I brought some incentive to get you to change your mind."

He grabbed the other chair that had fallen over before sitting and crossing his ankle over his thigh. I studied him the way he studied me. We had many similarities. People just didn't look hard enough. If they did, they'd have stumbled across the truth.

My eyelids fluttered, trying to stay open, but my body felt heavy. My head was getting lighter. My breathing staggered. The hand I was holding the gun with fell by my side.

"Just like you fucking spear chuckers to keep fucking fighting. That's the nigger blood in you, I suppose. You just have to keep beating a fucking dead horse until you just can't beat it no more. However . . . ," he said, then held up his finger.

My soul shook when I heard a blast in the distance. It came from the direction of an orphanage Claudette and I financed. I closed my eyes and took a deep breath, praying to God. . . .

"Ahhh," he said. "You heard that, huh? I have several more men positioned at different houses. Give up, King, or I'll take this whole piss-poor-ass town down. Light this bitch up like it was Black Wall Street all over again," he said with flair, then flicked the ashes of his cigar at me.

I tried to kick my leg out to topple his chair, but I was too weak and my leg was injured.

He laughed. "I told the old man that one day this would happen. He didn't listen to me. At the last summit meeting . . . to bring your black ass in there and parade you around like I didn't mean shit. You got too cocky, brother." He said the word brother *like it singed his* tongue to do so, then spit at my feet. He was taking a shot at my blackness. "Got too big for your breeches. Who the fuck are you to form a syndicate and then fashion it after the Commission, brother?"

I laughed. Well, I tried to. The sound that came out was more like that of a stalling train.

"We . . . we could have ruled this shit," I whispered. "But you couldn't get past my blackness. I trusted you," I croaked out.

"Trusted me? Ha. I guess what you're saying could have been true. We could have ruled the underworld, but what makes you think I don't already rule it? I sit at the table of the Commission."

"But for how long? That was what you were afraid of. Afraid I'd come after that seat," I said, then coughed erratically. "But what you d-don't get is . . . I never wanted it. I—I created my own path. I didn't need the pull on the old man's coattail."

The man in front of me turned his lips down at me. Before I could take my next breath, he drew back and slammed his fist into my face. It stung. I couldn't lie, but because bullet wounds had me damn near delirious, anyway, I laughed. I had to. Had we been on equal footing, I'd have beat the shit out of him, and he knew it.

I looked up, then hawked up a wad of bloodied mucus and spit in his face. I got a second wind from somewhere. I pulled myself up in the chair and glared at him. "Fuck you. I trusted you!" I yelled, and he used a handkerchief to wipe his face. "I gave you my loyalty, and you would betray me like this? And for what? Because I exist?"

My throat burned, and my vision blurred. I was teetering on the edge of death. Claudette . . . my baby. My life. My world. There was a secret I'd never told her. I didn't tell her, so I could keep her safe, and now it had come back to bite me in the ass.

My baby was smart as a whip. Some of my best moves had been because of her quick thinking and business savvy. I thought about that time in Vegas when because she was quick on her feet, the Syndicate solidified their status in the underworld. Baby had always been on her shit.

That move garnered us a lot of enemies, but in no way did I think the man in front of me would be one of them.

"Black piece of shit," he spat angrily. "How dare you walk around like you're not just another black bastard from the ghetto? Like you walk the same path as me? All your fancy suits, expensive shoes, and proper speech doesn't change that. You learned nothing from the man who claimed you as his. Nothing. We took that monkey down, and we're going to take you down and that piece of shit organization you call the Syndicate."

I thought about Claudette again. People had always underestimated her. That pretty face, round ass, and mesmerizing smile. I knew in my heart she wouldn't allow my legacy to go to waste. She wouldn't allow all our hard work to go to hell. Not with what I'd left her. Not with all the precautions put in place.

Quiet as kept, we had contingency plans, because she had always said that a black man with as much power as I had was, and would always be, a problem, no matter how many different white men we'd done business with.

"King, honey . . . baby, you walk in any room and shut shit down. With a fine brother like yourself melting the white women's drawers and having all that power, these white men may respect ya business savvy, but don't ever get it twisted, love. They will always keep their best interests at heart," she had said one night, as we lay in bed.

I had taken her words to heart, and the very next day, I had started journaling everything about the ins and outs of the Syndicate. Not a day passed that I didn't document the day and the business happenings. That was in tandem with just documenting my everyday life. Who knew? Maybe one day, one of the youngsters we had taken in would run my empire better because of said notes. But just as sure as I knew I was going to die, I knew the Syndicate would live on. Claudette would have it no other way.

Still, anger had me riled. I saw red spots in front of me. Before I knew what I was doing, I lunged forward and tackled the man in front of me. We went flying into the bookcase that had been pushed in front of the door. Like rams locked in a battle for dominance, I fought with the man whom I'd come to think of as a friend and brother.

His thick fist caught my cheek and sent me flat on my back. He laughed. It matched the madness in my laughter earlier. We were more alike than we were different. The only difference between us was the light golden hue of my skin. My mind screamed and told my body to move, but the bullet wounds from earlier kept me from moving as fast as I would have liked.

I cursed and scrambled to my feet as best I could with one leg wounded. My legs wobbled, and my vision turned bright red. He plowed into me like a raging bull. I drove my uninjured elbow into the back of his neck and dropped him to one knee. I used my good knee to attack his face. He grunted and growled, trying to get away. His anger from the blow had him lifting me into the air. I went airborne and slammed down on the floor hard. Whatever wind I had in me flew out.

I tried to crawl to my Glocks, which had fallen when he punched me in the face. I felt as if I was moving fast,

*but only at a snail's pace could I travel. Pain. More pain
than I'd ever known attacked my body. I no longer gave
a fuck about the guns. I used my arm to try to pull myself
to the phone. I needed to hear my wife's voice more now
than ever. Just her saying hello would do me good.*

*Tears burned my eyes. A foot came crashing down
on my spine. My stomach knotted as I yelled out and
flipped over.*

*"Where's your wife?" he barked at me before kicking
me in my side.*

*I grabbed ahold of his leg and tried to upend him, but
to no avail. My body was weak. His smile was malicious.
I saw my reflection staring back at me, though it was
mixed with a snarl. All the people I'd killed flashed
before my eyes. Then the night I'd met my wife. I'd met
the twenty-year-old spitfire, who was as beautiful as the
day was long, at a juke joint. Tall and built like a brick
house, she was mine as soon as I laid eyes on her.*

*She'd been there with another man. It had been a
meeting my father had taken me to. At thirty, he was
finally handing over the reins of his business to me. But,
damn, what they had been talking about. The beautiful
woman, with legs, hips, and thighs that had to have
been handcrafted by God himself, smiled at me.*

"Son, I want you to meet someone," Daddy had said.

I'd nodded, not giving a damn, really.

*"This here is Luciano Acardi," Daddy said. "The man
you gone be doing business with from now on. His
daddy is the Commission's lead chair. Luci here set to
take over soon."*

*I stopped staring at the woman with Luciano long
enough to pretend I had some kind of sense. I shook
hands with the man in front of me, a smooth-ass
Italian dude who looked like a playboy more than a
mobster's son.*

"Nice to meet you, Mr. Acardi. It's going to be a plea-sure doing business with you," I said.

Luci looked at me, then glanced at the woman next to him. He chuckled, then said, "I'm sure the pleasure will be all mine."

Daddy said, "Son, that there is Big Daddy Haynes's youngest daughter. She name Claudette. People call her Detty or Cece."

She smiled at me. "You can call me . . . whatever you like," she said.

I licked my lips, then smiled. I took her hand, then kissed the palm of it. "Name's Kingston. You can call me . . . anytime."

Her smile widened. Lush lips covered in ruby-red lipstick drew attention to her white teeth. I gave her the once-over. The black sequined dress she had on sparkled in the lighting of the club. Platform heels made her already statuesque frame even more appealing. Her hair had been pulled back into a puffy ponytail. I wanted to run my fingers through it. She was mine from that moment on.

My senses finally brought me back from the past when the heel of a shoe came crashing down on my face. I lay there as the man in the room with me stomped me until I stopped moving. A thousand shivers and cold chills crawled over my body. My wedding band burned on my finger. I focused the last of my energy on sending all my love to the woman I'd leave behind. I'd told her that I'd always be there for her, that I'd always be here. I'd failed.

"Fucking mook bastard," was the last thing I heard him say before he ordered someone to light my office up and before bullets from his gun ripped into my body.

I saw my parents, the people who'd taken me in and loved me when no one else would. I saw Claudette. . . .

I prayed to my ancestors that it would all be over soon. . . .

Chapter 24

Uncle Snap

"Javon, Cory, Snap, come in here for a minute. I need y'all to see something."

We'd been back at the hospital for about an hour. We'd all been patched up, minus Javon. He'd refused to let anybody touch him. Lucky and I had barely made it out of that damn club. If those blasts and explosions hadn't gone off, me and nephew would have been fucked with no damn lube. The blasts had created the distractions we needed to shoot our way out of that cesspool.

I looked at Javon and Cory, who looked just as haggard as I felt. Nephew Javon hadn't been quite right since he hit his head. Cory told me as much.

"I don't know, Unc. Something off about him," Cory said. "He keeps mumbling shit about Mama and King. Shit's freaking me out a bit."

I looked at Javon as he paced the small space. He'd been reading over King's and Mama's journals like he was waiting for something to jump out at him. He had looked up when Lucky came in the room, but hadn't made any moves to show he'd heard Lucky speak.

"Javon, you good, son?" I asked him.

He looked at me. There was a blank look in his eyes before clarity took root. "Yeah. I'm good. Just thinking. Got shit on my mind."

"Like what?" Lucky asked. He stood wide legged, then crossed his arms over his chest.

Javon looked at him, then glanced at me and Cory. "This Absolan shit too obvious," he said.

"What you mean, *kuya*?" Cory asked.

"Yeah, explain," I said. "I thought we'd pretty much narrowed it down to him, based on what—"

Javon shook his head, then walked over to stand near us. "Naw. If it's too obvious, it ain't right. Forget all that shit I just said back in the club. We're missing something. They killed Cavriel. Damn near killed Luci, but they wanted it to seem as if Absolan had been kidnapped. Why?"

Cory said, "Well, maybe he set that shit up that way."

"Maybe he thinks we're stupid enough to fall for the banana in the tailpipe," I said.

Javon shook his head in that crazy way again. "Naw, Unc. Someone is fucking with us. Lucky, what did you want us to see?"

I glanced at Cory. I saw what he was talking about. Javon was acting a bit off. Judging by the way Lucky was looking at Javon, he had picked up on it, too.

"We're prepping to move Uncle Luc—my *father*—out of here," Lucky said. "But I need to let you meet a few people."

We walked through the hall, down to what would have been a waiting area if the hospital were up and running. The room had a long rectangular table with about twelve chairs. There were three people in the room. They saw Lucky and stood. All looked to be biracial in some way.

"You guys, this is Javon. He's the leader of the Syndicate and is here to help us to sort this shit out. This is Cory, his brother, and Uncle Snap. They're his left and right hands," Lucky said.

The men nodded and shot out greetings. Javon stood there, nodding at the men.

"This here is Jules the Gent. We call him that because the nigga is always on some gentlemanly shit and dressed sharp." The man Lucky pointed out was indeed a pretty boy and smiled as he shook Javon's hand. "Next to him is Dapper Dan. You can look at him and see why we call him that."

I nodded. The bald brother was in a tailored suit that caressed the muscles in his upper body and legs. Shoes looked like he had them commissioned in Italy, and he had a smile that I was sure melted the drawers right off any woman he wanted.

Lucky continued as we shook his hand. "That one over there, we call her Switchblade Mary. You really don't want to catch her in a dark alley at night. She's hell in heels."

Jules and Dan chuckled as a short, petite biracial sister walked forward. She had a scar running from the right side of her eye to the right corner of her lip. Her eyes were so black, it was like you were staring into a pit of black ink. She had a low pageboy haircut, and she rocked cowboy boots, hip-hugging Levi's jeans, and a plaid shirt.

"Damn, Mama, what happened there?" Cory asked.

The boy ain't never had that much couth.

"Got jumped by some goons in an alley," she said, voice kind of deep, but it was the sexy kind a man would like to hear in the middle of the night.

Cory pointed. "And they did that to you?"

She nodded, with a sheepish grin.

Jules said, "Don't let that shy shit fool you. When they found those men, the families had to have closed casket funerals."

Mary dropped her eyes and looked away, like she was embarrassed.

Lucky said, "Let's just say if I had to choose between a gun battle with Shanelle and a knife fight with Mary, I'm going to just walk up and punch Javon in his shit."

Cory laughed. So did I, for that matter.

Javon smirked and nodded before saying, "Point made. So why are they here?"

"We're the throwaways," Jules said.

"Not all our dads are like Mr. Acardi," Dan added.

"We didn't get so lucky to have our fathers accept us," Mary said. "If not for Lucky, we'd be ass out."

Javon nodded his understanding, but the look in his eyes still asked what the fuck was the importance of them being here.

"They're my best killers, and I need you, Cory, and Uncle Snap protected at all times while here. You went into that club with only a few Thieves at your disposal. That can't happen again. Mama was good to me," Lucky explained. "She loved me in a way my own mother can't match. On those days when I didn't understand how to navigate between my Italian side and my black side—when my mama was too busy being selfish—Mama Claudette gave me lessons. She said I reminded her of King in a way she couldn't put her finger on. And because I loved her, and because I know without a doubt she loved the three of you, you can't get killed on my watch."

I respected him for that. I really did. And the kid was right; Mama had loved on him like she had with Javon and the rest of the kids. She loved all her children, but Javon was her favorite son, and we all knew it. Don't get me wrong. She favored them all, but Javon she kept close to her heart. Maybe it was because he was Toya's oldest child, and Mama had loved that girl until she couldn't anymore. When Toya had first birthed Javon, it was Mama who had to do the mothering.

Toya had wanted only to get back in the streets as soon as she could. Her husband at the time, that old Nam vet, couldn't do much of nothing for the boy. But Mama was right there, rocking and nursing him until Toya decided to bring her hot ass back in the house at three and four in the morning. When Toya yanked Javon out of Mama's life the first time, my woman was depressed as ever. Then Toya came back with another baby in her. This time it was Cory. Mama repeated the cycle all over again.

Lucky continued talking. "And you have a family to get back to. With a new baby, no way I'd be able to explain to Shanelle how I let you get killed while trying to help save me and my pops."

Javon nodded. "Thank you, fam. I appreciate that. No doubt. They're right on time too."

Cory looked at his brother. "Two things, bro. First, if you throw yourself in front of me again like you did in that club, once we get out, I'm busting you in ya jaw. Second thing, what the fuck you planning right now?"

Javon gave a slick smirk. "Just follow my lead. Lucky, I need to see the old man again. Is he up to it?"

Lucky nodded. "Yeah. The transport team won't be here for another thirty minutes. We're trying to be as incognito as possible."

"Good. I need a few minutes with him."

"Go ahead. Ma's in there, so . . ."

"No worries, my man. I got no words for her at the moment," Javon said. "Uncle Snap, walk with me. Cory, get acquainted with these three and then give me your feedback later. Lucky, something in this sewer smells like shit, and I intend to find out what."

Mary said, "Wait. If it's a sewer, it's supposed to smell like shit."

Javon smiled and said, "Exactly. You're smarter than a motherfucker right now."

Lucky and Cory quirked their brows. My head tilted to the side as I studied Javon. He paid us no mind and walked out of the room ahead of me. Cory was on to something. That hit to the head had nephew acting strange as hell.

I followed Javon down the hall toward Luci's room, wondering if nephew needed to see a medic himself.

"Nephew, you should let one of the docs check that hit you took on the dome," I said.

"I'm fine," was all he said. He had a brisk walk, and he kept running his hand across the back of his head.

I touched his shoulder to stop him. "Either you get checked out, or I'm calling Shanelle, nephew. I'm not jiving."

Javon glanced down at me. "Now, why would you do that? What have I done to you to cause such treachery?" he asked jokingly, then laughed as he pushed the door to Luci's room open.

I shook my head. He was going to see a fucking doctor, and I didn't give a fuck what he said. I walked into the room behind him to see Giana lying on the bed with her father. The Old Italian had his arms wrapped around his daughter, and she slept beside him. How she could sleep during a time of turmoil was beyond me.

Deedee sat in a chair next to the window. On a small table next to the window was the picture I'd seen earlier of a younger Luci, his siblings, and his father. Deedee had been sleeping until we walked into the room. She jerked awake and sat up to her full height when she saw us.

"Are we leaving now?" she asked.

"No," I said.

"What's taking so long? I feel like we're just sitting here, waiting to be attacked."

"Ask your son," was my response.

I didn't really have a lot to say to the woman. I still had a beef with her for what she used to do to Claudette. I'd never forgive her for breaking my woman's heart over and over again. Couple that with the fact she had known members of the Commission were in town on the day King was killed, and hadn't said a word to her sister about it. A dog had a higher place in my life than she did.

"Hey, old head," Javon said to Luci.

There was something kind of odd about the way he said this, but I just shook it off as him needing to see a doctor about his head.

Luci opened his eyes, then looked at Javon. He gave something of a smile. "Javon, I'm surprised you're still here and haven't run off yet."

"Why would I do that?" nephew asked. "Someone's trying to kill you and Lucky and tried to kill us all earlier. We got some toes to tag. Anyway, do you remember anything else about the day King died? Where were you? And before you ask, I'm starting to think all this shit is connected somehow."

Luci frowned, then coughed. "I . . . I was in Columbia. We had a big deal going down that day. I wanted to see it through by my own hands. Back then Columbia had pure, uncut white heat. I didn't want any fuckups."

"The first time we met face-to-face, you said Mama chose King over you," Javon said. "You didn't have any beefs about that?"

Luci frowned at Javon. "Are you crazy? Of course I did. When Claudette and I were doing what we were doing, it was an open thing. She was okay with that, as I didn't have no wife at the time. The moment King saw her, though, I seen something in Claudette's eyes I'd never really seen before."

"Which was?"

"Life. She came alive that night. That smooth motherfucker plucked her right out from under me," Luci said,
then laughed. "Me and some of the guys who kept black
jawns on the side often joked about how it was much
easier to control black men married to white women, as
opposed to trying to control black women who were with
us. That's why we never put up too much fuss when our
daughters marry the ones with money. It becomes
our money then. She has his son, and the son becomes
the heir. The son then marries white, and we get that for-
tune to stay right with us."

Luci stopped, coughed, then took haggard breaths
before continuing. "Black women, on the other hand,
they have this almost sick sense of loyalty to black men.
Once King had Claudette, wasn't nothing I could do to
sway her. She had no problems committing to him. And
he loved her. So yeah, I was slighted about that, but
Claudette had a way of making a man see things from
her point of view," the old head said, then looked at
me. "Right, Raphael? I lost her to you too . . . for a while,
anyway," he said, then chuckled.

I didn't miss the jab he threw at me. I was well aware
of what had happened between them on the day she was
shot. Me and my woman weren't right for almost a year
behind that. But, like Luci said, Claudette had a way of
making men see things from her point of view.

I didn't respond to the old man's low blow, though.
The nigga was damn near dead, anyway. And what the
fuck did he mean by a "sick sense of loyalty to black
men"? I could just take my gun out right now and blow
that bedridden ma'fucker to hell. Claudette wasn't here
to stop me this time.

Javon must have picked up on my mood. He nodded
his head to the left, telling me to move away from the bed.
I chuckled, thought about shooting Luci, again, and then
moved so as not to cause my nephew problems.

Javon smiled, then said to Luci, "That's nice. Anyway, why is Fabian O'Neil just chilling in a sex club when the man who adopted him has been kidnapped? Shit make much sense to you?"

"Fabian?"

Javon nodded.

"Is here?" Luci asked.

"Uh-huh," Javon said. "Now, why wouldn't he be out looking for the man who'd taken care of him his whole life?"

Giana sat up. "My guess is because Absolan is behind this madness. I do not believe he was kidnapped or taken or anything. He killed Uncle Cavriel and tried to kill my papa," she fussed, her voice croaking, as if she was about to cry.

I looked at Javon, and he was now looking at Deedee. Deedee looked uncomfortable. Javon knew something he wasn't telling me.

"Well, Luciano Acardi, you were wrong about one thing," Javon said.

Luci wiped at his daughter's eyes and then looked at Javon. "What's that?"

"Not all black women have a sick sense of loyalty to black men," Javon said, then smiled coolly at Deedee. "Some have only a sick sense of loyalty to themselves. Ain't that right, Ms. Deedee?"

Chapter 25

Shanelle

I sat in that dimly lit room, studying Mama's and King's journals. After I had a panic attack, I went on the offensive. Jojo had been right. We were sitting ducks, but we were also a team of crazy-ass kids who had come from violent and crazy-ass childhoods, until Mama took us in. I was also the wife of the head of a criminal enterprise. I didn't have time to have a mental breakdown when my husband was in trouble.

I looked at Honor as she slept in a bassinet next to the bed. Next to her lay Justice. In the room with me were all my siblings, Jai, Ms. Lily, Nighthawk, Creed, Montego, and Ming. I had called every last Syndicate member in. Lucky for me, they had all been in the United States and had made their way to me as soon as they could.

Ms. Lily sat stoically in a rocker right next to Honor and Justice. The old woman looked harmless, but I knew that with the blink of an eye, she could kill anybody dead.

"You sure about this?" Creed asked.

"I wouldn't have asked you here if I wasn't sure," I said.

Ming's light, melodic voice rang out. "Going up against the Commission could come back to haunt us."

"We're not going against the Commission. We're backing Javon. Think of it that way."

Montego said, "My men are in position. Ready when you are."

Montego was the head of what had once been his father's empire. He ran the Mexicans in the West and South, and he was the Syndicate's connection to the Mexican cartel. He'd come to assist me in aiding Javon, and he'd brought his best men along with him.

I looked at Creed. He nodded. Creed was the head of the MC Federation, which had connections on the East Coast and the West Coast.

"My men are good to go," he assured me.

"Of course, my people are ready to move when you say," Nighthawk said.

Nighthawk was our connection to the rez, and his men were best at hunting. Since I felt like my husband was being hunted, what better way to go from prey to predator?

"As are mine," Song added.

Song was a feisty little woman, but she packed a lot of heat. She was the leader of the Chinese crime ring, having taken over where her mother left off once she succumbed to her injuries a year ago. So I knew the men she'd come with were just as deadly as they were thorough.

I stood, then looked at my siblings and Jai. We were all dressed in black, with skull masks covering the bottom halves of our faces and hoodies covering our heads. I grabbed the sling to my assault rifle and threw it over my shoulder.

"If any of you get killed, I'll kill you," I said.

Jojo said, "We're like German cockroaches. It's going to take a whole lot more than Raid to get rid of us."

Chapter 26

Uncle Snap

Javon didn't give Deedee time to confirm whether or not she was loyal only to herself. He signaled to me, and we walked out of the room, then headed out of the hospital. The night was a bit windy for the summer. The air was humid. Rain was coming. Even though no one really knew where we were, standing outside that abandoned hospital made the hairs stand up on the back of my neck. Before he turned to me, Javon looked at his watch.

"He's lying, Unc," Javon said. "Just like he lied to me about—"

I turned to give him my full attention. "About what?"

"He wasn't in Columbia that day."

"How do you know?"

"King made an entry in his journal that said he'd spoken to Luci the day before. Said Luci had sent his best men to Columbia for a shipment. However, Luci stayed back to attend to his sick father. The old man is lying, and the only reason I can think of is that he's protecting somebody. Before I tell you what I think, you tell me what's got you spooked about me reading King's journal. It would be fucked up if you had anything to do with his death, Unc."

I gave Javon a slow blink. His words were like a sledgehammer to the chest. "That man was like a father to me."

"Mama was like a mother to Melissa."

"Fuck you, Javon," I barked out.

Nephew took a step back, which was probably in his best interest. I had a good mind to knock him clean on his ass.

"I was in Creek Town with your fucking mother, killing the nigga who had sexually violated her body." I was pissed at Javon, so fucking angry that he would even suggest such a crock of shit that my hands shook. "I think you hit ya fucking head harder than you think."

Javon tilted his head to the side, then studied me. "Answer my question, Unc," he said, like he didn't give a fuck about my anger.

The wind whipped around us like it was just as angry as I was. I wanted to lie, but I knew that I couldn't. Not when it was possible that Javon already knew the truth and was testing me.

"There was something King made me promise not to ever tell Mama," I said. "And I never did. I loved that woman with every breath of me, but out of loyalty and respect to King, I never revealed his secret, because even in death, he was the only father I'd ever known."

Javon licked his lips as he nodded.

I said, "That man plucked me from the streets. I was trying to steal from him, and he took me in. Fed me that night. Took me to Ms. Dutchess's place. Told me to rest and eat, because come morning, I was going to work to pay him what I'd stolen from him. He was my role model from that moment onward."

"I understand, Unc. You don't have to explain. However, I think it was that secret that got him killed."

"Wait. You think King Senior not being his real father got him killed?" I asked.

"It's logical, don't you think? He didn't tell Mama so he could keep her safe."

I nodded. "Yeah, he told me that if she ever knew his true lineage, it could get her killed. Hell, I didn't know his true lineage. I just knew King Sr. wasn't his father. And King had it coded in his journal. Mama was probably too grief stricken to pick up on it. She always had a tough time reading that thing."

Javon's eyes widened a bit. "So you're saying, you knew his father wasn't his father, but you didn't know who his real father was?"

"Yeah. He wouldn't tell me that. He only told me about King Sr. And that was only because I'd overheard them arguing one day. King Sr. was telling him not to trust *those* people. Said that his real father would never truly accept him, no matter how much he pretended to love him."

"What people?"

"I wasn't sure at the time, but I assumed he was talking about whoever King's real father was."

"What happened at the last summit meeting before King was killed?"

"That was a few months prior. Like, six months prior maybe. Same thing that normally happened at those meetings. A lot of posturing and shit talking. Territories got rearranged. Money was discussed and split accordingly. Capers were discussed. Cops and FBI agents on the payroll. By then they had the DEA and prosecutors on the books too. King was a big topic. Cristophano Acardi, Luci's father—"

Glass shattering and a man's loud yell interrupted our conversation. I looked up to see a man flying from the top floor of the hospital. Since Luci was on the basement level, that meant one of Lucky's men had been tossed. Just as that thought settled in, rapid gunfire erupted in the building and mixed with loud yells and screams.

My right arm was already jacked from the bullet I took to it earlier, and shooting with my left, even though I could do it, was taking some getting used to. I turned to lay my eyes on Javon. Nephew shoved me back into the building before taking aim at the hooded figures coming out of the shadows in the alley. I fell on the trash-littered floor just as Cory and Lucky came bolting up the stairs.

"Where my brother?" Cory yelled.

I got up in a fit of rage. "Crazy ass shoved me inside—"

I got cut off. This time by Javon's agitated yelling. "Motherfucker!" we heard Javon yell.

Lucky and Cory tore through the front doors. I was right behind them. Javon had a hooded figure on the ground and was pummeling his face, while another lay flat on his back, a bullet hole in his face the size of a crater on the moon.

Javon looked at us. "Nigga tried to cut me. You niggas just don't quit," Javon yelled as he shoved a knife in the man's throat, then proceeded to use his hand to open the wound further.

It looked like the nephew was trying to rip the man's head off. He looked like a fucking madman. Then again, people had been trying to kill us since we had stepped foot in New York. That was enough to drive anybody mad. I saw headlights coming down the street.

"Javon, get inside!" Lucky yelled.

Javon looked over his shoulder just before he rushed inside the building with the rest of us.

"Down to the basement," Lucky said as his men made a beeline to the doors.

By the time we got to the basement, the shit had hit the fan. We'd been invaded. Robed figures were all around. Mary had hunting knives in her hands and was working them like she was a chef at Benihana. After she stabbed one man with a backhand jab to his sternum, she yanked out the knife and hit another one with a quick dice to the throat.

I heard Cory grunt behind me. He'd taken a blow to the face. It angered the boy so much that he fell back into the wall, bounced right up, and shot his attacker point-blank in the face.

"Bitch-ass nigga," he snarled, wiping the man's brain matter from his face.

Lucky was hunkering down around a corner, shooting, trying to get to his father's room. Jules and Dan were flanking him, taking out hooded figures left and right. It was like the Wild Wild West in this place.

"Mom," Lucky yelled. "Giana."

He stepped out into the hall, two Desert Eagles in his hands, and shot his way through the melee. I heard maniacal laughter; I looked to my right to see Javon fighting with a man. He was blocking body shots. Once he got tired of doing that, he bounced on the heels of his feet and sent a rapid succession of punches to the man's face, and that was right before he shoved the man into Mary so she could give him a Zorro slice across the abdomen.

I saw all of that while I shot to kill anything in a robe that moved. At that point, Jesus could have caught a bullet if he had on a robe. I got football tackled into a wall. The hit knocked the wind out of me. Once I went down, the man faked at me. I jerked back. My arm was paining me to the point that I almost felt crippled by the injury. He kicked my gun away, then smiled down at me.

I didn't like being fucked with, so I found the strength to pull myself up. He let me get halfway to my feet before he tackled me again. The young buck laid my old ass out. I was getting way too old for this shit. Once I was down, he pulled out his guns, but a shotgun blast to the back stopped whatever he thought he was about to do.

The man fell face-first into the wall. I looked up at Javon. Nephew looked demented. Eyes were a bit wild. Gaze was off. He dropped the shotgun and did some kind of crazy dance.

"Nigga, are you doing the Dougie?" Cory asked as he looked his brother up and down like he was crazy.

Javon stopped the dance and shrugged. "Nothing like killing a nigga to get your blood flowing," was all he said as he picked up his other guns and walked toward Luci's room.

Mary giggled as she wiped blood from her face. "I like him. He's funny," she said. Mary looked like she had just come from Camp Crystal Lake, after killing young adults in the woods.

Cory mumbled, "The nigga needs to see a doctor and quick."

Lucky rushed into his father's room after kicking the door open to find Luci trying to crawl out. The man was bleeding from his face, and the wound on his chest was bleeding through the bandages.

"Pops, where're Mama and Giana?" Lucky asked, helping the old man up from the floor.

Luci really did look as if he was about to die at any moment. "T-took them," he said in a raspy voice.

"Who took them?" Lucky asked. Panic and fear laced his voice.

"Ab . . . solan."

Javon glanced at me, skepticism on his features. We didn't have time to think about that, though. The herd of feet we heard upstairs let us know we had more trouble.

Lucky looked at Jules and Dan. "Get my pops out of here," he said. "Go. Now!"

Chapter 27

Javon

See, why don't motherfuckers listen to a nigga when he's on to something? They pay attention only to what the fuck they wanna hear, and they do not look at all the pieces of the puzzle. I had hit my fucking head hard, but a nigga was thinking with clarity. I told everyone that this shit was inside, that these motherfuckers were going to come after Luci, but what the *fuck* did they do? Sat around for a *goddamned* hour, while patching up and not *listening* to the *fuck* I said about moving Luci out.

The Absolan link was solid on some level. That nigga was up to shit, and now here we were.

All I could do was laugh to myself, because this shit was like HDTV, clear and fucking concise. Everything I did was for a reason. *Everything.* Going into that club with a small backup was for a reason. It was to rip the Band-Aid off and get motherfuckers talking, which would help me see what the real deal was. Did I think it was possibly going to get us killed? Hell, the fuck yeah. Why? Because you always planned for the good and the bad. In this world, that was what came from drumming up intel and being a *goddamn* killer. You mixed it up in seedy locations and handled fucking business. Now here we were, looking dumb as fuck, with our location assed out because *no one was hearing me but angels*!

"Nephew, who the hell you talking to?" I heard Uncle Snap ask behind me.

Everyone was rushing around. Because of the oncoming bullets, we all had rushed into the nearest room that we could find to wait shit out just for a quick second and get Luciano situated. Behind us were three of our Forty Thieves, one being Alex, who made sure we were cleared.

"Don't flip ya wig now. We all are listening to you, nephew," Uncle Snap said by my side. "But you, ah . . . need to get to that doctor."

I paced back and forth, with my hands gripping the back of my neck. Stress had my hands sweaty. My breath was coming out in ragged gasps because I had just got done handling business. In all, I was little dizzy, but I was good. My mind was going a mile a minute. Seeing a doctor would only slow everything down, and I said as much.

"No disrespect, but does it look like I got time to lay up under some doctor?" I pointed my gun at the door and gave a haphazard chuckle while looking from my uncle to Cory. "Hell to the naw. So you both get that out ya mind for now. . . . If we make it up out of here . . ."

I thumbed my nose and glanced down at a haggard and gray-hued Luci. There was no doubt disappointment in me. Every original assumption was right, but my need to trust in Mama's words, her allies, had made me forget one thing. I was here, living and breathing, and I was a damn good judge of character. I had to be in order to keep myself and Cory safe in the streets. I was my brother's keeper, always. So, staring down at Luci—and I mean really staring down at him—all I could do was thumb my nose in disappointment. Something I felt when I thought about his wife— or baby mama, or whatever she was—Deedee.

There was a loud bang. Following that, I could hear Cory's cell buzzing.

"What's an easy exit out of here, Luci?" Cory asked while looking at his cell. He gave a brief smirk, began typing, then looked up while stuffing his cell back in his pocket.

Dust and debris from the old building began to fall around us like rain. Uncle Snap came over to my side. I pointed for him to flank the other side of the door, while we waited like a chicken ready to be baked in the oven. I rolled my shoulders, listening and counting feet.

Luci's wheezing then coughing signaled that he was ready to talk. "L-Lucky. Show them."

There was pain in Lucky's eyes. Everyone in the room could tell that he was worried about his mother and sister, so he was a little off kilter.

"Lucky, man," Cory stated. When Lucky kept standing there and not responding, Cory frowned. "Lucky."

"Yeah?" Lucky said in a daze, suddenly regaining his damned hearing.

"Grab those packs of ointment and wound gel. You need to smear that stuff on his wounds to clean them," Cory explained, pointing around the room. "Then grab that syringe. Squirt it over Luci's wound that's bleeding, and then press the sides of the wound together. Throw on some gloves, though. That shit is liquid stitches. It'll handle the blood trail he might leave if we move him. Be quick with that shit too. Once you do that, wrap him up with the gauze. Then grab that IV back and keep it attached to the old man."

Both Uncle Snap and I looked at Cory with questions in our eyes.

Cory chuckled, then kept his voice low when he said, "My baby Inez been teaching me some shit. She's a lifesaver."

"It's done," Lucky said hurriedly, looking around the room. He was kneeling at Luci's head, which he was propping up with his hand. The homie wiped Luci's wet brow and kept a hand on his chest. "We need to ride out now."

My gaze ran around the small room. Beside the stash of medical equipment and medicine were several wheelchairs. "Hey, grab a wheelchair. Dan and Jules, help Lucky with Luci. Luci, where the fuck can we go?"

Luci was coughing again, but he was awake. He pointed to a bare wall that had a glass case of medicines in it, then glanced at Lucky. "Like the wardrobe for your favorite book, son."

We watched Lucky frown; then his eyes lit up. Quickly, he flung open the large glass case. "Where's the switch?" He franticly moved bottles and ran his hand around the insides of the drawers of the cabinet.

"Don't know," Luci said tiredly. "Just look."

I stood there, getting antsy, so I rushed forward and helped Lucky. As soon as my hand touched the cabinet, the tips of my fingers found a hinge. You wouldn't know it was a button if you didn't know this was an exit. It felt like a regular screw, like the many screws that held the cabinet together.

"Got it," I said, then watched the inside open. Behind us, Cory and the Thieves were on their shit, lining the place with grenades.

"A'ight. Get him through," Lucky said.

And that was what we did.

While the inside slide to the side to an open exit, Dani and Jules lifted Luci on their shoulders, then waited for Alex to drop the wheelchair. Mary clicked her watch, which lit up and became a flashlight. She then walked into the tunnel to help with Luci. Once they settled him into the wheelchair, we all hustled into the tunnel. We left the cabinet looking untouched.

"This will get us out. B-but it'll drop us close to them," Luci struggled to say.

"It don't even matter. If they don't see us, then we're good," Cory said.

I kept my mouth quiet; my mind was still calculating and planning. I had questions, but every time I vocalized them, some shit popped up. So as a man who believed in happenstance, I shut the fuck up. We needed to get through this; then I could get my questions out.

"Ah, shit. The fuck was that?" Cory spat out. His locs went flying, and he stomped his feet while running a hand over his face.

"A roach? Spider? A rat?" Jules said, then laughed quietly. "I don't know, dude."

"Goddamn it. Warn a nigga," Cory said, then walked on. "Inez would cackle about this, so any of you talk, I'll shoot you in the asshole."

Dark walls surrounded us. Flashes of peppered light shouted out. We could hear our boots crunching on rubble while we moved. WWII was going on in the building, and we could hear it. Men and women screamed. Bullets began flying through our tunnel, which had us stopping mid-step until they ceased.

"This shit is a death trap," was all I said as we moved on. I was flanked by protection in the back and the front, as were Luci and Lucky.

"You ain't experienced a damn thing until you're stuck in the South, in the hot, humid heat, face flat in stinking swamp water and dirt while crawling through insect-infested swamp water," Uncle Snap said in front of me.

"Explain that shit. We need something to get through this shit," Cory said. I knew he was doing it for my sake. To get me to chill out, but I was too hyper, so fuck that. But I listened.

"Was right after I strung up that nigga who hurt ya mama," he explained. "There was something called sundown rules back in that old town."

Uncle Snap was talking in codes due to the people who were around us. "The rules was this. After you take ya pound of flesh—if that's what needs ta happen—you string 'em up in the middle of the town, by the station, for the town to see and understand that whateva the perp did wasn't gonna be tolerated."

"Those old tales weren't a joke," I heard Mary whisper.

"Damn. So you strung him up?" Cory asked.

"Like a fucking prize. Let his body bake while I worked him up and finished the slicing Mama put on him," Uncle Snap said solemnly.

In my mind, I could see it all. Mama never wrote that part out, but it was like I already knew it. I could see Uncle Snap dragging that nigga Lonnie by his neck out of the juke joint. Could see the man bloodied but still fighting for his life, because that was what humans did. Through it all, there was Uncle Snap, dragging him through the town as the elders watched on their porches and dogs barked in the distance.

"Mama watched on her porch," I heard him say solemnly. "Her pretty cheeks were covered in tears. Her eyes were red, and her hands were shaking at her sides. Back then, I thought it was because of what I was doing. When she fell to her knees on the porch, I learned that it wasn't, but I kept on. Kept on because I promised her I'd finish it. So I did."

Everyone stopped. We had come to a fork in the tunnels. We all listened to see where the most gunfire was, and then we went in the opposite direction.

"I gutted him like a fish. Made an offering to the ancestors and the children who were hurt by this man. After, the elders came from their homes, walked by him, spit on him. Then I took him down and dragged him to the swamps. Left him there fah the fish and gators. Made sure he was in there real deep too," Uncle Snap explained.

He went on. "After that, we left with yawl's mama and grandmama and Deedee. Yawl's mama was never the same after that. That nigga tainted her soul and her mind. Rewired it something fierce. Mama tried to help her, but ya mama couldn't trust anymore. Could only see using people as a means of survival, and yet—brokenhearted again and in deep grief— Mama still did all that she could for yawl's mama. As did I, for Mama's sake." Uncle Snap slowed his step and pointed at a door haloed in light. "See. I take care of Mama. Always have and always will. Be it in honor of King or for myself. I ain't no second with her, and she knew that. Knew that so well, she killed for me too."

His words helped fill in some missing info. I also knew what he said at the end was a jab at Luci.

Luci's wheezing became hard, and Uncle Snap chuckled.

After treading through the tunnels, we made it out on the first level of the old hospital. Glancing around, I noted that everything was like in a ghost town. Dust, dirt, rocks touched everything, from old welcome desks to old help stations and then some.

Several overhead signs were hanging from their hinges. On the walls were stock photos of medical staff grinning in their scrubs. PARISH HOSPITAL and the hospital's logo were stamped across the front of their shirts. Those photos were also coated in dust.

Everything was so quiet that it bothered my soul.

"This shit ain't right," I said, hearing the battle raging on below us. "Feels off. Feels like death."

"You ain't lying, *kuya*," Cory said, shifting on his feet.

My gaze traveled around. Through the broken panels of glass in the windows, I could see the masses of cars parked in front of this place. Felt like we had a million eyes on us, and it made the hairs on my nape stand on end. We were locked in, with no real way out without being noticed.

"I'm sorry," came from Luci, and we all gave him a look.

"Why?" Lucky asked.

"T-the hate runs bone deep. I—I'm sorry for not . . . correcting it," he said. "For thinking we were protected here. For . . ."

See, I knew some shit, so his words were falling on deaf ears. Shit was working me, but again, I kept quiet to get my thoughts right. It wasn't the time, and I let him know. "All things come to light when sloppy as fuck, and as the old die and the young discover all ain't right in these here woods."

"Von," I heard Cory say.

I gave him a quick glance, then thought, *Fuck it*. If we were going to die, then I was going out with a bang.

"No. See, all this shit seems to be the fault of Mr. Acardi," I began.

Lucky looked at me, then frowned. "Why are you going hard at Uncle . . . I mean, my father? Why now?"

"No disrespect to you, because you are still in the dark about who the Old Italian really is, but it's like this." I thumbed my nose, then moved around to stare Luci in the face.

Everything I read, all the pieces, all the running around this damned city, had me stewing. I wanted to cage the man I had come to trust myself, a man Mama had led me to. But I couldn't, because if I did, Lucky would put a bullet in the back of my skull before I could snatch his throat out, so I chilled.

"King trusted you, Luci. He trusted you with his life. It is all there in King's journal, all between the lines," I said. "See, King had said at the last summit, his father had personally told him how proud he was of him. Earlier entries had it documented that King Sr. had already been dead, by several years prior. Was no way that Mama's King was talking about a dead man. But above all that, Mama Claudette trusted you. Never would have suspected you'd turn on them both."

"Von, what you talking about, nephew?" Uncle Snap slowly inched up to me, his voice shaking.

"Naw . . . naw. Wait. He told you he had nothing to do with that, Von, so drop this shit," Lucky muttered as he stood between me and his ailing father.

"And? You're right. He told me." I gave a cold smirk and glared at Luci. "That don't mean that shit is true. See, pictures are a reflection of our souls and vessels of our memories. They sure do know how to tell on people too. Tell all the business." When I was in Luci's hospital room, the one thing that had caught my eye was the old fading picture of two Sicilians who looked oddly like King. Shit threw me for a loop, but then we were ambushed, and I didn't have time to gather my thoughts until the tunnels and now.

"I—I don't know what you're talking about, son," Luci wheezed. "I've been loyal."

"Chill the fuck out, Von," Lucky growled, being the protective former nephew and now son that he was.

That bond I understood well. *But on the real, fuck that shit*, I thought. The desire to put one between Luci's eyes was weighing heavily on me. But, really, it wasn't time for all of this.

So I did the hardest thing ever. I backed away, but not before I mouthed to Luci, "King's your blood brother, right?"

When Luci began coughing violently, to the point of spitting out blood, that answered my question. Anger rose in me. I wanted to put a bullet in the nigga's head, but one lesson I had learned was this: let the enemy stew in their own shit before you let them hang themselves. A bullet was coming, but it wouldn't be from me.

"Back up, Von. You're right. I don't get this shit, but I plan to, so back up." Lucky continued to block me.

An indifferent smirk spread on my face, and I backed up. "A'ight."

I had every intention to leave payback to the one man who was still around honoring the ghosts of Mama and Kingston, and I was staring him right in the eyes. No words were needed, as the look my face said it all, and Uncle Snap got the message clear and in living color.

As I walked past him, I whispered, "When this is done, handle it after I reveal the truth."

Uncle Snap's anger seeped from his aura. He gave me a curt nod; then an icy, apathetic mask appeared on his face. After that, I thumbed my nose, walked off, then motioned for us to move out. The love of my family was in my spirit. This felt like the walk of death, and in trying to help an ally, I had learned a lot about how scandal and secrets could corrupt a foundation. It was the sins of the past that were about to kill us all, and it pissed me the fuck off. I was a new father and still in the honeymoon phase with my wife. I had left the rest of the family as protected as I could get them.

I knew they felt they were sitting ducks, but they weren't. The Syndicate was there to protect them, along with the rest of our allies. My family was good. I had made sure of that before coming here, but after everything, even that had me feeling weak. It had me feeling worried. See, I didn't want to go out without being with my family one last time. I felt and related heavily to King's lessons.

I might not have known what his real words and thoughts were in his last hours, because there was no way for that man to record any of that in his journal after dying. But I knew this: the fight in a man who loved his family above all things could still be felt in those he had helped. King's life—his lessons, his strength, power, and love—had formed their own foundation and had been passed on through the blood of everyone he and Mama had touched. I felt his energy, and I even felt Mama's.

That was why I knew I didn't want to die and wasn't going to die today. No fucking way. I had a legacy to protect, and I planned to do just that.

Chapter 28

Javon

"We have a problem, people," Mary quipped. She jogged into my view, pointing her rifle away from her.

In the mix of everything, I hadn't paid attention to the fact that we weren't alone anymore. People in robes began spilling into the long main entrance area. Guns were pointed at us. People with swords, hammers, and other medieval-looking shit also pointed their weapons at us. I could hear some shit, like a hymn or a prayer, being said in Latin in the background. It sent a chill down my spine, and it also made me pissed the fuck off at the disrespect.

"Get Luci behind something and keep him covered," I ordered the Thieves and Dan while getting my gun ready. "We don't need that bast—" I cut myself off because I needed to look like a crazy person, and not a turncoat, to those who were devoted to him. "OG disappearing on us."

From in between the people dressed in robes, men in all-black military attire, including helmets, stepped forward. These men were Luci's own men, and their mission was to keep him protected. The fact that they had the unmitigated gall to stand with the Knights made me suck my teeth. Yet again, it proved my point. This shit was internal.

It also made Luci shout, "I protected all of you, from your family to burials of your dead loved ones. And you do this to me?"

I glanced over to see him pointing and almost falling out of his wheelchair at the disloyalty. His emotions didn't matter to them. It was clear from their blank stares. He had been betrayed, and now it was time for our deaths.

"Uncle Snap," I quietly muttered.

"Yes, nephew?"

"I need you to do something for me, to make a promise."

"Won't be no more promises from me, nephew. I ain't leaving ya side."

As I shifted on my feet, the rising anger in me made me grip my Glock. "Then get near an exit. Stay clear of bullets, because it ain't your time to die, and you'll break me if you do, regardless of how I feel about you lying to me, understood?" I gave one look at the old man who, I realized, was my world. "I never had a real pops. You're it and all I've ever known. Do me this solid, and whatever you do, find a safe exit out. Because if I go down and that nigga lives, you need to be the one."

After that, a silent standoff went on between me and Uncle Snap. I could feel Cory watching. He stood on the other side of me, with slight confusion on his face. Watching the wall of robes in front of us, I then decided to give a quick rundown as best as I could. It seemed like the whole area had become chilly, chilly in a way that signified rage.

For a second, I thought Cory was going to say fuck it and off Luci, but when he said, "Please, Uncle Snap. You're all we got," it made me see the change in my brother.

"Mama always said, 'Give an inch, and they'll hang themselves.'"

"She also said, 'Grab a knife and watch that guppy flap.'"

Uncle Snap gave a quiet grunt, then backed up slowly to stand to the far right of us, by the welcome desk, his eyes locked on Luciano.

Vengeance helped me focus. Something in my gut was saying Luciano was the final chess piece in all of this, so I needed to survive this shit. However, if I was going to die, I needed my thoughts to be clear. When I looked ahead, I shook my head to right myself and stop the sensation I had of the floor dipping, then stepped forward. In the sea of Knights, I saw death.

When the sound of more feet approaching made me turn, I curled my lips and said, "Fuck my life."

At my front and back were nothing but Knights.

"Looks like a showdown, motherfuckers," I said out loud. "Only thing about to be cleansed here is the shit that you all are. Let's rock out."

"Maximum effort," Lucky said near us. He gave a nod, then blazed the fuck up by lifting two hands and pointing in front of us and behind us. "I am the son of Acardi. This is my motherfucking world, you hear me? Mine. You all will die by our hand tonight."

Bullets went flying, shattering everything that was left in that old space, while hitting some of the bastards in front of us.

I ran forward, aiming my Glock at the sweet spot on each bitch's and bastard's clocked faces, their third eye. Sweat ran down my face as I ran. My heart pumped a mile a minute. Cory moved with me like my shadow. When he swung out over my head, I ducked low, pumped bullets into the enemy. The moment my gun went dry, Cory tossed me whatever he had on his body, and I used it to my end.

A sweet karambit-style folding knife was pressed against the palm of my hand. I deployed the blade with my thumb and felt that shit kinetically snap out, ready to slice into anyone who wanted this shit. This baby was so light and compact that it felt like a part of me as I reached out and sliced it across the stomach of one of the people in robes. My reward for being so close was a pummeling hit against my side with a crazy-looking hammer.

I fell back hard but still had my knife. Mama loved these things, and I realized why. They were the perfect weapon for close combat. When I fell on my back, I rolled left, and that hammer came down near me. I thought I was doing some shit, until I felt moisture against my fingers. It was blood. My thigh hurt, I could see that it had been grazed by a bullet.

"Bitch. Did you shoot me?" I shouted out, in pain. I looked from my leg to my assailant and then back to my leg. Incredulity was written all over my face.

What I said caught the person off guard, which I used to my advantage. Swinging my feet out, I knocked his legs out from under his, and he fell and cracked his head on the floor. A beautiful red puddle formed beneath his head. I pushed myself up to climb over him, then pressed my blade against his neck and pushed his hood back so that I would remember his face while I cut his throat.

There was satisfaction in the kill, but I wasn't done. More fools were coming at me. I grabbed a hammer I saw on the floor, got up, and went swinging. I could see Cory going ham on some folks. He found a way to choke some folks with their own beaded belts, while sticking them in their sides with his jagged-edge hunter's knife. To the other side of me, in the crowd, I could see that Lucky was surrounded. He was letting off rounds, then switching to his own blades. This shit was hectic.

Even though the Thieves were doing their magic, Dan was holding it down, and Luci was awake enough to slice at Knights with his blade from his wheelchair, I knew that there were too many of these resurrecting motherfuckers. The whole area was littered with bodies. When Alex and then Dan caught a bullet, I felt my blood boil even more.

Mary appeared, with Jules flanking her. They rushed forward as one. Mary took a loose steel pole and slammed it into the bodies of several of the Knights. Though her bloody face was a mask of rage, tears fell down her cheeks. Jules cleanly decapitated every Knight who got too close to Mary. I watched Jules take a bullet to his hand, but he kept on fighting.

Uncle Snap was blasting skulls. His face was a blank canvas of "Piss the hell off." He snarled, "Hold the hell up! This ain't *Enter the Dragon*, a'ight? When I kill you, stay the hell down and don't not nary one of yawl rosary-wearing bastards come into this room again. Ya feel me?"

He was right. The more men we killed, the more men came. And as blood from my thigh leaked out, I did my best to keep the grim reaper away.

Thank God for that.

Glass shattered and rained around us. Smoke appeared, and bullets that weren't from us or from the robes whizzed all around us, the sound mixing in with that of . . . Motorbikes?

Everyone stopped for a second, except me. I was busy cracking bones in the face of a Knight with my fist. This Knight had a chain on him. I wrapped it around my knuckles and began making ground beef. It was only when a massive collective of people in all black, their faces covered, came riding into the room on racing bikes that I stopped my face bashing.

I looked up from where I had moved, and kneeled next to a dead Knight. My thigh was on fire from the bullet wound there. As the chaos was going on around me, I watched as those bikes slammed into the Knights; then more gunplay followed.

From the design of some of the bikes, I knew they were the Forty Thieves. One of the ringleaders took off their mask, and my mouth dropped. Shanelle sat on the bike, frantically looking around.

Another rider, who was clearly male, came over to her, and she leaned in to hear what he wanted to tell her. "We're cornering Absolan now and reclaiming the lost stash," he said.

"Cory's message to you came just in time. Are you sure they are with Absolan?" she replied.

"Yes, ma'am."

I heard all of that through the chaos because I wasn't that far away. I watched as the second rider shifted on his bike and muttered more stuff. He removed his mask, and it was Sino. She pointed for him to go a specific way. Then she looked around again, grabbed something from her back, then swung it forward. It was one of Uncle Snap's semiautomatics.

On everything I felt pride and straight-up relief. I didn't have to die today. I watched my baby let that shit go off, spraying bullets. Bodies dropped without care due to her gun. Shanelle flung her foot out, kicking in the face of anyone who came at her. When she revved up her bike, she made that shit smoke, then lifted it to run down another target. I had to clear my throat.

Shanelle loved her bikes. Lost in the bloodlust, I watched her shoot off more rounds in a circle like Rambo, until she stopped shooting, turned the gun my way, then gasped, "Von."

My queen was here, and she wasn't alone. Marks on the bikes let me know that the Syndicate was here with her. My baby had the calvary and had ridden in like the boss she was. Had I not had to, you know, kill mother-fuckers, my dick woulda been all up through her body, while I shook her ass a little bit for stepping onto hell's battlefield. But for now, on a deep love level, a brotha was happy. Today had indeed turned into a good day.

I tried to stand the moment Shanelle rode up to me, but I couldn't. My fucking thigh was hard as fuck, tense and jerking at the pain inflicted on it.

"Baby, the fuck you doing here?" I tried to hide the pride I felt in seeing her and saving my ass, but I knew she saw it in my eyes.

"I figured something out and couldn't have you assed out. This is a trap. Luciano isn't—"

My hand went around Shanelle's waist. I gripped her so hard that she yelped, which stopped her in midsentence. I wasn't trying to shut her up, but fuck, I needed to kiss her, and I did. My mouth claimed hers, and I felt her lips soften and accept my tongue. I felt refreshed and energized by her touch. Felt pride that she had figured this shit out.

"Don't you ever in your life do anything like this again . . . unless you have backup like you do now." I smirked, then pulled on her back and removed twin guns from her hips. I pivoted, then sent two rounds into the skulls of approaching Knights.

It seemed that Shanelle and I were on the same wavelength, because she took her semi and let that bitch sing at the same time. Our gunplay was like a dance. I hopped on her bike and held my baby's waist as she started it up.

When she did so, my mouth almost dropped again. "You brought the family too?"

"You know I had to, baby. This is a family affair," Shanelle said with pride.

Ahead of me was a masked goon. I knew the body type from anywhere and the mask with the Joker face on it. Squatting on a bike was Jojo. That kid leaped off his bike to rush a towering Knight.

Like some type of demon, Jojo sent his fists hard into the bastard's face, tagging him left, then right, then leaped up to kick the Knight in his chest, sending the guy backward. When the Knight stumbled, Jojo followed by leaping on him and slicing him across the exposed areas of his uniform. Blood flew in the air, and Jojo didn't stop. Clutching his hands together, he brought his fisted hands down on the Knight's head, sending the guy's helmet flying and allowing Jojo to leave his blades in that dude's skull.

I was blown away. I hadn't seen Jojo in this light, with this much aggression. When Jojo continued bashing that dude's face in, I realized that I saw myself. I had just done the same only seconds ago. My baby brother was beasting, and though it worried me, I got it. He had a lot of angst to work out.

"Jojo, get low," shouted a female voice that I recognized. Looking in the direction from whence it came, I saw Inez. She was sprinting forward like the former track star she was. In her hand was a goddamned flamethrower.

"Where the hell did Inez get a flamethrower?" I shouted near Shanelle's ear.

My baby gave a laugh and kept riding through Knights. "Blame the Thieves and Cory."

All I could do was gape. Inez lit that shit up, set a bunch of Knights on fire, then removed a gun from her hip and pumped steel into the running bodies. To the left of her, I could see Cory rushing in toward her. He hooked her around his hand and spun her. I could see him mouthing something to her, and she grinned brightly, then let that flamethrower go off as they turned in a full circle, as if dancing.

No one was getting close to them, and no one was walking away unscathed from their flames.

"Von, jump and roll," Shanelle shouted. When she did, I made us lean, so the bike could slide over the flooring of the massive entryway. Both of us let off our guns, then leaped and rolled away, taking out a wall of Knights.

Sweat poured down my face, and in the chaos of smoke, fire, fighting, and shooting, I could see my whole family being flanked by Syndicate members, like Nighthawk and even Jai. Monty was by the doors, boxing like Ali, throwing his knee up in MMA style, then bringing down a pole. Near Jojo was Navy. That kid was a tactical one like me. His love was making shit go boom and, from what I was seeing, using a machete. He ran up on Knights, hit them with a one, two, three, then lined their bodies with grenades. After swinging his machete upward, to open up some throats, I watched him rush off. The second he did, whoever he'd touched blew up like a glass plate that had been sitting on a hot stove too long.

Everyone was handling business. I felt Shanelle come my way and help me up. As best we could, we fought our way out of the entryway. I swung left; she swung right. I managed to lift her up and toss her on the back of a Knight who ended up being a bulky-ass woman. Shanelle took the chick down with ease, choking the chick with her forearm.

The battle was of epic proportions, but when the smoke cleared, it was the Syndicate who was left standing. We fought our way out of hell, and we still had one level to stop on. Afterward, we headed out. Once we were in the clear, I spilled everything I had learned about Luci as fast as I could.

"Why? Why would he hurt Mama like that?" Shanelle asked, with anger in her eyes.

"That's what we need to find out, babe." I looked around for Luciano, but all I saw was his empty wheelchair and no Lucky. For that matter, I didn't see Uncle Snap, either.

"Baby, you see Uncle Snap? Lucky? Luciano?" I asked, trying to catch sight of them through the smoke.

Fresh air hit us, and I was thankful for it.

"Um . . . wait." My baby reached for something on her hip. In her hand was a tablet. There was a sudden *whoosh*, and I looked up. My baby was operating a drone.

"On everything, I'm in love with you woman," I said, impressed.

Shanelle chuckled and showed me her tablet. "They are by the old gardens. They're getting in a van. . . . It's the Knights. They have them."

Looking up at the sky in annoyance, I sighed. "Trail them. I need my thigh wrapped, and we need to go now."

"Already on it, baby."

And, sure enough, she was. Shanelle led us to a slick Audi. Several Thieves appeared. She gave them orders, and soon, after I had my thigh wrapped, we all were out on the street, trailing the van of Knights and ready to end this shit for the last time.

Chapter 29

Shanelle

"I'm still in shock at what you revealed," I said as rain started pelting the car.

I hit my wipers and maneuvered the Audi like I had been trained at NASCAR. Javon told me that along with Snap and Lucky, Lucky's mom, Deedee, and his sister, Giana, had been taken.

"Yeah, I was shocked too, and I'm trying to figure out how Mama didn't see it. Then again, there are so many possibilities why she wouldn't have noticed," Javon said.

"I had to look at Luci's father in order to see King in him. Luci clearly looks like his mother. King looked more like their father, Christophano. Luciano lied about a lot. When I first met him, he said Mama had come to New York in the late eighties, when she lost the baby. I assumed he meant around eighty-nine. However, it had to be in ninety. That's when Mama and Snap hooked up. Even then, he was lying to cover his tracks. And that ain't even the half of it."

I whipped the car around a slower-moving vehicle, looked in my rearview to see Creed and his men right behind me. Their bikes were in a cardinal-point formation, which showed they were in fight mode. Song had already sent her people. A car revved up beside me. Montego let his window down, then gave a hand signal that he was speeding ahead. I nodded. Mixed in with

Creed's people were our siblings, who were riding their
bikes like they were warriors.

"Did he say why he did it?" I asked, glancing at Javon,
then back at the road. I felt as if Absolan's men were
leading us someplace. They were speeding, but not in the
sense that they were trying to get away.

"No," Javon said. "Slow down. I think . . . I think
Absolan wants us to come to him. Just slow to a normal
speed and follow the van, baby."

I did as he said. And it was weird the way upstate New
York was set up. Most people thought it was all hicks and
farms, but as we raced behind the van with Uncle Snap,
Lucky, and Luci, we passed several upscale suburbs.
Maybe those who were wealthy didn't always like the
hustle and bustle of major cities like New York City.
Anyway, it was clear that the area wasn't all farmland and
Amish people.

However, as we continued on, Amish country did
come into view. Houses that were clearly lit by candles
and lanterns made me feel as if I'd driven onto the set
of *Little House on the Prairie*. Montego's and Creed's
men stopped when I did. The van we had been following
turned down a dirt road that led to several small houses.
The area was surrounded by robed figures.

"Quiet as fucking kept," Javon said. "We need to get our
security game on this level. These niggas multiply like
fucking maggots and roaches. Pull in, baby, but slowly."

I nodded as I saw Song sitting atop a hill, hair whipping
in the wind as she held her helmet under her arm. All her
people were sitting on their bikes and were lined up like
they were ready to run into battle.

"Damn, baby, you really brought in the cavalry," Javon
said.

I looked at him and smiled. "Honor wouldn't stop
crying. She was insisting I come to get her father."

Javon chuckled as he rubbed his injured leg. His face was bruised. He had scratches and cuts littering his neck. He was dirty and kind of smelled, as if he had walked through a sewer. Baby looked like he'd been in all-out war. I reached out to cup the back of his head. My fingers hit a knot. He winced, then moved my hand.

"Chill, baby. Took a hit back there. Shit hurts," he said, then kissed my palm.

"Did a medic look at you?" I asked.

He placed my hand on my thigh, then exited the car. I was going to kick his ass. Rain drenched him, and he didn't seem to care. I hopped out behind him, set to fuss a little, until I saw the doors open to the van. Uncle Snap and Lucky were shoved out, with their hands tied in front of them. Luci was just kicked out of the van. The old man fell to the ground, hard.

Lucky growled, then tackled the guard who had done it. For his affront, the guard got the butt of a rifle to the back of his head. He went down on his knees, then was out like sack of potatoes. Blood trickled down his neck. A shrill cry lit up the night. Giana fumbled down the steps to her father. She fell and rolled down the last step, then crawled in the mud to Luciano.

"Papa," she cried, cradling his head, trying to pull him closer. "Papa!"

He was alive, but barely.

"Call off your people," said a voice at the door.

I looked up to see Absolan looking at Javon. He also looked like he was dancing with death. He was beaten and bruised, but the look of determination as he held a gun to . . . Who the fuck was that?

"Mama?" I said, damn near gasping.

I made a move toward the steps. Javon snatched me back. I felt our siblings rush forward.

"Stop," Uncle Snap yelled. His voice was clear and crisp. Something else was there that I couldn't put my finger on.

Since Javon had snatched me back, I held out my hand to stop the rest of them. Jojo damn near plowed into my back, causing me to stumble and Javon to grunt in pain, as I'd bumped into his leg.

"That's not Mama," Javon said. "That's her sister."

It clicked for me then. I'd read about Mama's sister, Deedee, in her journal after Javon had told me about seeing her last year when he visited New York.

"Her sister?" Inez repeated, like she hadn't heard him the first time, gazing up at Deedee like she was seeing a ghost. "Looks just like Mama . . ."

Deedee looked stressed. Her hands were cuffed behind her back, and her silky straight gray hair got tossed around by the wind. Blood was leaking from her mouth. Her dress was ripped, and her feet were bare. She looked like she had been in a fight too. She was Mama's sister, so I knew she had some fight in her.

"Mama got a sister?" Navy asked.

Clearly, he was just as shocked as I was, to the point where he'd forgotten I told him Mama had a sister.

"She looks just like Mama," Monty whispered.

Jojo tried to move forward again. Cory jumped in front of him.

"I—I just need to see for myself," Jojo said, trying to move around Cory. "Just let me see for myself."

Cory shoved him back. "Not now. Now ain't the time, Jojo. Chill."

Tears rolled down Jojo's face. "I just need to see. . . ."

Javon looked at Jojo. "Later. A'ight? Later. Get yourself together out here. We're in the middle of a war zone."

"Call them off, Javon," Absolan shouted again.

I turned to see Creed, Montego, and Nighthawk walk up to flank Javon. The message was clear. The Syndicate came as a unit. You messed with one, you messed with all.

"Can't do that, Ab. See, I'm not too hot on that chick next to you, but you have my uncle Snap here, and you have Lucky. That poses a problem for me and for the Syndicate," Javon said.

Absolan looked at Luci; a flicker of pain and regret crossed his eyes before they turned to slits.

"Fine. I'll let them go. Leave Luciano," Absolan said.

"No," Giana cried.

Javon tsk-tsked, then said, "See, I would, but then Lucky would just find his way back here, guns blazing and shit, and we all know what would happen."

"Let him, then. He can die beside his treacherous father," Absolan spat.

Javon moved forward a bit, and a shot rang out at his feet. My husband threw his hands up and did a three-sixty spin.

Damn near foaming at the mouth, he yelled, "Stop fucking shooting at me, nigga. I'm about sick of you troll-ass motherfuckers." He turned back to Absolan. "If another motherfucker takes a shot at me, we gone turn these here goddamn farm hills into World War III. Try me!"

I cocked my head to the side and stared at him.

"Just walk away, Javon. Take your people, your family, and walk away. You don't understand what is going on. You are a good kid—"

Javon tilted his head. "I know very well what's going on, old head."

Absolan cut his gaze at Luci and then back at Javon. I turned my attention to Lucky, who moaned on the ground. He was finally coming to. One of the men in robes yanked him up. Another dragged Giana, who was kicking and screaming, away from her father.

"Pick him up, Fabian," Absolan said to someone.

A big, tall, brawny man with a messy man bun pushed the hood of his robe back, then yanked a frail Luci from the ground. Fabian walked Luci to the front of the porch. Deedee dropped her head and sobbed. Uncle Snap stood statue still, hands still behind his back. He looked more like a soldier than a hostage.

"I take it this has something, well, everything, to do with that day in the summer of nineteen eighty-five, correct?" Javon asked.

Absolan nodded once, then looked at Snap. "I had nothing to do with that. In fact, I told Luciano to let it go. But he was young and stupid, as we all were at one time. He is—was—my friend, and I'd have taken his secret to the grave with me, but old age has made him an even bigger fool."

"What happened to Cavriel?" Javon asked.

"We were to meet to discuss the Commission, as we always did. The time had come for us to relinquish seats to the younger generation. Cavriel made the mistake of saying Lucky didn't get to have a seat, because of his bloodline. Luci got upset about that. Then Cavriel reminded him of the brother he'd killed because of the very same thing. He threatened to tell you and Lucky. Told Luciano that he and I had already discussed the matter privately and that another of the sons should get the seat."

"I didn't even want a fucking seat," Lucky shouted. "I made my own fucking way. I never asked any of you motherfuckers for shit," he spat. Anger had his wet face red. "All these fucking years y'all pretended to love me, care for me, but as soon as you think I wanted that seat of power, my fucking bloodline is a problem?"

Lucky was hurt. I could tell by the way he sent Absolan a long pained look.

"So Luci killed Cavriel?" Javon asked.

"Sliced him like he was an enemy. Then he came after me," Absolan said.

"So all this shit is because the Old Italian wanted to keep his secrets buried. Here we were thinking someone had come and declared an all-out war on the Commission," Javon said, then chuckled.

Luci croaked out, "It wasn't supposed to play out like this."

The old man looked sickly as rain pelted him. Blood seeped down his upper body and soaked the thin pants he had on. If Fabian let him go, he'd fall to the ground.

Lucky said, "I thought someone was trying to kill you and us. What did you do, Pops?"

Luci gave his son a pained look. "King was my brother," he said. "I killed him," he finally admitted.

Deedee sobbed louder. The woman sounded as if she was choking on her own tears.

"Why?" Lucky asked. "Mama was good to you. She was always good to you. She jumped in front of a fucking bullet for you. She lost a child because of you."

Uncle Snap's head whipped around so quick, I was sure he had whiplash. "What?" His question came out as a hard demand.

I looked at Javon. Clearly, he had never revealed to Uncle Snap what he'd found out upon first meeting the Old Italian. Just like he hadn't told our siblings about Mama's sister. Over the last year, things had been hectic and chaotic. I knew we wouldn't hold it against him. Uncle Snap might be a different story. Lucky glanced at Uncle Snap, then looked at Javon, wondering if he had revealed too much. Uncle Snap followed Lucky's gaze. He looked at Javon with bewilderment in his eyes.

Javon shook his head, then stumbled a bit, like he was trying to get his thoughts together. He looked at Mama's sister. "You knew, didn't you? You may not have always known, but at some point, he told you. And he told you while Mama was alive."

The woman neither confirmed nor denied it. She just sobbed harder. Regret was written all over her features.

Luci looked at his son, then said, "I couldn't tell you. You were too close to Claudette. Your loyalty to her would have caused you to—"

Before Luci could finish, with his hand still locked behind his back, Uncle Snap rushed forward and kicked Luci in the sternum like he was a Spartan. The old man went flying backward from Fabian's hold. Luci hit the steps of the small house so hard, it sounded as if his spine had broken.

Giana broke free of the men holding her and went after Uncle Snap like a madwoman. Mama's sister yelled for her daughter to stop. Inez rushed forward and yanked Giana off the only man we knew as a positive father figure. She tossed Giana by her hair and yelled for her to stay away. Giana went Frisbee flying into the mud, her jet-black, wavy hair sticking to her face.

"Get these fucking cuffs off me," Uncle spat. "Out of all the people in the fucking world, you, Luciano? And then to be in her presence, to be the cause of another loss of life for her? For me? I'm going to murder this motherfucker." Uncle Snap was damn near foaming at the mouth as he tried to get past Cory, who had to pull him back.

Javon said, "I need everybody to pipe the fuck down. Absolan, you can't have Luci. That's my family's kill. You were okay with keeping his secret because, hey, King was just another nigger who had to be put down, right? But as soon as Luci wanted his son, who's half black, to have his seat, then all hell broke loose, huh? Y'all some funny ma'fuckers. You feel me? My family needs that pound of flesh."

Javon paced, rubbing the back of his head. "So let me make you a deal. You take the cuffs off Lucky and Snap. Call off your people. Because this shit is basically over. We can all walk away from this free and clear."

Absolan shook his head.

Javon stopped pacing. "I'm not going to offer this deal again, especially since your son and your men tried to kill me and the rest of my family in that club."

Fabian said, "I came to rescue my father. I assumed that you were batting for Luci since I saw you with Lucky. My father was in that club, bound and gagged in that basement."

"I foolishly assumed that Lucky had been in on this," Absolan spat.

I didn't know if Lucky was crying or if it was the rain, but he was visibly shaken up. His face was bloodred as he stared ahead, with hatred in his eyes. He inhaled and exhaled heavily.

"Y'all got me out here looking stupid as fuck in front of my faction," he yelled. "All because you thought I wanted something I never even once dreamed of fucking having. Why do you think I took a seat at the table of the Syndicate after meeting with Javon? I paved my own fucking way, and I'll continue to do so. Ask Uncle Luci what I ever asked from him in this fucking game. Nothing. Not a motherfucking thing. Anything he's given to me is because he wanted to," he yelled at Absolan. He turned to the guards and shouted, "Get these fucking cuffs off me."

I kind of got what Lucky was saying. This whole time we had been thinking one thing, when it was another. I had literally wrecked my mind by searching and putting clues together, trying to figure shit out. I'd left my daughter and niece in the care of an assassin just so I could come and help my husband, because I'd thought someone had put a target on his back, and the whole time we'd been fighting another man's war. We'd been unintentionally helping another man to hide his secrets. We'd been played.

I looked to my husband, who, surprisingly, looked less than amused but not angry in the least.

"Absolan, man to man, leader to leader, you know that by rights of war, Luciano belongs to me. And if you really want to get serious, I got the right and the manpower to take out you and your men right now."

As soon as Javon said that, Absolan's men cocked and aimed their weapons. Nighthawk stepped forward and whispered something in Javon's ear. Javon gave something that was supposed to be a smile, but it was anything but friendly.

"I am not amused, but I am losing my fucking patience," Javon said coolly while watching Absolan. He raised his hand. As soon as he did, headlights lit up the road and the foothills. There were so many lights, it looked like daylight.

"Now, my lovely activated a panic button when she called in all members of the Syndicate," Javon revealed. "As you know, my hands stretch far and wide. Over the past year, with all the business moves made, I've made a lot of . . . let's say, friends. You're surrounded, and I don't think you want this fight anymore. Now, again, walk away."

What Javon had proposed seemed reasonable, but Absolan was old, and his pride had been wounded. There was such a thing as a fool, and then there was an old fool. I prayed Absolan would be neither. I watched as the old priest lifted his chin. He still had a hold on Deedee's arm. Her sobs weren't as loud as they had been.

"Okay," Absolan finally said to Javon. "On one condition."

"I'm not really in the mood to negotiate at this point," Javon said.

"Just one small thing."

"Speak."

"Once we leave, you will hold no ill will toward my son or Cavriel's grandson. They fought only to avenge Cavriel and to find me. We don't want a war with the Syndicate," Absolan said.

"I have a better deal. You and your men leave now, and we can all meet at a later date to discuss this. Until then, you have my word that no war will be with the Commission."

There was something unspoken in Javon's words. Maybe no one else picked up on it, but I did. I studied my husband the way a woman would when she knew there was something that was not being said.

Chapter 30

Claudette

The summer of '85 . . .

That drive home had to be the longest one I'd ever taken. My heart was in my stomach. My head wouldn't stop spinning, and my soul was bleeding. During that drive, there were times when I wanted Snap to pull over and let my tears fall. My spirit was screaming at me that Kingston wasn't on this earth anymore. My emotions were crashing against my mind like a wave of oppression, and the tightness of my heart wouldn't go away, especially with the sound of Toya's tears against her mother, Betsy's chest. They sat in the back, heading to their new life.

I was on the verge of a nervous breakdown. That was why Snap was driving for me. Deedee flittered only once in my mind. I hadn't wanted to collect her ignorant, traitorous ass, but I planned to ship her off promptly to Luciano's. After that, I would be done with her. I knew that I'd never understand her, or why she was how she was, or why she loved to hurt me. My only hope was in my faith in God and karma. I prayed she remembered that even during those times I hated her, I was loyal to her.

*Once we made it to Atlanta and Snap dropped Toya
and Betsy off at Ms. Dutchess's house and Deedee at my
place, we sped off as quickly as we could. As soon as
we pulled into downtown Jonesboro, I knew something
was wrong. My gut had been right.*

"Lawd Jesus," I whispered when I saw the carnage.

*Before Snap could even stop the car, I jumped out.
King's office and the surrounding area were up in flames.
Lord knew, I couldn't breathe. Couldn't do nothing. My
legs got weak. I hadn't felt pain like that in all my life.
I couldn't feel him. Couldn't feel my heart beat in sync
with his.*

"King," I yelled in the middle of the turmoil. "King!"

*Sirens blared in the distance. People came running
from wherever they'd been hiding. Snap or somebody
tried to grab me, but I shoved him off of me as I ran
toward King's burning office.*

*"My Kingston," I cried. "No, no, no. Lord, Jesus, no.
Baby!"*

*I hadn't been there for him. He'd died alone. He had
always been afraid of dying alone. My hands balled into
fists. I let out a cry that would have probably stilled the
night had I been in the jungle. Sweat and tears pooled
down my face. My whole body went cold with shivers.*

*I was so far gone that I didn't even notice when Snap
ran into the burning office. My world spun and then
tilted. It wasn't until I saw Snap dragging a body out of
the office that reality set in. Snap coughed like his lungs
were on fire. My heart was on fire. I kneeled down to the
body that I knew was husband . . . Kingston.*

*I was so weak that I fell flat on my ass while pulling
his body haphazardly onto my lap. He was hot, and his
clothes had been scorched, so they looked like they'd
been burned into his skin. I could tell where bullets had
entered his upper torso. The skin on his face had been*

so scorched, his eyes were melted shut. Kingston looked like one of those mummies in National Geographic, *but charred. The image shattered my heart.*

Oh, dear God in heaven, why would you do this to me? *my soul cried.* Why? Why?

As durable as I was as a queen pin, nothing had prepared me for the sight of King the way he was. My man had been tough. He'd been so strong. In my eyes, he could take on anything, and he had. He done some bad things, but he'd done so much good to counter them. What would I do? What would the kids do? What about the Syndicate? What about me? How would I fucking go on now that he was gone?

I didn't want to. I couldn't imagine going a day or night when he wasn't by my side. Why did he send me away? Did he know his time had come? "My fucking God, why did you do this to me?" *I yelled.*

I didn't even realize I'd yelled that aloud. Most the whole town was out there looking at me, and I didn't give a damn. I gazed up through my tears to see Snap sitting across from me. The young man looked the way I felt. King had been the only father he'd known. Same could be said for so many of the kids.

"They killed all of 'em," *Snap said, voice cracking.* "They all in there. They all dead."

They'd taken him out. They'd taken out the young men he'd made his sons. A rage filled me like one I'd never felt before. I thought I took leave of my senses. Somewhere in the back of my mind, the sane me took a seat. As I sat there rocking back and forth, cradling the body of the only man I'd ever loved, I felt the break in my mental well-being. My life was forever altered by the murder of my King. Someone would pay. People would pay . . . and they would pay with their lives.

Chapter 31

Lucky

The cuffs had come off me and Snap. Absolan took his son and his men, and he left the premises. It was just us family now. Just us, our demons, and unanswered questions. Javon and I stood face-to-face, man-to-man. I had no qualms about what had to be done. There had been so many secrets for so long. I didn't know the man I'd assumed was my uncle for years. I had to stop kidding myself, though. The rumors had been rampant. So somewhere in the back of my mind, I had known he was my father. I just hadn't wanted to accept it for some reason.

The rain had let up, and the wind whipped around us. I wanted to talk. Wanted to say so much, but nothing came out. Nothing. The McPhearsons and Snap, especially Snap, were owed their pound of flesh. Those were the rules of the game. I turned to look at my mother and my sister, who were doing all they could to help a dead man. I lowered my head and pressed my lips tightly together. I turned to Snap and gave him a bitter smile.

Regardless of what the old man had done, it was still a tough pill to swallow, knowing he would be executed. But to an honorable leader, that was a rule of war. To the victor went the spoils. There was really no victor and no war—just old skeletons that had finally fallen out of the closet.

Snap's expression was set in stone. He had a Desert Eagle clutched in his hand. I knew there would be no talking to him, no asking him to just let the old man die of old age and his wounds. I trudged up the steps to where my mother, sister, and father were. I signaled for Jules and Mary to follow me.

My mother looked up at me, questions in her eyes. "What?" she asked.

"Come on, Ma," I said, my voice having no emotion.

"No," she whined. "What are you . . . What do you mean, come on?"

"Ma, you know what has to happen. Don't do this."

The old man coughed. Blood coated his lips as he looked up at us from the chair with hooded eyes.

My mother had a look of panic in her eyes. "You can't just let them kill him," she fussed, eyes wide.

"Take her out," I told Jules and Mary as Giana wrapped herself around our father's waist.

"Lucky," my mother yelled as Jules and Mary escorted her out. Jules had to use all his strength to hold her. "Lucky, he's your father!" she cried.

I looked down at my sister. "Giana."

"No," she said. "They have to kill me too."

"Giana," my father said, "you . . . you have to go."

As soon as he said that, Giana cried harder.

"Take her," he ordered me.

With ease, I grabbed Giana around her waist. I carried her, kicking and screaming, as Snap walked past me into the house. My soul was burdened. . . .

Chapter 32

Javon

It was always amazing the shit one could find out if one dug deep enough. Coming into New York, I'd assumed that one of our allies and fellow Syndicate members was in trouble. In the end, I'd found out so much more. Envy was a powerful drug, and the more I had read King's journal and compared it to Mama's, the more I had found that some things just didn't fucking add up.

Initially, it looked as if Absolan had been the culprit, but that shit was too obvious. I'd learned in life that if it was too obvious, then one needed to take a second look. I mean, don't get a nigga wrong. Sometimes it was the obvious; however, in this case, not so much.

I shook my head, trying to keep my wits about me as much as I could. With Shanelle by my side, I was barely conscious. I wondered if she could pick up on that shit, so I looked to see if she was looking at me. Sure enough, the woman I'd married had her eyes square on me.

"Swear to God, I'm kicking your fucking ass," she spat low, so only she and I could hear.

"Couldn't see a doctor. Too much shit was going on. Way too much shit. I'm cool, though," I lied.

"You're lying, and I know you are."

"Where's my daughter?" I asked to divert shit.

"With her fairy godmother."

I quirked an eyebrow. "And my niece?"

"The same place Honor is."

I nodded, then turned my attention back to the house, where Lucky was dragging Giana out. He tossed his sister into a car with his mother. I watched Uncle Snap walk up the stairs. Luciano looked up at him. The light from the house was dim, but with the cars lighting up the area, we could see well.

Uncle Snap said, "For years you betrayed her trust, knowing you'd been the one to cause her the greatest pain she'd ever known."

"I regretted it," Luci croaked out. He sounded older than he had before.

"He trusted you. You were his brother, and you killed him. The Cain to his Abel."

Luci said nothing. His face was a mask of fading life and was devoid of emotion. I could have been wrong, but I didn't believe that nigga had no fucking regrets about what he'd done. He was the cold case for being pathological, and it sickened me. Frankly, it reminded me of Melissa, and it made my jaw clench from constrained hurt and anger. Luci sat straight up, as much as he could.

Snap moved a few feet across from Luci. We couldn't see him from where we were standing, but we saw and heard when he emptied the gun into the Old Italian. Fate was a cruel bitch.

The rest of the Syndicate and I pulled back after that. There was nothing more to be done. All grievances had finally been brought out into the open and made right on both ends, though I knew the sins of our family in this world might not ever be done. That just made me stay up on game and not relax my resolve. Also, it reminded me never, ever to believe that trust could be maintained with Lucky's sister, and definitely not with his piece of work of a mother.

We left Lucky standing over his mother and sister after his men dragged his father's body from the house and laid it in the yard. Just like Mama had described in her journal how she had held King during his death, Deedee sat cradling Luciano's head in her lap. Her face was wet with her pain. Maybe now she knew what pain was. Maybe now she'd understand all the pain she'd caused her sister.

After we left those Amish farm hills, we headed back to the hotel where Shanelle had left Ms. Lily, Honor, and Justice. I hugged Ms. Lily. She seemed so small under my weight and smelled of whiskey. I smiled when her accent came through as she greeted me.

"Good grief, Javon. You smell like you been wrestling with hogs," she fussed. "Don't touch my babies until you wash."

I chuckled. "I just need to look at her for a minute, is all."

There she was, staring up at me. Everyone claimed she looked like me. I thought she looked like her mother. I wanted to pick her up but knew I couldn't. Behind me, Shanelle had opened the door to let Jojo in. He and I had to talk. That ruthless aggression he had displayed earlier was new. I mean, he'd shown it once before, when he got locked up over a year ago, but this seemed different.

I went to shower. My head was spinning. Eyes burned. I was so out of it that the fact that I had a bullet wound on my leg had all but escaped a nigga's mind, until I saw the heavy stream of blood leaking from my leg and going down the drain. This whole fucking shit had drained me to the point where I wanted to rethink my decision to take on this fucking lifestyle.

I looked up when Shanelle walked into the bathroom. I didn't really feel like talking. Because she knew me, she knew that. Baby just got naked and stepped her pretty ass into the shower with me. I stood against the wall and let her wash me from head to toe. She was careful with me because of all the injuries.

Once she was done, I held her close to me and kissed her like I never would again. Learning all this new shit about Mama and King had been rough, but what stood out to me the most, what a lot of hood novels and movies didn't tell or show, was that it was possible for a drug dealer—a kingpin, a bad man—to love one woman and one woman only.

That nigga King was the epitome of that. He had found a true queen in Mama and had treated her as such. The nigga was a fucking alpha who had no problem with marrying an alpha woman. Shit, reading King's words about Mama made a nigga want to step his game up with Shanelle. Shit made me take a look at myself and examine my thought process.

There was a time when I felt Shanelle needed to focus on bringing more women in so she could run that part of things, but shit, King had allowed Mama to sit at the table right next to him. And because of that, he'd been able to secure his faction in a way that nobody else could. I took note of that shit.

"I'm going to call in Inez so she can patch you up. She was working on Cory and Uncle Snap. She should be ready for you now," Shanelle said once we had stepped from the shower. "Ms. Lily went to Jojo and Navy's room to help Jojo get Justice ready for bed."

I wanted to chuckle but was too tired to. "That old woman is something else," I said.

"Tell me about it."

"Monty . . . did you know Nighthawk was his father?"

I gawked down at my wife, who had kneeled to examine the bullet wound on my thigh.

"No, no, I didn't. Wow. Some more shit we have to look into," I said.

"I learned a lot while you were away, and it wasn't even that long. Ms. Lily was like a gatekeeper. She knew a lot of shit."

"I have to tell her who killed King."

"That's going to break her heart," Shanelle said.

I needed a drink. Preferably something strong, but then Honor cried out. I needed to get to her. Needed to hold her in my arms. I took a step, and my whole world rotated on a 360-degree axis. Before I got a chance to hold my daughter in my arms again, I passed out on the hotel room floor, my injuries finally getting the better of me.

I woke up two days later, back in Atlanta. I was hooked up to an IV, my head throbbed, and my body ached in places I didn't know there should have been fucking places. My throat was fucking dry, and I had a catheter in my dick. That was the most painful, uncomfortable shit a man could endure.

One of the doctors for the Syndicate had come in and doctored me up. Apparently, she had flown in with us from New York on a private jet chartered by my wife. I still owed Shanelle some good loving—dick—for the way she'd held a brother down. As soon as she thought I was in trouble, she'd come running. She hadn't waited for me to call or anything. She had dropped everything and had come to my side, and she'd left nobody behind. Not even Ms. Lily. Shanelle was my Wonder Woman.

"Yo, can I get this shit out my dick?" I snapped. "Where's my daughter? I need to see my baby."

"What you need to do," Shanelle said as she came from the bathroom, "is lie there and relax."

Baby was dressed in biker shorts that cupped her ass and a sports bra. Her hair was in a messy bun. The sensual image made my dick come to life. She stuck her head out the door, then called the doctor to tell her I was awake. I had to lie there while some broad I didn't know handled my dick. Once that was done, she checked a brother's vitals to make sure I was good.

"The hit on the head was serious. You did good not to go to sleep, but if your wife hadn't had medics on standby once you passed out, you could have been in serious trouble, Mr. McPhearson," the doc said. "You're lucky, and thank your sister Inez as well. She did a good job keeping you stable until I could make it to you in that hotel."

The thought made me smile. My siblings were back on the path, getting the education Mama had always wanted for them. We might be the people who made things go bump in the night, but we had learned how to blend in from the best. I took it that Mama and King could finally be at peace now.

Epilogue

Javon

It took another week for me to be back to what I considered full health. I spent that time with my family. Everything else took a backseat. Over the next three months, Nighthawk and Monty had big blowups, but that was to be expected. Monty was hurt. He had a lot of questions, and once he and Nighthawk stopped butting heads, father and son were able to talk.

Lucky and I hadn't spoken in that time. He'd reached out to me a few days after his father was killed to tell me he needed space and time to process everything that had happened. Once the dust settled, shit was real touch and go for a while after that. I didn't know if Lucky would vacate his seat at the table of the Syndicate or what. As the leader of the crime ring, it was my duty to keep shit together, even when it appeared to be falling apart. Even if those who sat at the table asked me about it in the future, I'd be prepared to give them an answer they'd be satisfied with. For now, I just didn't know.

It was on a late Sunday afternoon that the family got a few surprises.

"I don't know about this," I heard a woman say.

Shanelle had been cooking dinner. She and I peeped out the window of the back porch to see Uncle Snap standing with a younger woman. All the women I'd seen him with had some kind of similarity to Mama. This one was no different.

"What's bothering you about it, Ro?" Uncle Snap asked her.

"I'm a whore, Raphael. Men don't normally invite whores to dinner. Families don't normally throw out the welcome mat for my kind."

"These kids, they don't care about shit like that. They come from rough upbringings, anyhow. They will see you as the person you present to them."

The woman had on tight jeans that showed a bubble butt and thick thighs. Her blouse was thin, and her bra pushed her big breasts front and center. Her hair flowed down her back. She had red lipstick on her thick lips and diamond earrings in her ears. Her nails were painted red and were pointy. And she had on six-inch pumps. Her butterscotch skin glowed in the sun.

"She is kind of dressed like a hooker," I said in a low voice to Shanelle, who elbowed me in the side.

I chuckled as Honor lay against my chest.

The woman looked at Uncle, her brows bunched. "You sure? I don't want no problems."

Uncle Snap kissed her forehead. "I'm sure," he said, then turned to the door.

Shanelle rushed back to the oven. I pretended to be walking Honor around.

"Hey, Uncle Snap," Shanelle said with a smile when he walked in. "I didn't think we'd be seeing you until early morning."

"What up, Unc?" I asked, jerking my head upward.

Uncle Snap smiled as he ushered the woman inside with a hand on the small of her back. "I don't think I'ma ever be used to seeing you as a daddy, boy," he quipped.

Just as he said that, Jojo walked into the kitchen with Justice. He had the same baby carrier that I did, and his daughter was lying on his chest as well.

"I ain't gon' ever get used to seeing that shit, either," Uncle Snap said about Jojo, then laughed. "Anyway, where everybody at? Want y'all to meet somebody."

"Cory and Inez were down the street. They stopped to get some drinks. Navy was out back, macking on one of Rize's female guards. Monty and Trin are in his room, arguing again," Jojo said.

Shanelle sighed and shook her head. "They got that fight-and-fuck thing down, huh?" she said, then turned back to the oven. She untied her apron and walked over to extend her hand to the woman. "Hello. I'm Shanelle. How are you?"

The woman took Shanelle's hand in a firm grip. "Hello. I'm Rowena, but you can call me Ro."

After Jojo and I introduced ourselves, he yelled out back for Navy to come in, then shouted down to the basement for Monty and Trin to come up. They were all pretty shocked to see Uncle with a woman too, but everybody smiled and introduced themselves. Soon after, Cory and Inez walked in, with Ms. Lily in tow. They, too, introduced themselves, and all was well. . . .

Until Ms. Lily looked at Ro and said, "You's a whore, ain't you?"

"Oh, dear Jesus," Shanelle whispered.

Inez turned around to keep from laughing. I scratched the back of my head and glanced at Uncle Snap. Cory coughed to keep from laughing. Uncle Snap's eyes widened. Navy, Jojo, and Monty walked from the room just to be respectful enough not to laugh in Ro's face. Trin, however, outright cackled.

Ro swallowed and glanced at Uncle Snap. For a minute, she looked like she was going to run away and fast. But then the woman stood straight up, shoulders back, and declared, "Why, yes. Yes, I am. Is that a problem?"

Ms. Lily stared up at the woman. "Naw. Not 'less you make it one. Are you whoring now? Or are ya here because Ralphy boy likes ya? If ya whoring, you eat and go on." She pointed a stern finger at the woman. "And don't touch nothing. If ya here because he likes ya and you like him past his wallet, then you can stay and bond. Mama didn't like no thieving whores around her place, and because she ain't like it, King ain't like it, either. You be an honest ho, and you's welcome here," the old woman said, then grabbed place mats from the counter. Then she walked into the dining room and started setting the table, as if she hadn't just insulted the woman.

"You have to get used to Ms. Lily," I said. "She's old, and she doesn't give a fuck what comes outta her mouth." I shrugged, then grabbed the plates and walked into the dining room behind Ms. Lily. We loved that old lady around these parts, and we had gotten used to her loose lips.

Dinner was served. It included Ms. Lily's favorites: oxtails, rice and beans, steamed cabbage, coco bread, plantains, and German chocolate cake.

"I want y'all to know King went out fighting. He ain't lay there and take that shit. He fought, even with bullets riddling his body," Ms. Lily said out of the blue.

She did that often. She would get a faraway look in her eyes, and then she'd blurt out something about the past. She was her most lucid when she was sitting with the babies. After we'd told her about who'd really killed King, the old lady broke down like we'd never seen. It took her days to come out of her house again.

"Last thing he said was, 'Take care of my woman,' and I did. For thirty more years, I did," she said, wiping her mouth. "Shanelle, why you keep feeding me all this ethnic food? I told you I don't like it," she then fussed.

Shanelle looked across at Ms. Lily with a smile. "Sorry, Ms. Lily. Tomorrow I'll bake you some salmon and asparagus."

Ms. Lily frowned. "I guess. Sounds nasty, but okay." Then she mumbled, "Better be seasoned."

We laughed, and everything was all good, until Jojo's cell phone rang. When his smile faded, we all knew who it was. Anytime Dani had called over the past three months, she'd always brought Jojo's mood down. She'd promise to come see Justice and then never show up. Jojo would be excited. He'd get their daughter ready, only for Dani to go back on her word. I was actually tired of seeing the hurt and pain in his eyes behind it.

"Hello," Jojo answered just as music outside the house blasted from a car.

The Thieves and members of Rize were on duty, so I wasn't worried about who it was.

"I'm outside. Come open the door," I heard someone at the front door say.

"Dani, we're eating—"

"I came to see my baby, so I don't care what you doing. Open the door and bring me my child," I heard her snap on the other end of the phone.

Jojo adjusted his glasses as stress lines took up residence across his forehead. He hadn't been the same since Dani walked out on him. It showed in the way he walked, talked, and the way he did business. There was an edge to him these days.

Jojo sighed as he stood. Justice was in her swing next to Ms. Lily, who had a look of utter disdain on her face. I followed Jojo to the door, just so he knew I had his back. I felt Shanelle walk up behind me. Dani banged on the door before Jojo snatched it open.

Dani was dressed like she had walked out of a hip-hop video shoot. Her pussy was damn near eating her denim shorts. She had on combat boots and a shirt that had been ripped to show her breasts.

"Where my baby?" she spat at Jojo as soon as he opened the door. She looked at me and Shanelle, sucked her teeth, then rolled her eyes. "You had to bring your mama and daddy to the door with you?" she asked sarcastically.

"Where are you taking her, and what time will you be bringing her back?" Jojo asked, his voice calm—too calm, actually.

Dani jerked her head back, with a scowl on her face, like she was offended. "I'm taking her to my place, and she'll be back when I bring her back," she snapped.

Jojo shook his head. "That ain't going to work, Dani. I need an address, a phone number, and a specific time to expect her home."

"Nigga, you outta your fucking mind," Dani said, then tried to push past Jojo.

He didn't move, which forced her to step back. "Dani," he said, "we can do this the easy way or the hard way. You pick."

"Oh, so you jumping big and bad since those two flanking you? You wasn't this tough a few months ago, fuck nigga."

Shanelle dug her nails into my back. That was a signal she was losing her patience and wanted to fight. I held my hand back, keeping her at bay. I wanted to see Jojo handle it. It was amazing how Dani had come into our family, pretending she was one thing and turning out to be another.

"Yo, Dani, what the fuck taking so long?" I heard a nigga yell from behind Dani.

I smirked.

Shanelle said, "Oh, hell no," as she tried to move around me.

I grabbed her by her waist and said, "Watch. A man can take only so much before he snaps."

I knew without a doubt that Jojo wanted to lay hands on Dani, but he had been raised better than that. However, since Dani had been stupid enough to bring another nigga to the house, he now had someone to take his anger out on. Jojo shoved past Dani. He scratched the back of his head, then adjusted his glasses before pulling his jeans up as he moved toward the stupid motherfucker who had stepped outside the car. I didn't say a word as Jojo kicked the door of the car so hard, the man's throat hit the top of the door before he hit the ground.

Jojo didn't even take his glasses of as he yanked the baggy jeans–wearing man from behind the door. I peeped Cory and Navy watching from the right side of the house. Saw Monty and Uncle Snap on the left. Jojo was covered at all angles. So if Dani's new nigga had any backup in his car, they would be handled swiftly.

It wasn't really a fight, if I were to be honest. It was just Jojo beating a nigga into a bloody pulp. Dani screamed for Jojo to stop before running to jump on his back. I politely moved to the left and let my wife out of the cage. I guessed Cory had been holding Inez back as well. Because she came running from the right side of the house like she was floating on air.

She and Shanelle grabbed a handful of Dani's wild hair and yanked her off Jojo's back. She slammed to the ground so hard, her scream got caught in her throat. Just like old times, when we were kids and Mama was sick of our shit when it came to fighting, I watched Shanelle and Inez beat a bitch's ass.

It was comical to me. There we were, all of us grown now, but at any flip of a switch, we could revert to those same kids who had bonded over trauma and the love of Mama. We might not have been blood, but we had shed blood and had made others bleed in the name of family. If that wasn't related by blood, I didn't know what was.

I watched Cory and Uncle Snap pull Shanelle and Inez off Dani, who was in a bloody heap on the ground. Dani pulled herself up slowly, holding her bloodied mouth, and walked to lean against the car. It was odd, but in that moment, I missed Melissa. I knew we would always miss her. Even Shanelle, who had all but written Melissa off. I still caught Shanelle staring at old photos of them.

Monty and Navy called Jojo off of whoever the nigga was who had driven Dani over. Jojo stopped fighting, adjusted his glasses, then got in Dani's face. He put his hands around her neck, damn near lifted her from the ground.

"Jojo," Uncle Snap and I called out at the same time.

"You ain't that kind of young man," Uncle Snap said to him.

"And you never will be," I added, walking onto the porch.

"Put her down, nephew."

I said, "Jojo, li'l bro, take your hands off her."

Jojo dropped Dani, then turned to stare the nigga down before strolling angrily onto the porch. "Don't come back, Dani," he said over his shoulder. "Don't ever fucking come back," he added, then stalked into the house.

My little brother was a changed man. Dani had chewed him up and spit him out. That would be another story for another time.

When my love, Shanelle, reached for her gun, I swore I heard Mama's voice in my mind saying, *Shoot that gal in her foot. Then she'll act right.*

She said to Dani, "You get your shit together before you come back this way. Jojo is angry, and he has every right to be. But I'm a woman and a mother. Daughters need their mothers as much as they need their fathers and vice versa. But if you bring your hood-rat ass back over here, disrespecting my family or my little brother, the young man who you left to be a single father for the past three months, I'm going to shoot you right in your damn foot."

Family connected us to the Syndicate, but trust me, family was the root that ran this game, and I'd never want my life to be without any of them. Just as Mama had taught us.

My dearest children,

These words come to you all in pure love, pride, and hope in who you all will one day be as adults. In your lives, you may stumble. You may fall, and life may whup your behinds, but know, when you got this family, ain't nothing foul gonna take what you have in your hearts—that fight, tenacity, and love. Now, Mama has something she has to share, and that's this: Mama doesn't know everything, but Mama has gone through fires to get the understanding she does have. This has helped me train you all up as best as I could.

Babies, the streets ain't a comforter. I hope y'all understand what I mean by that. That means don't let it smother y'all. I know each and every one of you all has what it takes to make it in whatever your unique personal abilities will allow ya, and that's why I took you all in my home. Mama's little warriors. I sit here now writing this, watching this little bigheaded, hardheaded boy Vo yell at his equally hardheaded muskrat brother Cory in the front of my lawn.

Von, the day you and Cory showed up against the side my house, the spirit of my long-lost son seemed to be all through you both. I don't know why, but one day, I hope to understand it. By the time y'all came to me, I had fostered many children. Only a few could remind me of my purpose. I thank you both for that, my sweethearts. I truly do.

Shanelle, my little bossy, smart gal, I see a lot of myself in you. Gal, if you were back in the day, I know my own father would take you out in the back and teach you how to shoot like he did me. I could see you coming from my home, see you growing like a strong weed of my own line. You, baby girl, are something powerful, so don't you ever doubt your own thoughts, worth, or actions, ever. No man has a right to what you were born to do. They don't even have a right to your heart. I need all my girls to remember that.

Now, don't think I'm giving praise to only my eldest, 'cus that ain't the deal here. Each of you reflects the best in me.

Inez, my dear precious girl, my own mother would love you with all her heart. You remind me of her, I promise you, and one day, I hope to help you see the brightness that I see in you, baby girl. You are a fighter too, and not just a healer. Know that and never forget it.

Melissa, even as I write this, I see the spark of fear in you, fear that you are alone, and I hope one day, you will see that the other side of yourself is so much more than your fear. You are like someone I hope to introduce you to, a woman who is like a second sister to me because of how she's helped in protecting me. But I know that if I don't catch you fast enough, you might leave me. For now, you are a carefree child, even with that glint of fear. I just hope that in my small way, in raising you, that you will have all that you need and love. I want the best for you.

Now, my three youngest, Monty, Jojo, and Navy. Y'all my little babies, don't you know it? Even with the sadness in your eyes, I see a future so bright for you. I can't even express it in my words as I write it. My heart overflows with what I see in y'all, and though you three are too young right now to discern who you all will be, I just know that the brilliance of your minds is incredible.

Lastly, my Cory. I did this on purpose because I spoil you enough. I got only this to say: I'll whup your behind even when I'm in heaven. Boy, you are something else, but you are a protector, and I love that about you. I know you're in your wild days, but one day you'll trust your own spirit, and when you do, the man you will become will make me weep in joy.

I love my children. Each and every one of you came to me when I thought I'd have no children to love. So, Mama is thankful.

So, I need y'all to remember my words always, and the words of my Kingston and of ya Uncle Snap. If you do, I promise you all, the foundation might shake, but the family will always stay strong. Now, get my loving from your uncle Snap. Let that grumpy man know that my love is in you all.

As Kingston F. McPhearson would say, "The merit of a man and a woman is their ability to take ownership of their own bullshit, while not making excuses for their deplorable actions." Y'all remember that, each and every one of y'all. Because in life it also takes the merit of a man and a woman to have the ability to walk away from conflict. Unless that conflict means to end your life, as Snap would say. So, I know I'm talking too much, because Snap is glaring at me from under his hat, so I'll end this for now. I have so much more to write you all as you grow, and if I never get to finish my words, just know I tried.

Family ain't always perfect, but even when we don't like or love each other, we always have to remember our family, however we build it. Because they always can get that ass dragged and tagged.

With love always,
Claudette Haynes-McPhearson